CW01086722

Singing Home the Whale

MANDY HAGER

RANDOM HOUSE
NEW ZEALAND

For Luna

The assistance of Creative New Zealand is gratefully acknowledged by the publisher.

A RANDOM HOUSE BOOK published by Random House New Zealand
18 Poland Road, Glenfield, Auckland, New Zealand

For more information about our titles go to www.randomhouse.co.nz

A catalogue record for this book is available from the National Library of New Zealand

Random House New Zealand is part of the Random House Group
New York   London   Sydney   Auckland   Delhi   Johannesburg

First published 2014

© 2014 Mandy Hager

The moral rights of the author have been asserted

ISBN 978 1 77553 657 4
eISBN 978 1 77553 658 1

Design and cover illustration: Carla Sy
Cover photograph: Shutterstock/Rich Carey
Chapter page illustrations: Rose Lawson

Printed in Australia by Griffin Press an Accredited ISO AS/NZS 14001:2004

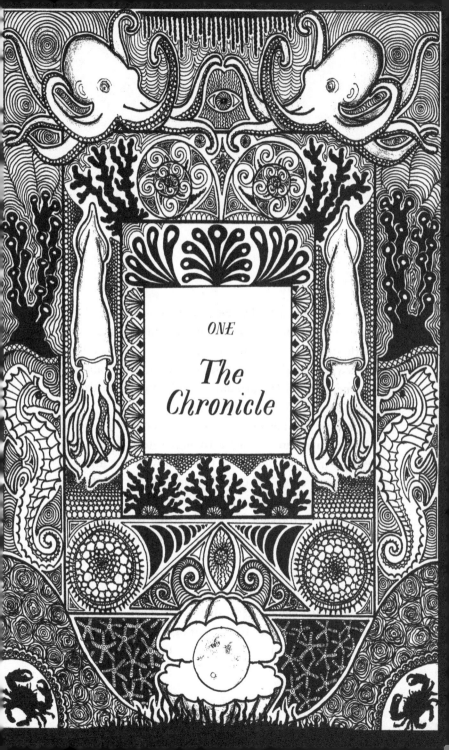

ONE

The Chronicle

I was born on a night the moon drew the sea high towards her face. As the swell lifted my mother I slid into the tide tail first, the cord snapping as she nudged me skywards to the icy air. Below me rang my family's welcome, lapping love around me as I nosed towards my mother's milk.

For those first few hours, days, weeks, months, I clung to her calm company, never roving from the reach of her all-seeing eyes. When we travelled with our group I nestled in the curve of her slick satin side, her slipstream aiding any feeble efforts of my own. At two months my top teeth broke through; by four the lower row took root. My first flesh food was salty squid. I can still recall its death-throe tickle on my tongue.

It took some time to learn the breadth of all my family's store of sounds. Their songs told tales of times long past; their wails, our wash of woes. They showed me how to pulse our notes to cut through the great swathes of sea; how to send clicks and calls to sense the secrets of the other beings who share our sea-bound world. But the markers that made plain my family's moods I never had to learn. Oh no, these I always knew. Each yearning bleeds an inborn stippled charge — and when it hits I feel it as my own.

Right from the start I was a seeker; wanted to explore the workings of the waters we called home. I glided between peaks and spurs, rocky spines, and boiling vents that bubbled from the belly of the ocean's core. I was the minnow of my mother's clan, pandered to by parents, uncles, aunts; and with my cousins by my side, we cruised through coral coves, skimmed stands of kelp and bladderwrack, and swam through swaying sea-grass meadows that split to single stems as we eased through.

Our days were filled with feeding, feeling, floating, amid the currents' great convergence and the pull of moon and tide. We goaded flying fish, dangled driftwood from our snouts, racing, chasing, breaching: such playing taught me how to grace the gifts of my sleek shape.

From the rush of air above to the press of trenches, pits and chasms in the lightless lands below, I wondered at the beauty. I felt no one had ever known such sweet fortune as the likes of me. So if a ship stormed through the waters where we passed I found myself drawn to its throaty call. I paid no heed to my dear mother's fear. In my eyes she was all-powerful, while the Hungry Ones who trod the decks seemed small and weak. I could not grasp how they might ever do us harm.

My mother said that in the early times we watched the Hungry Ones when they first crowded to the coast. She said we listened and we learned and matched their sounds with what was trickling from their thoughts. But we have lost this melding of our minds; must, drop by drop, relearn if we are once again to live in peace.

I am The Chronicle, and this will be my last song. Like the ones who came before me and the ones who will come after, in my final hours it is my duty — no, my joy — to share all I have learned in my long swim through life.

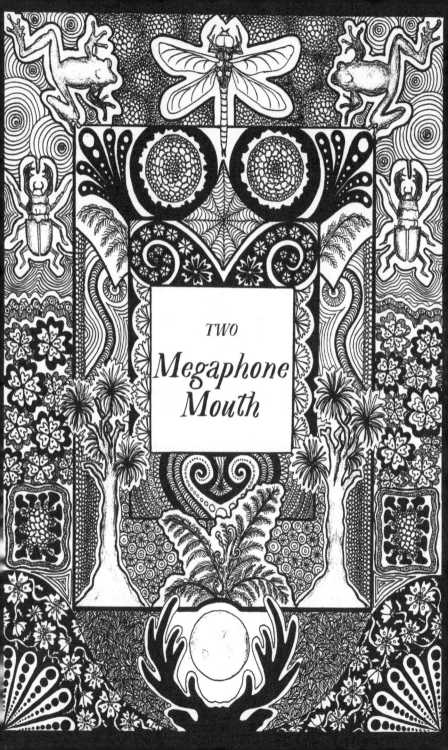

TWO

Megaphone Mouth

Will hovered outside Blythe's general store, the plastic envelope sweaty in his hand. He'd already learnt to steel himself before he took on Gabby Taylor.

His first day here, six weeks ago, she'd cornered him.

'So *you're* Dean's boy.' She hadn't even tried to hide the sneer that curled her upper lip. She'd eyed him head to toe.

'Nephew,' he'd said, heat swarming up his face. Though probably not much older, she had the power to switch his ever-present nausea to high gear.

She'd reached under the counter and fished out Dean's mail, her small brown eyes bright with gossiper's fervour.

'So, what's your name?'

'Will Jackson.'

'Where're you from?'

'Up north.' Dean had warned Will to keep the fact he came from Wellington under his belt. The locals down here hated it; said it was full of politicians and greenies who had no understanding of the real world.

'How long're you here for?'

'Dunno.'

Her nostrils pinched like he'd dropped a fart. 'Well, best you get over yourself, Will Jackson. We've got no call for freaks down here.'

'What the hell did *that* mean?' he'd asked when his uncle came home from work that night.

'Well, doh! You dress like that, they're going to react.'

'Like what?'

Dean rolled his eyes. 'Jesus, Will, you look like you're the bloody Prince of Darkness.' He held up a hand to temper the insult. 'Hey, I don't care what you look like, mate, but this place is a time warp — the last time they saw someone pierced and tattooed was in the Māori wars. You might recall it didn't turn out too flash for them.'

Still, Will was buggered if he'd ditch the piercings — they were part of him, proof that he'd once had a life. But he'd tied his long black hair back and stuck with plain black tees and jeans from there on in. Better to be bland than take more shit. His nerves were still as shot as hell.

Now he leaned against a lamppost, watching as a family of tourists eased out of a camper van, their over-sized shorts and tourist T-shirts revealing folds of dimpled sunburnt flesh. *Perfect!* He slunk in after them, careful not to catch Gabby's eye, and nudged the envelope of completed assignments over the counter, hopefully just out of her line of sight.

She was busy poring over a map with the two parents, pointing out the 'must see' sights of Pelorus Sound.

'. . . and then, of course, there are the salmon farms. My uncle . . .' She stopped and stared straight up at Will. He felt his balls retract. 'I saw you,' she said, a smirking great white shark. 'On the internet.' Glee and scorn shot off her like a volley of poisoned darts.

Will turned and bolted from the store. Ran all the way back to Dean's shabby wooden house on legs that threatened to give way. *Goddamn.* Now the megaphone mouth of Pelorus Sound had seen the clip, he was twice doomed.

He collapsed on the doorstep, shaking as he struggled to regain control. He tried the breathing exercise the counsellor had shown him. *In, one two three, out, one two three* . . . Even so the YouTube clip materialised in his mind in all its gothic splendour. The angry mottled swelling of his eyes. The bruising around his throat. His broken nose. The unfocused — concussed — struggle with his words. Viral in the real sense, jumping from one user to the next, each new posting another kick in his already battered guts. And while the producers of *A Star Is Born* denied all knowledge of who was waging this attack, they must have loved it all the same. A heap of free publicity for their shitty, parasitic show.

THREE

*An Ancient
Ailing Bag*

When we left behind the White World for the warmer waters in my second year, we young ones were a brazen band, given to rough and tumble games. Our elders, betters, bore us for the most part, with only the odd side-swipe from a flipper or fluke to hinder our hot-headed play.

I learned the joys of cruising in the company of the ones I love: the shared rhythm that settles in once we are under way. Warm bodies brush past in casual caress. Feelings and minds merge. It is this harmony that forms the backbone of our world; connects us to each other — and to all else. This, too, I learned.

Then came the day my mother taught me to track through the seas. *There is a Pulse*, she sent, *that weaves its way beneath the oceans and the land. Pathways of Pulse. North, south, east, west; as charged as the gleam that washes White World's midnight skies.* Her steady eye met mine. *Clear your mind now. Try to hold off other thought. Just listen . . . listen and feel.*

At first all I felt was the twitch of my tail and the hammer of my heart, and the crush of currents in the sea's embrace. Nothing else. I wiped away all thought and drew a mighty breath and dived. Five times I dived and four times failed to feel the planet's pulse. But the fifth time . . . ah, the fifth time . . . It came upon me suddenly, a feeling like fingers of kelp sliding along my spine. Then every pulsing part of me fell into line with it and I could feel its tingling charge.

I raced from one pulse to the next, breaching with pure delight. Plain foolishness! The current I was chasing drew me back towards the ice. I did not hear my mother's worried warnings until, at last, she overtook and barred my way. How long had I been speeding through the sea? So long my cherished clan were simply sprigs of spume.

My mother called the clan to tell them I was safe. *Swim on*, she sent, *we'll catch you up.* My aunt bounced back an offer to return. *No need . . . Be happy . . . He has felt The Pulse!* The whole group sang with pleasure and I plumped with pride.

So when I heard the distant drumming of a ship I sped to it, arguing with my mother, wheedling, pleading, to take a closer look. I ignored the worry washing off her as she tried to steer me back on course. I would have none of it. I was a fat little calf who thought he owned the seas.

Just as the ship was well within my sights, crawling with hairy Hungry Ones up on the deck, my mother bit me by the fluke — not hard, but firm enough for me to falter. *Can you not feel the threat?* Her thoughts were steeped with such a dread it haunts me still.

But did I listen? No, not I. I spy-hopped, splaying fins to hover upright and (to my never-ending shame) exposed.

Dive! my mother moaned, but I was too intent on trying to read the twinkling lights now trained on me. She knocked me off my axis. *In the name of the Great Mother, dive!*

Already there was a shift in the thrumming of the ship, as if its heart was speeding up. While seabirds squabbled in its wake, it changed its course and started making straight for us.

I heaved in air and dived down after her, seeking out her slipstream as her tail threshed to pick up speed. I had no chance of keeping up; was bludgeoned in the backwash of her wake. She circled back and clutched me to her side, and I could feel every muscle, every sinew, strain beneath her silken skin as she steered me on.

Hush, she sent. *Put your will into the task and do not look behind.*

A fearsome pounding pocked the air, growing ever louder until it drowned her urgings out. My mother's eyes had never shone so bright, as if by force of will she could conceal me in their protective pool. But as I spat my blowhole open to expel the stale air the maelstrom roared right over us. I risked one backward glance: the ship was speeding to us fast, but, worse, a whirling creature buzzed low to the sea, the source of this unearthly roar.

My mother's wail was like the winter winds that howl through White World's ice. She pushed me down, tail slapping as she tried to bolster me beneath her bulk.

A crack of thunder split the sky. I felt her jolt and heard a grunt. Read her shock before she rolled. Time crawled, so slow I heard the water shift as blood bloomed from her broad black back.

I was flummoxed by the pain and desperation flooding

off her. Circled, calling, crying, as the sea stained red. I nudged her, stroked her, pressed my flippers to her flesh. *Go,* she groaned. *Leave me now.* But I could not.

So rising from her pain she fought, lob-tailing with the full force of her fluke before she shot skywards to confront this flying foe. Mid breach, the thunder struck again. It tore into her lower jaw. Smashed bone and flesh right down her throat.

The ship was nearly on us now. *Mother, come. Mother, please.* I nuzzled, seeking comfort, but no milk came forth. Instead, I felt the terror as her pain-filled heart pumped out her life.

Tell them, warn them. Go.

As if this plea stole her last leaking air, I felt her shock as something detonated deep inside. She shuddered once. Her heartbeat stopped. The very motion of the sea stopped too.

I couldn't understand her silence. Couldn't grasp the void. I circled, prodding, pleading, when she failed to answer back. I lost all track of time.

I hid beneath my mother's blood shroud as the flying fiend descended to the ship. The Hungry Ones fired hooks into her flesh and hauled her up its shell-encrusted side. Blood sweated from her skin. Red against white. Crimson against black.

They hung her by her tail, her shattered face lapped by the swell. She looked so small. Reduced. One thrust a blade in her and heaved on it, stiff-armed, the tool splitting her belly open, fore to aft. All the workings of her bundled out.

Ah . . . Forgive me. I had wished for my last song to be as calm as those of the wise Chronicles who came before

— I have told it many times without this hurting heart, shared all my secrets — but this day the memory bobs around me like a bloated corpse. Grief never leaves. Nor pain. Nor the licking loneliness of loss. They only ever limp towards accommodation.

And so you see me as I truly am: an ancient ailing bag of wretchedness and thorny love still pricked by anger and regrets. I am the unwise wise one tasked with passing on my past. Life flees as fast as foam upon a windswept wave.

Be still. Bear with me, travellers. These are the wanderings of a dying mind . . .

After the ship had fled, I drifted in a nightmare world of windborne tricks: I'd hear my mother call, and race towards the sound, only to find nothing, no one in the formless sea. Time and time again those taunts would snare me. Time and time again I ended up alone, and wished the Hungry Ones would take me too. But on the fourth day I sensed land, and I was torn between two tides of thought: the urge to hide did battle with the need to rest with something solid at my back. Rest won.

The sun rose to full force as I passed landforms skinned with grass and trees. Between the leaves, small buildings blinked. I hugged the coast and wished this world was fashioned from a pressing of warm bodies; I craved my mother and my clan. I could not eat. Each time I tried to swallow, my mother's death swelled in my throat. Sluggishness stalked me now.

I rounded still another spit of land and thought those teasing trickster winds were back.

I heard a song. It soared — tuneful and fully voiced — a sweeping, airborne song that steeped into my skin. Its bleakness spoke to me. Its grief akin to mine.

Drawn by a need I had no strength to fight I slipped into a sheltered bay. Lush trees lined rocky outcrops; a stony beach lay to one side. The sunlight licked the leaves deep coral-gold. I edged around a shingle bank, the unknown song enthralling as I rose for air.

That's when I saw the boy.

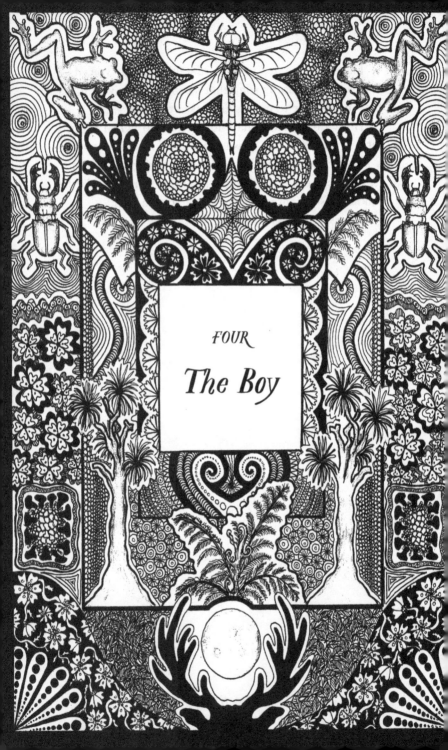

FOUR

The Boy

Will trundled the old Z-class yacht down to the slipway and rigged it up. Six weeks of daily practice (thanks to Dean's expert tutoring) had cured his greenhorn fumblings, and he pushed off now and jumped aboard, sliding in the centreboard as soon as he cleared the mud. He guided it out into the channel between the mudflats without a hitch. Sailing was one of the few times since he'd moved here that he felt in control. He loved the tug-of-war with the sail as he worked the sheet rope, and the slap of water as it hit the sailing dinghy's prow.

By the time he'd cleared the bay, his nausea was easing. He stretched his spindly legs; leaned back and drew in a deep breath. *Get a grip.* Maybe Gabby wouldn't talk. Though, how'd she even found the clip? And who else knew? Could Dean have told? It was all so incestuous down here: Dean working for Bruce Godsill, Gabby being Bruce's niece — hell, half the town were interbred.

He stewed over this as he tacked his way up the main channel of the Sound, setting his course for the salmon farm near Franklin's Cove. Twenty-five minutes later he pulled up alongside the main pontoon, brandishing the bag of sandwiches his uncle had left behind.

'Special delivery for Dean,' he said to Hunter Godsill, the boss's sullen son, who caught hold of the bow of the Zeddie to hold the yacht in place.

'Deano!' Hunter roared, ignoring the proffered bag. 'Your lunch is here.'

Dean emerged from the crate-like shed, grinning as he walked over. 'Thanks, mate. You get your schoolwork sent off?'

'Yeah.' Will eyed Hunter, who didn't seem to take the hint to move away. People round here talked as if the guy was thick — and there was no denying that he looked it. Big hands. Big head. And wing-commander ears. The awful haircut didn't help: it looked as if he'd been attacked with hedge clippers.

As Dean reached down to take his lunch, Will murmured in his ear: 'Gabby Taylor's seen the video.'

Dean nodded, clearly not at all surprised. 'Yeah, Bruce said.' Pity lurked behind his eyes.

'You knew?' The betrayal stung. 'Why the hell didn't you warn me?'

Dean shrugged, lowering his voice as Hunter watched with a disconcertingly blank gaze. 'What good would that do, mate? As it is, you hardly leave the house.'

'Not true! I come out here. I sail every—'

'Listen, Will. Running away—'

'How can you say that when you know what happened?'

Dean straightened up and rubbed his hand across the back of his neck. 'Let's talk about this tonight, eh?

Meantime, how about you concentrate on catching us a decent cod for tea?'

Will merely grunted as he pushed the Zeddie off the pontoon.

'See ya,' Hunter Godsill called. He waved his giant hand and blushed as red as lethal sunburn. Will nodded back.

He drove the yacht hard into the wind, tacking tight to outrun the anger pulsing in his head. He had to let such feelings out, that's what the counsellor told him, or else the headaches would continue to drive him nuts. *You need to avoid stress,* she'd said, as if the calls for Will to top himself, to 'rid the world of freakish losers', were in his head alone. What he needed was anonymity. A safe place where he could let go all the hurt. And he thought he'd found it, too — exiled down here, away from everyone he knew — but if Gabby lived up to her name, he was screwed.

He sailed out towards the head of the Sound, a further hour's zigzag past the other salmon farms and baches, the exclusive private lodges and the run-down farms. The place was beautiful, no doubt of that; drowned river valleys formed after the last big ice age, with steeply wooded hills between the fertile strips of land. A tourist mecca, though the only people rich enough to stay and not merely pass through these days were all from overseas. Meanwhile the locals (with the exception of bosses like Bruce Godsill) were feeling the recession hard.

Will knew all about *that*. One moment his life was all happy families in the capital city up north, wanting for nothing, performing in shows at school and hanging out with a great group of friends; next thing his parents lost their public-service jobs — austerity to 'help' the banks — and they'd had to rent their house out just to keep afloat.

It might've been all right if they'd both found new jobs. But when neither had any luck they'd ended up staying with friends, not even able to rent some rat-shit dump or they'd default on the mortgage for their own house.

This is what those pricks who thought they knew him from the YouTube clip just didn't get: he could've won — could've eased his parents' problems and they'd not have ended up slogging it out, helping shift truck-loads of toxic waste from Aussie's Ranger Mine. Goddamn, he missed his mother's reassuring smile, his father's try-hard jokes.

Coming here was meant to be a break from all the flak after the clip had aired. He'd been amazed what pleasure people took in watching others fail. Over and over, millions of hits. Good old social media. Pretty damn anti-social, when the chips were down.

It was his own fault. He'd signed up on the day the producers announced the try-outs. *A Star Is Born.* Nice irony, in the light of what came next. He'd lapped it up when people said he should apply. Had hoped it was his first step on the road to fame — and, better, that the hundred grand would save the house.

All this because he had a crazy inbuilt urge to sing. Perfect pitch by three — and once puberty had done its worst he grew into a clear full-bodied tenor voice.

The thrill — the sense of utter calm — that overtook him when he sang was almost indescribable. All he had to do was open up his mouth and breathe. He loved opera, always had, since he was small, loved pure emotion synthesised through sound, though not so much the cheesy plots, which were the musical equivalents of daytime soaps. It was the music that he loved. He wanted to be part of it — the sounds, the drama, the feeling of elation and control when he stepped onto the stage — not trapped here like a head-case with a bunch of small-town hicks.

At Brookes Bay he lowered the sail, eyeing the gnarly trees and wind-frayed ferns that lined the rocky shore. He dropped the anchor on the leeside of a shingle bank and baited a hook with scraps of octopus still chilly from Dean's freezer. Cast the line and wedged it through a cleat, then stood balanced in the centre of the yacht and closed his eyes. The lapping water beat a rhythm; birdsong tuned his ear. He filled his diaphragm, ribs stretched wide. Drew the air low into his belly until it pressed against his spine. Now he opened his mouth and released a steady flow, feeling the first note reverberate through his skull. *Ah, home.*

With eyes fixed on the sunlit hills he sang his doomed audition piece from *La Bohème*. '*Che gelida manina! Se la lasci riscaldar . . .*' All the hurt poured out of him: his parents' forced eviction, their departure overseas, the YouTube clip, the headaches, anger, paranoia, the sad farewell to all his friends . . . Weeks and weeks of humiliation wrapping the bay in heartfelt song.

He was halfway through the second verse when something moved. He turned just as a dorsal fin slipped beneath the yacht.

Will lurched backwards, his foot caught in the sheet rope. Stumbled, a comic-book pratfall of flailing limbs as he scrabbled to regain his balance. Instead, the rocking yacht pitched him straight overboard. As he resurfaced, something brushed past his thigh. He lunged upwards and vaulted the gunwale, all the time expecting the whomp of jaws connecting with his skin, his bones.

That was way too close. He raised himself and peered over the side to see how big a shark it was. A head burst from the water, rounded, soft lined, black and white. *Holy shit!*

It was an orca, a young one, bobbing right in front of him, mewing like a baby in need of milk. Its body mass was not much bigger than a full-grown dolphin. Its mouth, which curled up at the edges, looked for all the world like it was smiling — and that smile served to split the border between black and white. Black above, over its blowhole to its slightly cock-eyed dorsal fin, a yellow-tinged white below, and white-on-black in two neat patches just behind its eyes. Those eyes: they studied him with such intensity, emitted such a desperate loneliness, they drew Will close.

They were like no other eyes he'd ever seen; their oily coating glistened as it held his gaze. The shifting liquids changed the colour of its pupil, a subtle kaleidoscope, one moment blue, the next a brownish grey. Longing and sadness lingered there. He dragged his gaze away and scoured the bay and open water for the rest of its pod. The seascape was deserted.

'Where's your mum?'

It dipped its head to one side, holding his gaze, and nudged closer. Its reply — almost a whistle — formed a melodic cavatina. Will sang the notes back to it but it slid under the water. Disappeared. He cursed himself for frightening it, then heard a splash behind him and spun around. The little orca exposed sharp baby teeth and shrilled again.

Will pitched across the deck, echoing the orca's call, and it lifted itself high enough to rest its head on the side of the hull. Before he even thought it through, Will reached over and rubbed its rounded rostrum. The skin was pleasantly warm and lush. He held its searching gaze and ran his hand towards the blowhole further back. Stroked it, fondling its alien skin.

He crooned, the kind of voice his mum would use to reassure a flighty kid. 'What's happened to your family?'

It bunted at his arm and squeaked. He laughed and it quivered as if laughing back.

Behind Will, the fishing line clattered. 'You stay there.' He reeled it in as fast as he was able, singing something from last year's school production to distract the whale from the struggling fish. '*A wandering minstrel I — A thing of shreds and patches, Of ballads, songs and snatches . . .*' The words had never seemed more apt.

He landed the fish, a good-sized cod, before the orca twigged. Slammed it on the deck like Dean had shown him, stunning it before he killed it with a quick jab in the head. Next, Will dislodged the hook, all the time still singing under the orca's watchful eye. It seemed the most natural thing to offer the cod, which he dangled by its tail over the side of the yacht.

The orca nosed up to the fresh fish and Will released it into the whale's open mouth. The fish flashed silver against the baby pink of its wide serrated tongue before it swallowed the cod down.

'There you go, mate, a tiny offering.'

It rolled onto its back, lounging beside him with its pale belly skyward. He could feel the need radiating off it, like a puppy angling for a scratch. He leaned right out and ran his hand along its strip of white. The little creature blew bubbles, squeaking like a waterlogged Donald Duck.

Will dropped his head down and blew a series of watery raspberries in return. It rolled and sprayed Will with fine mist as it exhaled.

He laughed again, amazed by its dexterity as it rose out of the water to meet him eye to eye. Its head jerked backwards as if urging Will to join it in the sea. Why not? If it was out to eat him, surely it would've made a grab for him by now? What the hell . . . it couldn't be any more dangerous than a run-in with three meth-heads on a cold dark night.

He stripped down to his boxers and slipped over the gunwale, his heart beating staccato quavers. But as the orca edged towards him — looming large, now that Will's head was all that bobbed above the surface — Will panicked. He spun around to haul himself back on board. Too late. The orca bumped against him, dense flesh velvet against his own.

He turned to face it as it bunted him again — shy, enquiring, maybe even a little scared. He held his breath as it caressed the whole length of his body with its own. It emitted little mews and clicks, as though scanning the mass of him, his shape, his human make-up. When it circled back and nudged against him on its second sweep he reached over and wrapped his arms around its meaty form.

He could feel the orca's warmth and soft surrender as it stilled beneath his stroking touch. He swallowed back a sob. It was the most amazing thing, to offer such a wild creature comfort — and to feel, oddly, like the orca gave it back. Its pectoral flipper curled around his neck just like a baby clasps its hand around a finger. That's all it was: a baby. As frightened and helpless as any toddler cast adrift — except he couldn't simply pick it up and take it home.

'What am I going to do with you?'

He could have sworn the orca sighed.

FIVE

Further In

It may seem strange I put my trust in him, a boy formed from the same species — same blood and bones — as those who stole my mother's life. These fifty-one years on, all I can say is that he filled a need. Warm flesh. Kind eyes. A sense he shared my pain.

He wrapped me in his reedy upper limbs, my hurting heart banging to the beat of his. I hoped he'd never let me go. But when we each came to a place of peace then we began to play. I flapped my fluke, he lashed his limbs. I breached to bury him beneath a spray of sea. He bunted me back to the surface like a callow calf.

When he was spent he climbed back in the tiny boat and stroked my snout, crooning, chuckling, calling sounds I did not understand. But I could feel the good-will gushing off him and it helped to ease my grief.

As the day started to dim — shadows shifting, currents cooling — he heaved aboard the heavy weight that tethered him. The boat bucked in the breathy breeze, its white wing waving as he hauled it high above his head.

All the time he called I heard the ripples of regret that threaded through his strange sad sounds. He was leaving, I could tell, and I was swept by pangs of panic so intense my insides ached.

Perhaps he sensed my great forlornness: as the boat began to pick up speed, another of his soothing songs skimmed on the air. It egged me on, delving deep into the break between the hump of hills. I took the risk of following, my muddled mind still far too tired to fight the urge. The further in, the more I felt the thrust of other thinking minds — of Hungry Ones — but fear of being so soon parted from this kindness kept me in his thrall.

Trust me, my friends, our kind were never meant to be alone.

Between the limbs of land we started passing structures sunk into the sea, with scores of salmon so hemmed in I took a closer look. It set my gut a-grumbling, so much food in such a penned-in place. But the nearer in, the more I felt the hate-cloud of the Hungry Ones, smothering my senses like storm-spread silt. It mingled with the misery of all those swarming salmon, dark as deep-sea ditches and as foreboding as the flying thing that struck my mother down.

I shied away, back to the boy, relieved to chase his calming call. The sun was sinking, shadows shifting, seabirds stirring as they sensed the nearing of the night. He led me through a channel between fallow flats of mud, into a bay where boats branched out and dwelling places poured out lightning from within.

The boy bundled in the wing and beached the boat as I hung back. He hauled it up onto the shore then swam to me to say goodbye. One last caress.

He spoke in soothing tones and pressed his strange flat face to mine. I sent a plea for him to stay but, though I sensed he understood, instead he sang — a sweet slow song, so very soothing — and then he waded from the water. Left.

I waited as the night turned dark. Could feel the Hungry Ones' thought-traces hanging in the chill night air. Their minds were still so strange to me; I could not match their blood-lust to that feeling boy. My mother said that some among our tribes were known to hunt the other Warm-bloods, single-minded, cunning, killing with no care. They merely wished to sate their guts while we, who feel our prey's panic and pain, maintain more mercy. In this the Hungry Ones are much the same. Some good. Some bad. Some scratching to survive. Back then, so filled with fear, abandoned in that inky waste-filled water, all I could think to do was call — keening for my family, and then, when no one answered, for the boy.

In truth, I thought no Being had ever suffered such a loss as me. And though I now know differently, I find no comfort in the fact my pain was shared by so, so many, over such a stretch of time. In the dreadful Days of Blood the Hungry Ones hunted us — we were bludgeoned, stabbed, exploded, drowned, defiled, cleaved in two. And they grew fat upon the killing of our kind, slaughtering on such a scale our many tribes were broken, driven to the brink. Whole families gone. Whole generations lost. My mother's death was but one drop in the ocean of our blood.

I waited, panicked, in that place, with hunger gnawing at my gut. My loneliness, my fretful fear, arose again inside, the horror of the Hungry Ones bleeding back into my bones. It drove me off, back out towards the bay where I first met the boy.

I passed the pens of salmon, the feelings of those frightened fish storming me. They knew that I was stalking them; grew fidgety. I could have broken through the barriers but, in the end, their distress drove me off. My nerves were still too shattered; my hunger no match for the memories meddling with my mind.

At last I slept, and the boy's song melded with my mother's in my moonstruck dreams. I felt so warmed I did not want to wake.

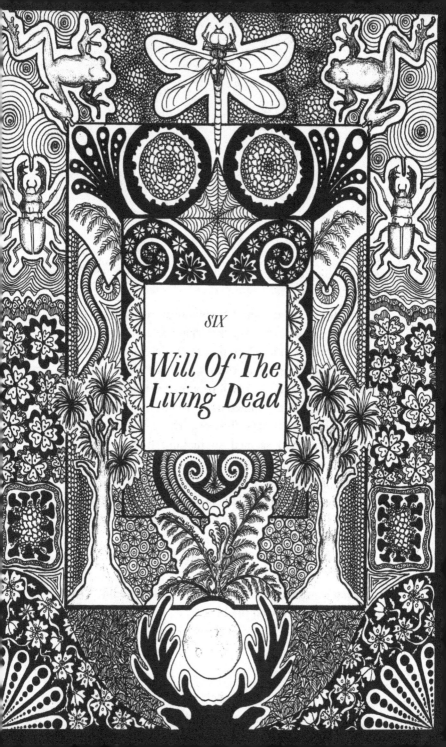

SIX

Will Of The Living Dead

Will ran up the slipway, bursting to share his news with Dean. He quickly changed into dry clothes and mopped the floor. Peered in the fridge, relieved to find a bacon pack stashed at the back. Dean would be tired and hungry, and the cod Will promised was now digesting in the orca's gut. He smiled as he went out to the chicken coop to fetch fresh eggs. The way that little orca looked into his eyes had seemed so human. It was the most uplifting experience he'd ever had — even more fulfilling than playing the male lead in *The Mikado* last year.

He shoved the cooked bacon into the warming drawer as Dean's car pulled up. Went out to greet him before he came inside.

'You have to come!' Will said. 'Now! Down by the slipway!'

Dean slammed the car door shut and locked it. 'Don't tell me you've screwed the boat?'

Will grinned. 'Come on, you're not going to believe this!'

He raced ahead of Dean, down towards the water. As Dean trailed after him, Will began to sing the Handel aria he'd crooned to the orca as he'd said goodbye.

'*Lascia ch'io pianga mia cruda sorte, e che sospiri la libertà . . .*' He loved this one, even though it was first written for a female voice. *Let me weep for my cruel fate, and sigh for liberty. May sorrow break these chains of my sufferings, for pity's sake . . .* He knew so many lyrics now they formed a constant soundtrack to his thoughts. Sometimes it drove him nuts.

'What the hell is going on?' Dean said.

'I was out at Brookes Bay and there was this little baby orca—'

'An orca?'

'Yeah, and it was all on its own and really bloody lonely. I sang to it and played with it — you wouldn't believe it, Dean, it wasn't scared of me at all. And when I sailed home it followed me.' He squinted towards the dark water, hoping for a sign.

'Jesus, you brought a frickin' orca right into the Sound?'

'I think it's been deserted. It was—'

'You'd better hope it's got more sense than you and buggered off.'

Defensiveness balled in Will's chest. 'Why?'

'Why? Christ, Will, there's a good twelve million dollars' worth of sea cages out there full of salmon, and you invite the sea's most deadly predator to play?'

Will's joy evaporated. He could hear Gabby Taylor snarl *bloody townie* in his head. 'It was abandoned, man. No more than a baby.'

'Then pray that baby pisses off before Bruce gets wind of it.'

Dean turned and trudged towards the house. His shoulders slumped, tiredness radiating off him like torpid heat. Will cast around one last time, but if the orca was still there it wasn't showing. *Damn.* Why did everything that felt so full of promise turn into a crock of shit?

He finished cooking while Dean took a shower. Placed a cold beer beside Dean's plate when he sat down to eat. They ate in silence, only the scraping of knives and forks on plates and the chewing of crisp toast to break the loaded hush.

Dean stared unwaveringly at his meal while Will studied his face. Dean shared his sister's — Will's mother's — eyes, the loamy brown of fertile soil, as did Will. They also shared the same sharp cheek bones and lank black hair, but where Dean's lips had thinned to a perpetual frown, Will had been told he had his father's mouth — that teasing elevation at the corners, as if a joke was only ever a breath away. Trouble was, these days the joke was always on him.

Only once Dean had finished eating and scraped his chair back to smoke a cigarette did he look up at Will and speak.

'Listen mate, you can't keep on freaking every time someone mentions that bloody clip. It's been a year—'

'Eight months, one week.' *And two days.*

'Whatever. You have to face the fact it's out there in the world.'

Will had to force himself not to bite back. He picked up his fork and traced a treble clef in the dregs of yolk. 'Easy for you to say.'

'I know it is. But you've been here six weeks now and you've hardly said a word to anyone. Your mother's worried—'

'She always worries. What does she know?'

Unfair, he knew, to diss his mum when she was stuck wrangling trucks in a uranium mine, but they all seemed to think he could just forget the shame and pain. *They* hadn't been labelled as a laughing stock. *They* hadn't been beaten to a pulp. The headaches and the mood swings were bad enough, thanks to those bastards fracturing his skull, but no one bothered to warn him he'd be swept by waves of hopelessness and nervous paranoia — and nausea to boot. He was a mess, he knew. Was so bloody sick of feeling vulnerable and weak. That's why the business with the orca had been such a treat. For those few short hours he'd forgotten his own misery. But now the little guy was gone it flooded back.

Dean shifted in his seat. 'Maybe it's time to see the head doctor again?'

Will sighed. 'What's the point? They'll only say to get more rest. Or go on medication.'

'If you think it'd help—'

'Forget it. So long as Gabby Taylor keeps her mouth shut, I'll be fine.'

'And what if she doesn't, mate? At some point you have to put that all behind you and get on with your life.'

'Look, if you want me to leave—'

'I'm not saying that, Will. I just hate to see you moping. It's all very well doing Correspondence to avoid the local school, but you should be out there having fun. Seeing people. Making friends.'

'Yeah, right. Who the hell can I relate to here? Hunter bloody Godsill? I bet he knows a thing or two about opera. Probably has a poster of Pavarotti hanging above his bed.'

Dean snorted smoke. 'You might be quite surprised. He's not a bad kid once you get to know him. God knows he's had a lot to put up with too.'

Will rose from the table and started clearing the dishes. Dean wasn't bad either, he just didn't understand the world outside this one-horse town. He hardly used the internet and had no clue at all about the curse of social media. Dean thought it could be ignored; that if Will didn't look then it would go away. But Will knew differently. His clip would be out there forever and he'd never live it down. Would always be the sad loser who drew a laugh.

When he'd done the dishes he retreated to his room. Logged on to the internet, unable to resist his daily ritual of checking the latest stats. The views had risen again, another sixty-three since he last checked. He resisted the urge to play it; already knew every awful detail off by heart.

The real tragedy was that the first try-out had gone so well. '*Che gelida manina*', the perfect song, a student falling for a dying girl. The judges had lapped it up, tears spilling down their cheeks by that final haunting note. A standing ovation. A definite 'yes'. They'd loved the way he looked: his tattoos, piercings, fingerless gloves, black nail polish and long black goth-inspired leather coat. Had talked to him for an extra ten minutes past his allotted time. They were excited, he could tell. He'd seen the look at other competitions where he'd won: a hungry energy. But in this case, they ate him up then spat him out.

He was such a goddamned fool to have agreed to go out with his friends the night before the first filming session. He'd let audition nerves get the better of him and sculled far too much bourbon and Coke. Had dropped his guard. Got halfway through the shortcut at the back of the old hospital and tripped over those three evil meth-heads, too drunk to get the hell away. He'd mouthed off something stupid and they took violent exception. Couldn't remember what he said, but next thing he was on the ground, robbed of wallet, phone and shoes, his leather coat slashed with a knife. One of them pinned him by the throat before the final parting shot that broke his nose and cracked his skull.

He should've gone straight to the hospital. Called off the audition and waited for the swelling to go down. But he was desperate. Concussed. Hid from his parents and turned up to the filming the next day looking like he'd walked out of a zombie flick, still half-cut and dazed from the crack to his head. They'd tried to send him home, but he'd insisted on singing as they escorted him towards the door. He sounded like a geriatric yodeller with a dose of flu. Goodbye stardom, hello YouTube out-takes. Some prick had filmed the whole sorry performance on their phone. They dubbed the clip '*Will of the Living Dead*' and he'd often wished he *was* dead; it would've pleased the jerks who taunted him online. Of course it was an instant hit. And every time his parents' lawyer hassled someone to take it down, it popped up somewhere else. With money so short, he had no choice but leave it be — and stew.

Old history. Dean was right: he somehow had to shake it off. The trouble was, the bumps and bruises may have faded but the nausea still screwed his gut. And the doctors said it could take years before his head came right.

He spent an hour browsing through clips and photo-graphs of orcas, listening to the different sounds and finding out their purposes: pulsed calls for recognition and coordination of their groups, whistles that they mainly used when in the company of their clan, clicks and squeaks for echolocation . . . What amazed him was the discovery that each group had its distinct dialect, a repertoire of calls that pods could identify as their own. And, while no one came out straight and said the whales had a shared language, it seemed their soundings were so complex and mysterious that it was hard to argue otherwise. That had to mean that if they shared a universal language and regional dialects, they had a brain at least as complex as his own.

At ten-thirty the day's excitement finally caught up with him, the words blurring and shifting as his eyelids drooped. He shut down the computer and stretched out on his bed, conjuring up the encounter with the orca as he felt himself pulled into sleep. He dreamed of an enormous pod swimming in through his window, lifting him, nudging up against him with their dense warm flesh. He sang '*Vesti la giubba*', dressed like the clown he was, and they accompanied him with their haunting harmonies. *Put on your costume, and powder your face. The people pay to be here, and they want to laugh . . .*

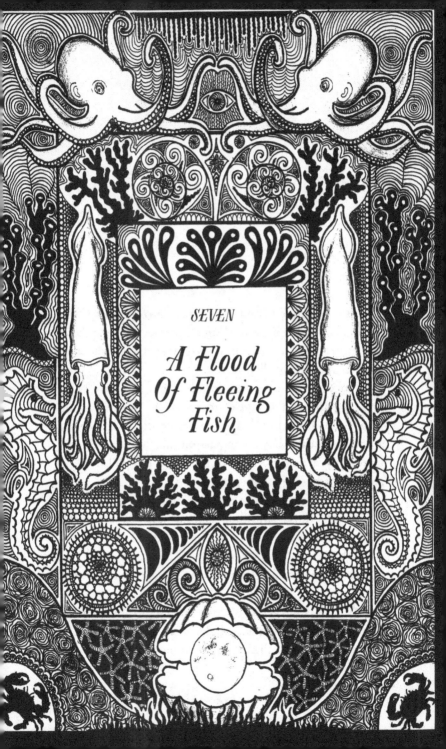

SEVEN

A Flood
Of Fleeing
Fish

As I descended from my dreams into the soft silver of early dawn, panic drummed inside. Gulls stalked the shore, shrieked shanties as they skewered shellfish from the flotsam at their feet.

Hunger nagged me now, the bawling from my belly breaking through my grief to goad me on. I did not want to feed, yet I no longer wished to die — there was a comfort in the boy's compassion and he'd sensed my youthful yearning for a fill of fun. I felt the pull to play, an untamed energy that egged me on.

I left the shelter of the shingle bank where I had slept, and sought those swarming salmon out. I nosed up to the weir that barred my way, but could not catch them through the cracks. Beyond, the fish fought to escape me. I slipped beneath to try to snatch them from below. I ached to eat.

My teeth could get no traction on that threaded thatch, and so I bunted, butted, bludgeoned, until the barrier broke. I backed off then, sank down into the sludge, and waited for the salmon to swim out. They teemed, a flood of fleeing fish, no match for my sharp-tipped teeth. But the festering that flooded off them — pricked by parasites, stressed and poxed — put me off.

Instead I played — corralling, chasing, catching them, then spitting them back out to start the game again. The gulls soon swarmed right over us, their cries recalling the brawl over my mother's meat. I fled.

As I caught cleaner cod out in the centre of the channel I sensed a ship. I swerved, and slipped into a sheltered cove. Two tiny waifs waded there, reedy voices ringing in the arrested air. I scanned the feelings flowing off them, found a softness like the singing boy's.

I edged as close as I could chance, and stretched up to show myself. They shrieked and stumbled from the sea, limbs flailing, faces flushed with fear; I'd yet to learn the Hungry Ones might mistrust me too. They teetered on the tide-line. Threw a wedge of wood to ward me off. I scooped it up and shot it back. They tossed it out and I returned it, time and time again, until their worry waned.

I sang, then, for them to swim with me, but at that moment a maddened man burst from the bush. He bellowed, breaking up our back and forth, and tugged those two small souls further up the shore. I slipped beneath the swell and sank, blowing bubbles, basking on the seabed amid the anxious fish.

Eventually I nosed back north, returning to the place where I had spent my nights. There was the boy! His voice was bouncing on the breeze, long notes and lengthy runs pouring from his frail frame. I breached to tell him I was there, and sped over to share my sounds.

For those whose daily thoughts are dull, they fail to

follow our most splendid songs — while we, who marvel at the many melded webs within our minds, are filled with thankfulness. We think, we feel, we love, we sing. It is our way.

And, so, to sing with one who walked the world, and feel the sharing of his spirit through his sounds, hooked my heart. Our calls collided, music mingled, two tongues tried to make us one. The wind whispered our wanting; the seaweed swayed along in time. I felt a fondness fix in me. A thankfulness. I may have lost my mother and my family, but now I strongly sensed that I had found a friend.

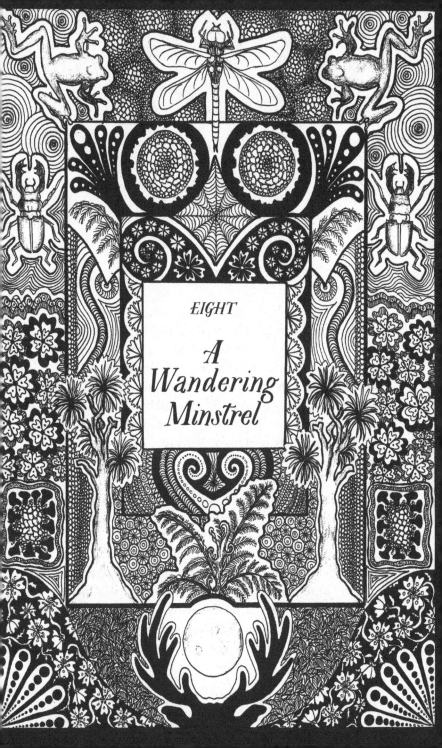

EIGHT

A Wandering Minstrel

Will was halfway through his song when the orca showed itself. His heart clattered as the little creature rushed over and flipped onto its back. Its gaze met Will's and held it as he kept on singing. Soon the orca's tuneful calls began to weave into his own.

The sound was doleful, like the gibbons who called across the valley every morning, voices rising from the city zoo near where he'd lived. And pure, a ringing crystal glass rubbed round its rim. All the hairs on Will's arms and neck sat up.

He closed his eyes, his voice ascending through bone and skin to meet the orca's in the late morning air. Tears pricked his eyes. Music did this to him every time. It tapped into the part of him that was hard to articulate. The side he tried to hide, for fear of being ostracised. *Poofter. Bum bandit. Knob jockey. Fag.* The comments on YouTube left him in no doubt of what they thought — and, though he had no problem with gays (had several close friends that way inclined), he resented being labelled one merely because he'd cried. But that was then — not anymore. He'd rather die than be sprung for blubbing again. Yet here he was, right now, tears spilling down his cheeks just like his mother when she watched a soppy film. Pathetic.

He squatted down to greet the orca face to face. It rolled, not breaking its accompaniment, and bumped its snout against Will's outstretched hand.

'Hey, you.'

The orca sprayed him with fine mist, emitting the little creaking sounds that he knew, from last night's web search, were for echolocation. Was it trying to read him? If only the bastards who'd judged him for his failure had bothered trying that, instead of writing off his life.

'What'm I going to call you?'

Beneath his hand the orca squealed, a girly giggle like *The Mikado*'s Three Little Maids'. He'd played the hero, Nanki-Poo, the wandering minstrel out to win sweet Yum-Yum's heart. Such stupid names. And yet . . .

'What about Minstrel, eh?' The orca's noise continued unabated. 'Or maybe Minor?' It *was* the relative key that underscored virtually all its sounds. 'Nah. Too obscure. Though Min's okay. What if I call you Min?' He liked the associations that came with this; it conjured up old black jazz singers in smoky bars. Little Min. Big Mo. *Will of the Living Dead*.

The orca seemed to grin, revealing spiky teeth. It nosed up to a dangling rope and took it up as tenderly as a mother cat carries her young. Floated backwards, feeding out the line.

Will scrabbled for the rope and gently tugged. Min squealed again and yanked a little harder in return. The

Zeddie swung around as they played tug-of-war, Will's laughter and Min's caterwauling chiming off the bush-clad hills.

When the game grew stale Will ditched the rope. He stripped down to his boxers and jumped into the sea. Before he'd even cleared his eyes Min was right there, brushing along him, blowing a series of noisy bubbles as Will studied its markings to figure out its sex. One of the pages he'd read online showed mammary slits, but nothing broke the velvet smoothness of its abdomen.

'So you're a boy?' He reached for Min's flipper and shook it like a hand, surprised to feel the knobs of bone within. 'How do you do, sir! I am Will!'

Min gurgled like a drain and dived, resurfacing right under Will. He joggled Will onto his back, Will clutching the slippery dorsal fin, fair crapping himself. He had flashes of *Whale Rider* as he was piggybacked around the bay, whooping his joy. Beneath him, Min's firm fat body swayed. For such a little guy he had surprising speed and strength.

Will burst out with the first thing that popped in his head. *'Away, away! My heart's on fire!'* He wished his mum and dad were here! It was his mum who'd stoked his musical theatre addiction. She'd played Gilbert and Sullivan endlessly since he was small. He'd even taken a CD with his favourite *Pirates of Penzance* song 'Tarantara! Tarantara!' to primary school for his morning talk. His mates were not impressed — to put it mildly. He'd soon learnt to keep it quiet — and, later, to shut up about serious opera as well. They reckoned it was for old fogies. And, anyway, most people thought music was a product, not an art. Only in Year 11 did he find a few like-minded friends — but they were all back home, too busy now, it seemed, to keep in touch with a screwed-up recluse like him.

After nearly two circuits, Will slid off beside the yacht. He floated on his back until Min came to rest beside him, and then flapped his feet. Min flapped his tail, so Will replied by slapping at the water with his hands. Right away Min aped him with his flippers. It was incredible. Surreal. Will folded at the waist and sank. Lightning quick, Min slipped below the water to blow a giant raspberry. Will shot back to the surface, laughing so hard-out he choked. Meanwhile, his small fat friend sounded like a strangled duck. The little sod was mocking him!

Will hauled himself aboard the Zeddie and wrung the water from his ponytail, stiffening when a movement up on shore drew his eye. Three hikers lingered by the bush, phones in hand.

He turned his back, elation souring. Min was *his* secret. He didn't want to share him with the haters of the world. He dredged up the anchor. Whistled a high B flat, the note closest to Min's default cry. Immediately Min answered back.

Will set the sail and urged the Zeddie out to sea, one hand on the tiller as he wrestled clothes over dripping skin. Ahead, Min kept perfect pace. As they approached the headland Will glanced back. The hikers had advanced down to the shore, phones aloft as if they were filming. *Goddamn.* Privacy meant *nothing*, not now every arsehole had a camera on his phone.

Beside him Min bounced through the water peeling off the bow as sunlight splintered all around. He was so at one with his world Will felt a pang of jealousy. *He* was the fish out of water here, always off-side, gut screwing up when someone even looked at him.

He never used to be like this. When he was young his parents gave him unconditional love. He used to sing his heart out, even as a little kid, at the supermarket, on the way to school, in the car . . . The world felt safe and reassuring with his parents always there to cheer him on. Of course, they *did* still love him, but the distance made it feel like they were dead. Even when he Skyped them or his friends it didn't feel real. And right now it felt as if he'd washed up in a weird new dimension . . . here, in a yacht, out at sea — romping with a singing orca! Maybe he *was* crazy after all.

The yacht had reached the channel now. To the south the mail boat ploughed up the Sound. Will back-winded the sail and threw the tiller over hard until the yacht hove to. Min bobbed up next to him, head listing.

'You need to skedaddle, mate.' Though he'd ignored Dean's parting shot this morning to 'stay the hell away from that black fish', Will also figured Dean was right. If Bruce Godsill got wind of Min then things could easily turn to shit.

But Min was performing again, back-flipping and tail-slapping like the show-off kid Will once had been. He had no idea how to return to Blythe without Min following. It wasn't like he was a dog that could be told to 'stay'.

He leaned over the gunwale and slapped his fist down in the drink. Min swivelled mid-breach and smashed down next to the yacht, completely soaking Will. *Damn.* Min thought it was a game. What the hell to do? He could try to scare him — drive him off — but that was cruel. Min was a baby. He had no one else.

But first things first: the mail boat was gaining on them fast. Will eased the tiller off and tacked out of its path, hoping Min would trail along without creating too much splash. As if. Min was clearly out for fun, racing on ahead then breaching before doubling back. The boat drew nearer, shifting from its normal course, heading straight for Will.

The boat, an aluminium launch, powered down and slowed until it idled a few short metres from the yacht. A crowd of tourists gathered at its rail, chattering and pointing as Min continued with his tricks.

Will tacked again to draw Min off, but the orca was spy-hopping, vertical in the water with his head right out. Cameras clicked. Hands reached. When someone's cap blew in the sea Min scooped it onto his nose and tossed it in the air to rapturous applause. Will groaned. His lonely mate had turned into a circus performer overnight.

He slipped away, chickening out of trying to lure Min with a song. If Min had cast his lot in with the tourists then Will could only hope they wouldn't do him harm. His chest ached like the key to happiness had slipped between his hands.

When he neared the salmon farm at Whitlaw's Bay, he saw Dean standing on the pontoon at the cage's edge. This wasn't where Dean usually worked. Will changed his tack and cruised over.

'Dean!' he called. 'Hey man. Wassup?'

Dean's jaw was tight. 'It looks like your little mate came visiting last night.'

Fate punched Will in the gut. 'What?' Beyond Dean's livid face the salmon cage was empty.

'I told you that thing would do no good. There's a metre-long tear in the mesh.'

'That doesn't mean he did it. It could just be a co-incidence.'

'Big bloody coincidence.'

Bruce Godsill stormed up the pontoon. *Oh great.* 'You've found the tear?' His tone was sharp. Discordant.

Dean glanced at Will then looked away. 'Yeah. Hunter's had a scout around — we can probably net a few but most are gone.'

'Put everyone on overnight shifts. If there's a greenie on the rampage I want them hung.' He thundered back towards his boat, snapping out instructions to the other workers as he passed.

'Is it still around?' Dean shot at Will.

Will shrugged. As soon as *The Daily Mail* returned, the whole damn town would know. 'He's putting on a free show for the mail boat just off Buckley's Head.'

'Perfect. Now we'll have bloody Fisheries sticking their nose in as well.' Dean kneaded at the worry lines on his forehead. 'Best you get the hell home, boy. When Bruce finds out he's going to blow.'

'Look, Dean, I didn't mean—'

'Yeah, yeah.' He swatted the air between them. 'Go on, bugger off.' Dean kicked the Zeddie away and turned his back, scratching his head as he stared down at the empty cage.

~

WILL STOWED THE BOAT AND set to work weeding the garden. It was Dean's pride and joy — what he lacked in housework skills he made up for here — they never had to buy in extra veggies and the fruit trees produced bumper crops. He worked his way along the potatoes, then threw the weeds in for the chickens and set to work thinning carrots and spring onions for brownie points. Though even weeding couldn't take away the fact he'd be in knee-deep shit if Dean let slip. He felt stupid. Naive. Did he really think Min would ignore those poor imprisoned fish?

God, he wished he could speak to his mum; she was the only one who'd understand. She'd taught him not to walk away when someone — something — needed help. And he bet she'd do the same if she'd found Min. Anyway, how the hell was Min to know the salmon were farmed? Not that Will would eat them, even if he had the chance. He'd read enough about the crap they fed those frankenfish — but they were Dean's livelihood and, with his parents' wages funnelled straight into two mortgages, now Dean's livelihood was his as well. *Ka-boom.*

An hour later, Will stretched his back. He picked basil, courgettes and ripe tomatoes to make a pasta sauce. He owed his cooking skills to his mum as well. Dean was always mellower once he'd had a decent feed.

But the clock still seemed to crawl. Will tried to get a head start on his next history assignment — something about the Treaty of Versailles — but until the bag came back from the Correspondence School with the course booklets there was stuff-all he could do. Besides, his mind kept sliding back to Min — and Bruce Godsill. He flicked back to Google and searched out orca sites.

It was hard to reconcile the term 'killer whale' with Min, although the other name he found, 'wolves of the sea', he kind of liked. It seemed they lived in family groups, ruled by the females of the line — some staying with their mother for their entire life. So what had happened to Min's mum? His pod? There were stories of other orphaned orcas around the world, most of the poor little things killed by boats or rounded up and put in tanks. It sickened him. And clearly didn't do the orcas any good: from what he could make out, the only times they'd ever attacked a human was in captivity — and who could blame them? Some tanks were so small the orcas could hardly move.

At five-forty-five Dean finally came home. He grunted once and locked himself into the bathroom. Will's nerves were so on edge he barely registered the first few items on the TV news. He was picking at his thumbnail when the presenter said, '*It was all smiles today in Pelorus Sound, when passengers on the local mail boat were treated to a close encounter with a small orca . . .*' There was Min, performing for the cameras like SeaWorld's Shamu.

Behind him Dean snorted. 'Smiles?'

Will nearly wet himself. How long had Dean been standing there?

'. . . *It seems the little visitor has already made at least one friend. Ron Allison, who's with a party walking the Pelorus Track, sent in these mobile images, shot earlier . . .*'

Will's heart thudded. *Please god, no.* But there he was, frolicking with Min, half naked. The only consolation was that the footage had been shot from so far back Will's features were blurred.

'Jesus spare me!' Dean slapped his forehead. 'I thought I told you to keep the hell away? Bruce will go ballistic when he sees this. Shit!'

'He'll never guess it's me. The picture's—'

'Oh for Christ's sake, Will, there's my bloody boat. *Everyone* will know it's you.'

Will swallowed back a rising lump. *Bloody small towns.* He was still scrabbling for a new line of defence when the next bomb dropped.

'. . . *Fisheries spokesman for the Pelorus Sound area, Marine Mammal Officer Harley Andrews, spoke to us earlier . . .*' A middle-aged bald guy sporting an unruly moustache filled the screen. '*It is against the law for anyone to approach a whale in the water at a distance less than 100 metres . . .*' Will's washing-machine stomach cycled to spin. '*. . . nor a vessel approach within 50 metres, unless authorised by the Director-General. Anyone not complying with this regulation is liable for a fine of up to ten thousand dollars for each offence . . .*'

There was more, but Will couldn't take it in. *Twenty grand for comforting an abandoned baby?* He was still trying to shake this number from his head when the phone rang. He glanced over at Dean, who rolled his eyes before picking up.

'Yeah, what?'

Will watched Dean's face. The lines between his eyes puckered then set into his usual Shar Pei frown. The voice on the other end was so loud it buzzed through the room.

'I know, boss. I already—' He stopped as the voice railed on. 'Yeah, okay, okay. But you have to—' Another barrage came down the phone. 'Yeah, gotcha. Right.' He slammed it down. Turned on his heel to confront Will.

'No prizes for guessing who *that* was.'

'Does he know it's me?' The words could barely make it past the barbed wire in his throat.

'Does a bear shit in the woods?' Dean collapsed into

his favourite chair. 'He's gonna dob you in to Harley. Says that if we have more damage he's gonna hold you personally responsible.'

'But that's not fair! I can't be held responsible for what Min does. He's wild.'

'Min? You've even fucking named it?' The incredulity on Dean's face sent heat swarming up Will's neck. Dean blew out a slow jerky breath. 'You're not in bloody Guatemala now, Dr Ropata.'

The old *Shortland Street* line, one of his father's overused jokes, shocked Will into a tentative smile, even if it was Dean's way of calling him a townie. 'What happens when I can't pay?' *That* would turn into another nightmare fast.

'Harley's not going to do anything, mate. He's a pretty reasonable guy — well, for now. We went to school together. He owes me big-time for some information way back when. But you'd better keep the hell away. So far as Fisheries is concerned there's a "wall" that has to be maintained. Ask the Whale Watch guys at Kaikoura; they've been doing a balancing act around the protocols for years.'

'But what about — the orca?'

'Forget it, mate. Hopefully it'll bugger off before it's KOed by a boat prop — or someone shoots it on a cold dark night.'

'But that's ridiculous! It's all alone! They have the same life span as human beings — it's like he's barely out of nappies.'

'Fuck's sake, Will. It's a goddamned fish!' Dean scooped up the remote and changed the channel. 'I don't make the rules, just try my best to live by them — and you should too.' He turned up the sound. A clear full stop.

For the next two hours Will sat there, staring at the action on the TV screen, but took in nothing. His mind churned over all the stories he'd read online. If Min hung around, he'd end up dead, no argument with Dean on that. But how the hell could they force Min to go? *That* question did his head in.

Eventually he washed the dishes, just to do something, then went to bed. His book — an airport thriller of Dean's — was so ridiculous it didn't matter that he couldn't properly take it in. At ten he finally turned off the light. He lay there in the dark and listened to Dean's snoring rumble through the house — a nasal E breath in; a rolling lip-percussion out. And once he'd noticed this, his brain could not help trying to hum along. He had to get out of there. Walk off his frustration.

He snuck out the back door and walked down to the slipway where he'd sung to Min the night before. The moon lit up the ripples on the water as the tide came in, the sea's steady in-and-out a background chorus to the night noises: the distant buzz of television sets, the slamming of a door, a souped-up car doing burn-outs somewhere over near the park, two barking dogs. He scooped up a handful of pebbles from the high-tide line and skimmed them out into the channel.

As his eyes adjusted he noticed the ripples were being stirred up by a dorsal fin. Min eased between the channel markers, the white patches behind his eyes glowing as he made his way towards the slip. He was calling, sounding desperate, and Will sent forth one tiny answering whistle back. Min's head popped up, as though to verify it was Will. He splashed his tail, the noise loud in the night, and squealed in return.

Despite himself, Will's spirits rose. He watched as Min approached; heard Dean's lecture resounding in his head: *forget it, mate* — as if Min could be ignored. He kicked off his shoes and started rolling up his jeans. He'd just wade out and say goodnight, surely that couldn't hurt?

A voice shot from the darkness. 'Thought it was you!'

He jumped a mile as Gabby Taylor and two friends emerged from bushes near the walkway. Her cigarette trailed noxious smoke. He shrugged and turned to leave, praying they hadn't noticed Min.

'My uncle's really pissed off with you.' Gabby placed herself between Will and his escape route. 'He says you bloody townies should be driven out.'

A skinny blonde girl chortled while the other, dark-skinned, maybe Māori, stood silent, arms crossed, guarded, staring like he was a specimen in a jar. Out in the water Min exhaled spume. All three girls spun around, mouths gaping as Min spy-hopped and cried out. His need, his loneliness, spiked at Will's heart.

'You gonna get your kit off again?' Gabby snorted smoke as Will silently begged the darkness to mask his raging blush.

He pushed past her, hating to desert Min. His heart was thrumming, sweat prickling his temples, the smell of her cigarette summoning unwanted flashes of that other night. The clink of bottles as they came at him. The mad-eyed fury when he foolishly mouthed off. He could hear the schlick of the knife as it tore right through his coat, grazing his skin. Could almost taste the blood. Behind him Min continued calling over the girls' rough laughter.

He raced up the unlit road, sure he heard those meth-heads running up behind. He glanced around. Had to.

Jesus! There *was* a figure charging after him. He picked up speed, cursing his stupidity for leaving his shoes.

'Hey wait!' It was a girl's voice, but not the drawl of Gabby Taylor.

Will forced himself to stop. He stood stock still, breathing hard as she caught up. It was the darker girl, clasping his shoes in her hand.

'You left these.' She thrust the trainers at him. Her voice was low, perhaps the G below middle C. Melodic. Nice.

'Thanks.' He took the shoes from her. Turned to leave.

'What was it like?' she said.

He swung back around. 'Pardon?'

'Te kera wēra. The little whale. What was it like to swim with it?' Her head hung low, as if she didn't want to meet his eye.

'Amazing,' he conceded. 'He's so smart.'

'My nanny says it's the return of our māhuri tōtara — my brother Kingi. He passed away in Afghanistan last year.' She glanced up for a moment and the moonlight's cool silver cast her pain quite clearly.

'Maybe,' he said, not sure how to respond. 'I don't know. But I'm pretty sure he's a boy.' He'd heard about her brother's death — Dean reckoned they were related to her family in some way. Turned out the guy had been killed in what the army had called 'friendly' fire. Sick irony. The whole town had been in mourning for months, Dean said.

'Do you think—'

'Pania!' Gabby Taylor's voice split the night, harsh as a gull. 'We're going now!'

The girl, Pania, shuddered and wrapped her arms

around herself. 'I'd better go.' She walked towards the slip.

'Hey!' Will waited until she looked back over her shoulder. 'I'm really sorry about your brother.'

'Thanks.' She sniffed. 'Did you know we're second cousins?'

'We are?' He wasn't very clear on how that worked.

'Yeah.' She walked away, all turned in on herself. Her loss made Will's feel selfish. He'd always wished he had a sibling — now he figured the loss of one would hurt beyond belief. And then there was Min . . . To be so small and so alone; it got to him.

He stood in the empty street, the girls' babble slowly fading into the night. As soon as he was sure they'd gone, he backtracked past the slip and out onto one of the fingers where the commercial boats were moored. A down-light threw long shadows as he walked right out. Here the water was deep enough for Min to swim. He checked over his shoulder before he whistled softly. Nothing.

He lay down on the wooden planks and leaned out over the dark water. Patted its surface with his hand. Somewhere close by he heard the spitting of Min's blowhole. He whistled louder. Min emerged from the gloom like a piebald wraith.

Will reached out until his hand connected with Min's dorsal fin. He ignored his noisy chat, instead patting his back in long firm strokes. His mother used to do this when he was small and woke up crying in the night. The stroking soothed him too. He pressed his growing calm down through his fingers to quieten Min.

After an uncomfortable ten or so minutes the orca stilled. Will could no longer see the light reflecting from its eyes. It slept, floating in the oily water, connected to Will by the comfort of his hand.

He stayed until his muscles screamed for him to stop. Then, with a new sense of resolve, he stumbled off to bed.

NINÆ

Fellowship
Foundering

Young minds, my friends, they flit like lanternfish, never pausing in one place. One moment down, the next one up. From dark to light. And in those murky days my moods flip-flopped. I was either starved for solace or pulled to play.

It is sung, though it still tests me so to fathom it, that back before the landmass moved and split, there was a time our kin once strode the earth. We walked, we fed, we drank from water which was fresh. But as the planets cycled, age on age, our ties to the great ocean kept us clinging to the coast. When we, at last, forsook all living on the land, we found freedom as we floated in the ocean's outstretched arms.

But we never forgot our ache for air. Oh no, we live in a watery world while we crave the life force of our past. We yearn — *I* yearn — to take my last breath in the land's sweet light. So hear me now! I have a natural need. Do not allow me to be swallowed by a sea-bound grave. Drowning is still our deepest fear.

Ah, you wonder why I sing of this? Dear friends, through the misplaced mercy of the Hungry Ones they first showed their hoard of hidden love. We would wash ashore, seeking an airy end, and the Hungry Ones came to comfort us — caressing, chiding, calming as our spark grew slight. Whole families flung themselves forward, yoked by love to share their fate.

And yet these Hungry Ones would choke upon our chosen early end. They laved us, loved us, mourned our loss, sang soothing songs into our ears. And, when the tide returned, they shook us free and shooed us back to sea. They could not understand our urge to die as One. We would return, they'd lead us out. Death lingering. Fellowship foundering.

But we learned from this how deeply they could feel. That, just as we can choose to curb our worst, so too the Hungry Ones can call their cruelty in. Take heed of this. It is a lesson for us all. A warning and a blessing, both.

All those years ago, on my own, I thought my mother called on me — was sure I heard her — chasing me to make a choice: hide away, for fear of being felled like her, or sharpen up my skills for sensing deep inside. I had to find a way to feel when the Hungry Ones were *for* me — or against.

Into the stiff silence of an early dawn, I awoke alone. I floated off in search of play and found an unknown boy, a broad and brooding boy, whose outbound breaths misted the air as he swung a water-stream towards the sides of a big silver boat. I swam to it, showered by spray, and sent this boy a song. Shock pulsed off him, but I saw goodness in his eager eyes. I sensed a shyness too. A wary wakefulness.

He splattered me, fun flying off him as I gargled the sweet water. He splashed, I slapped. He threw the water-maker down; I took it in my teeth and soaked him in return. A great guffaw flew from his lips, a lively laugh. We played until the sun lit up the dawn-side hills.

But with the day came hordes of Hungry Ones, some among them steeped with spite. I shied away, sank in between the bobbing boats, and wallowed down below there, wishing for my friend. Water murky, seabed bleak, its skin oozed oil, weed slick with slime.

It shames me now to say but I grew bored and began bothering the fish below. Before I knew it I was breaking out beyond the boats, sightseers spying on my private play. Some came at me in crafts while others ogled, long lines of limbs leaning out, nosey, needy — yes, yes, I know — my pride puffed up. I broached, I breached, I bounced on cue. Their wonder worked to spur me on.

But when my first friend came again (bless him, yes he did) I sensed he saw my gaming as a grave mistake. He loaded up his boat, heaped it high, and called for me. Of course I went, and when we left behind the fuss he shed his sulk. Oh, how I calmed when he started to sing. Oh buoyant bliss! I thought that all was well within my world . . . but I was wrong.

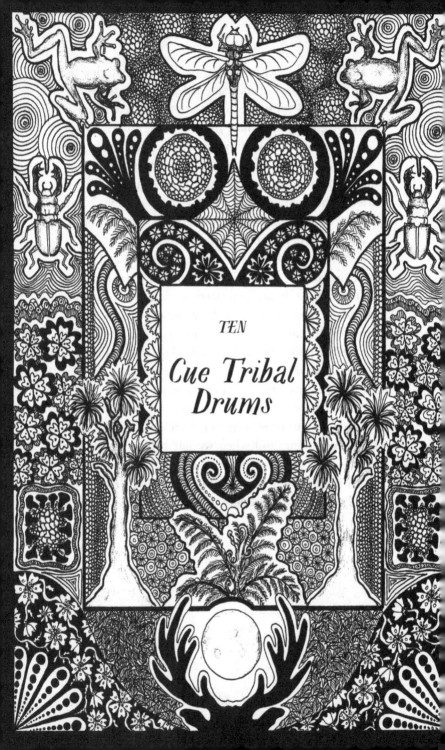

TEN

*Cue Tribal
Drums*

Will hunched over his computer, cold and stiff, hardly able to keep his eyes open. He flicked through site after site, scanning down the lines of text to soak in every bit of useful information. Physical characteristics, scientific classifications, habitat, clan distinctions . . . so many facts he knew he'd hardly remember a third of them. But it was the stories that stayed with him: the beluga who made sounds like human conversation; the huge captive male orca who killed his trainer and injured others while the aquarium tried to cover it up. How the different clans or tribes all ate different things, communicated in different dialects, played different games, devised their own techniques to hunt. Dolphins saving people from sharks. Whales seeking to be freed from fishing lines by human hands. Orcas sweeping seals off ice floes, hunting them in clever, deadly packs.

He felt like an alien anthropologist; that the notes he was making could've been about the different tribes of human beings. Loving, emotional creatures, with an innate capacity for killing — or not. The most depressing part of all was the discovery that people were the only real threat to lone orca like Min — while, in return, an orca had never hurt a person in the wild. It pissed him off that even those whose job it was to protect them sometimes got it wrong — standing back, procrastinating, sticklers for protocols that could do more harm than good.

There'd been a little guy, Luna, found alone in Puget Sound, loved by the locals, protected, befriended. The clips on YouTube could've been of Min. The same playful nature; same desperate need. He'd got in the midst of all these rugged logger types and won them over with his games, pushing logs around for them like a seaborne lumberjack. If handed a hose he washed down boats; if a fender was thrown out the back he raced along after it like he was being towed. In one clip he could even be seen 'talking' to a dog aboard a boat! It was the humour and goodwill of the little guy that stayed with Will. He was just like Min.

And, freakily, the local First Nations tribe thought he was the reincarnation of their chief — exactly like that girl Pania had said of Min. When the authorities tried to net the little fella to transport him back to his pod, the tribe took to the water — not trusting a word the government had to say. They paddled their canoes into the path of the official boats, calm and dignified as they chanted and beat their drums. It was one of the most moving things Will had ever watched, all the drama of *Madame Butterfly* — the same heartbreaking beauty played out in Puget Sound.

It did no good though. By the time everyone had pissed around, arguing over who should take control of him, the poor little sod had been accidentally killed by the propeller of a boat. As the locals talked about their pain, how much they missed Luna, Will ached for them. He'd be gutted if Min died. Felt hollowed by the thought.

He shut down his computer and fell into bed, restless until a plan slowly began to hatch. When his alarm went off at six a.m., he staggered up to catch Dean before he left.

Dean was already downing his porridge.

'Hey.' Will drew out the chair opposite and sat down.

'You're up early, mate. On a mission?'

'Kind of. I met this girl Pania yesterday — the one whose brother died. You know her, right?'

'Sure do. Her mother Cathy is our cuz — mine and your mum's. I guess that makes Pania your — your second cousin? Yeah, I think that's right.'

'How come you never mentioned they were Māori?'

Dean's spoon paused halfway to his mouth. 'You got a problem with that?'

'Hell no.' Jesus, what did Dean take him for? 'Would you introduce me to them?'

'Why now, all of a sudden? When I suggested it last month you cut me dead.'

Dean's suspicion hurt, even though it was deserved. But if he told Dean it was about Min he'd probably blow his stack. 'They're family, man. It seems rude not to say hello.'

Dean scooped up the last mouthful of porridge and swallowed it. 'Okay. I'll give Cathy a call tonight.' He scraped his chair back and stood up. 'Good to see you making an effort.'

'Cool. Thanks.' *Perfect!* 'Oh — and I'm gonna camp out tonight.'

'Eh?'

'Tonight. Thought I'd stay up at Gleneden.'

Dean's eyes narrowed as he scratched his chin. 'This isn't about that frickin' orca is it?'

'Jesus, Dean. You spend six weeks hassling me to get out more, and when I do, you go all weird?'

Dean's eyebrow rose. He dropped his bowl into the sink and collected up his lunch. 'Suit yourself. There's camping gear in the shed. Just don't do anything stupid, okay?'

It was a relief to hear Dean leave. He'd got off lightly. When it came to fish and animals, Dean and all the other locals shared a completely different world view from Will. Min threatened Bruce Godsill's bottom line, simple as that, and the success or failure of the fish farms touched everyone who lived down here. Min was a predator to them. To Dean. Full stop. Why couldn't they see that some things had more value left alone?

Will threw together an overnight bag and grabbed the blankets from his bed. Filled a box with frozen sausages, apples and a loaf of bread, all of which he lugged, along with Dean's tent and sleeping bag, down to the yacht. The marina was so lined with onlookers Will had to elbow through to see the fuss. *Damn it*. Min was at his circus tricks. He threw his gear into the Zeddie and quickly set the sail.

Once on the water he whistled and Min charged over, drawing the eye of every person in the crowd. As soon as they had cleared the channel, out of the public gaze, Will sang. He needed to distract Min while they passed Bruce Godsill's floating farms.

They reached Brookes Bay just after ten. Twenty

minutes further north, the entrance to Gleneden came into view, a tiny blip in the corner of Pitford Cove, one of the last stops before the ropey waters that split the two main islands. Will steered the yacht in through a natural arch of rock; inside, a perfect strip of beach unfolded, tūī and bellbirds flitting in the overhanging trees.

Will anchored right in the middle and tethered the yacht to a pōhutukawa tree each side. He lashed the boom, ready to support the fly of the tent when night fell. Somehow he was going to try to sleep there. If he was right, and Min behaved like Luna, then all he had to do was keep him occupied until he'd sounded out the tribe — or he was arrested by that guy from Fisheries.

He gave himself over to Min's demands, singing till his vocal chords ached. As the heat of the day condensed, he lolled in the yacht, one hand sifting the water as Min pottered close. It was uncomfortable as hell, his body too long to fit between the seats, but he was so calm, so happy, he almost felt like he used to before his world went mad. Heat and birdsong lulled him into a fitful doze. He was dreaming of his mother flirting with the Fisheries guy when something bumped the hull.

Will startled. Spun around. He came nose to nose with Hunter Godsill, whose overheated face clashed with the orange of his kayak and the ugly mottled bruising of one eye.

'Gidday!'

Will scrabbled up and cast around. No Min. *Good . . . and bad.* 'Gidday.' Despite his friendly smile, the fact that Hunter was a Godsill put him firmly in the hostile camp. 'Did you paddle all the way from Blythe?'

Hunter grinned. 'Bugger off! I've been up since five! I

got one of the farm boats to drop me off near Brookes Bay.'

He hooked his oar up onto the Zeddie's side and slithered from the kayak straight into the water. Will sent a silent plea for Min to stay away.

Hunter dived under, no mean feat in a lifejacket, then bobbed back up. 'Mind if I come aboard?' When Will shrugged, he clambered up, dripping on the blankets.

'Here.' Will tossed a towel.

'Ta.' Hunter dried himself then sat down on the gunwale. 'Hey, by the way, it's out in Pitford Cove, if you were wondering.'

Will tensed. 'What is?'

'The orca. It's out there stirring up a run of kahawai.'

'Oh, right.' What the hell was this about? A spy for his control-freak dad? Or Dean?

'It played with me this morning. Sprayed me with the bloody hose!' Hunter's voice lifted by at least two tones. 'I've never been so close to one.'

'You've seen others in the Sound?'

'Once, years ago. Dad reckons they come in every three years or so but that's the only one I've seen. He's paranoid about them.' The scorn that tightened his face took Will by surprise.

'I think it's a male,' Will said. 'I googled it.'

'Cool. Just us blokes then.' His grin grew wider. 'Anyway, I saw you on TV with him last night.'

Hunter was watching him so avidly that Will felt obliged to answer. 'Yeah, it was pretty wild,' he said. 'He's strong, and really smart.'

'You think he'd swim with me?'

Ah ha — a test! 'You heard the Fisheries guy. There's a massive fine.'

Hunter's grin twisted. 'So?'

'So, it's against the law.'

'What they don't know won't hurt — oh, look!' Hunter pointed towards the arch as Min cruised in through the gap. 'Far out!' He nearly overturned the yacht by lunging to the other side. 'He looks bigger this close up!' Excitement radiated off him like a wave of heat.

Will clicked his fingers and Min edged over to bump his hand. *What the hell.* 'Stroke him,' he said. 'Go on. Just do it real calm.'

Hunter reached out and brushed his hand along Min's snout. Min started up a barrage of clicks.

'He's just getting the feel of you,' Will said. 'That's how they sense things. Echolocation.'

Hunter nodded. 'Yeah, I know. I didn't expect it to be so loud.' He leaned closer to Min, who rolled over to study him with one oily eye. 'Come on, boy, I won't hurt you.'

Min snorted mist.

Hunter laughed, glowing with pleasure, and the tension bled off him as he stroked Min's exposed belly. It was this — Hunter's rapt attention, his aura of amazement — that finally won Will over. He knew that feeling; was pleased to meet someone who shared his excitement. 'Get in with him. He won't hurt you.'

'No shit? You sure it's safe?'

Will hooked off his T-shirt. 'Here, I'll go first.' He dived, shocked by the chill of the water after baking in the sun.

Min started sounding off, his Donald Duck impersonation sending Hunter into fits. He tore off his lifejacket and jumped in too. Min came right up and scanned as Hunter hung there in the water, an ecstatic giant.

Will dug out his empty water bottle and tossed it towards the arch. When Min had nosed it back over to the Zeddie, Will left the game to Hunter and clambered back on board the yacht. He lounged in the late afternoon sun, enjoying the wonder that lit Hunter's face.

About twenty minutes later Hunter hauled himself aboard. 'That was awesome!'

'Just don't tell Fisheries,' Will said. 'And, for god's sake, please don't tell your father.'

'Are you kidding? I stopped telling him anything important years ago.'

Will's gaze flitted to Hunter's swollen eye. 'You don't get on with him?'

Hunter shrugged. 'He's a total prick.'

'Fair enough.' Will closed his eyes and tipped his face towards the sun. The light shone pink through his eyelids. Somewhere close by a pair of tūī sang a rough duet, accompanied by Min's percussive blowhole.

Hunter's voice broke through. 'You gonna stay the night out here?'

Will opened one eye. Saw Hunter eyeing the tent and bedding. 'Maybe.'

'Don't suppose you'd like some company? I haven't camped out for months.' There was a shyness there, and loneliness.

The old familiar tension boiled in Will's gut. He'd grown accustomed to his own company. Preferred it. 'I was thinking of sleeping in the yacht . . .'

'So I could use Dean's tent?'

'You recognise it?'

'He's taken me camping a few times. He usually makes me put it up.'

'How come?'

'Whenever Dad has one of his psycho fits, we take off somewhere for a couple of days till he's cooled off.'

'O—kay.' Good old Saint Dean, protector of underdogs and social misfits. Had he sent Hunter here to keep an eye on him? Bugger that. If Dean thought for one— but, hold on . . . What if Dean had sent Hunter to escape from Bruce?

'How'd you get the shiner?' he asked.

Hunter fingered the swelling. 'Not fast enough.' His face closed off.

It certainly wasn't a stretch to believe Bruce Godsill beat his son. Even though Hunter was built like a brick shithouse, so was Bruce. Will cleared his throat. 'Your dad must be pissed off about losing all those salmon.'

Hunter snorted. 'He'll screw some more out of the insurance.' He reached over the side of the yacht and hooked a bag out of the kayak. Produced a can of beer. He popped the tab and took a swig. 'You want one?'

'If you've got one.' Not that he liked it much — bourbon and Coke was his drink of choice — but it seemed unfriendly not to join him.

Hunter hooked out another can and tossed it over. They sat in silence, sipping away until both cans were empty, then drank another each as Min played acrobat with streamers of kelp. The heat was leaching from the day, sun sinking behind the western hills. Even if Hunter left straight away he'd end up kayaking in the dark.

'Stay if you want,' Will said at last. 'I've got some snags to cook over a fire and heaps of bread.'

'You sure?'

Hunter looked so goddamned pleased, relieved, what

could Will say? 'Yeah, no worries.'

'Choice!' Hunter's grin switched to high-beam.

They ferried the tent and food ashore in the kayak, and set about scavenging wood to light a fire. When it built up enough heat they speared the sausages with sharpened sticks and cooked them over red-hot embers, then ate them between thick slices of gluey white bread.

After they'd demolished the lot, Will cleared his throat. 'So, do you like working on the farms?'

Hunter grunted. 'Only when Dad's not there.' He wandered over to the kayak and retrieved two more cans of beer from his stash of supplies.

Will swilled a mouthful to rinse the bread from his teeth. 'Thanks.'

'I bet you hate it here,' said Hunter. 'I do, and I was born here.'

'I like Dean,' Will said. 'And the privacy.'

'Yeah — Gabby showed me that YouTube thing. You sure as hell looked munted.'

Will tensed.

'At least you had the guts to try. Me, I'd rather die than sing in front of other people.' Hunter burped. 'I guess you had lessons for that, huh?'

'Twice a week for the last three years.' Until the plug was pulled. Too pricey.

'Wow, that's hardcore. I was in the school choir at primary school — quite liked it — but Dad said I sounded like a tomcat having its nuts ripped off.'

'He'd be an expert, would he?' It was out before Will could stop it. Sarky as hell.

Hunter's snorting laugh dislodged a string of snot. He swiped it with his arm, leaving a silver snail's trail across his cheek. 'He's the expert of bloody everything — or so he thinks.' He wiped the trail away. 'So, what's it like living in Wellington?'

'Better than Blythe,' Will said. 'Though it's nice out here.'

'Not bad, eh?' Hunter gestured to encompass the cove. 'Though I'd kiss it all goodbye to get out of that shithole town.'

'Why?'

'Are you kidding?' He drew his neck in, until the double chins he'd made looked exactly like his dad's. *'There have been Godsills here since 1893,'* he said in Bruce's bullish twang. *'And you're the biggest disappointment of them all.'* He sighed, shaking off his father's mantle. 'I'd go, except the fish farm is the only job I know.'

Will couldn't help it, he was warming to the guy. There was a lot more to him than he presented to the world. 'How long have you worked for him?'

'All my holidays till I turned sixteen, then Dad made me quit school.'

'When was that?'

'Last year.'

So they were roughly the same age, though Hunter was twice his bulk. 'You like working with salmon?' He couldn't think of anything worse.

'What do you think?' Hunter shook his head. 'I wanted to go to uni — find more sustainable ways to manage the fish — but Dad said he wasn't going to waste his hard-earned cash on someone like me.'

'That's harsh.'

'Yeah, but probably true. I'm dyslexic. In Dad's world that equals thick.'

'That's crap, man. My friend Tim, back home, he's dyslexic and he's bright as hell. Just needs some extra help for the exams.'

'My school dean tried to tell Dad that — he even called him in to try to talk him round.'

'No luck?'

Hunter laughed. 'Yeah, like *that* was going to work.' He pointed to his eye. 'You think this looks bad, you should've seen me after that.'

'So, why do you put up with it, man? I'd leave.' Thank god his parents didn't believe in physical punishment.

'My mother made me promise I'd stick around.'

'Why? He treats you like shit.'

'She said the farms were my inheritance and I had to promise to stay until Dad passed them on to me. It was just before she died.'

'She died?' *What was it with this place? First Pania, now him.* 'Sorry to hear that, man.'

'I was eight,' Hunter said. 'She drank herself to death.'

'Jesus! That's terrible.' He didn't even *want* to imagine how Hunter must have felt.

'To be honest, my memory of her's a bit patchy — though I can remember a few brutal fights.'

'I don't mean to sound harsh, dude . . .' Will swallowed. He wasn't quite sure how to word it. The poor bastard was being beaten by that prick and he needed an out. 'But you were only eight. I don't think she'd hold you to that promise now.'

Hunter picked at a scab on his foot. 'It's complicated. There's Dean to think about too. And, besides, it's one of the only conversations I still remember. If I backed out now I'd be betraying her.'

It was clearly such a messy, personal thing, Will realised, it didn't matter how illogical it was. 'What's Dean got to do with it? Wouldn't he just be pleased you'd got the hell out?'

'If Dean can stick it out then so can I.' There was a decisiveness in his voice now. It was clear he wouldn't budge. 'Where are your parents?'

'Australia.' It sounded like bragging after Hunter's tragic tale. 'They're in the shit financially.'

'You miss them?'

What was he supposed to say? His loss was nothing compared to Hunter's. 'Sometimes. Mostly my mum.'

'Dad's sister tries to mother me. You know her? Selma Taylor. She runs the store.' Hunter rolled his eyes.

'Gabby's mum?'

Hunter smiled. 'You've met my cousin Gabby, then?'

Will crossed his index fingers to avert the evil eye. 'Afraid so. Looks like you *really* lucked out on the family stakes!'

Hunter let rip with a belly-laugh. 'Dude, Gabby's a wicked witch.'

'D'you know my cousin Pania?'

'She's your cousin?'

'Second cousin, apparently.'

'Sweet. She's really brainy. Nice too — even if she does hang out with Gabby.' He tossed a stone into the sea. 'You met her friend Simone?'

Will pictured the three girls from the night before. 'Is she blonde and giggly?'

'Yeah, that's the one. She's okay when Gabby's not around.'

'You fancy her?'

'Stupid, eh? When we were young we used to get on really good. Now every time I try to talk to her I screw it up.'

Now it was Will's turn to laugh. 'I know the feeling, man. I used to sing in front of hundreds of strangers, but when I'm near a girl I freeze.'

'Dean says you could've won that competition if they'd given you another chance.'

Gratitude filled Will's chest. 'Maybe.'

'Give us a song then!' Hunter turned to him, all expectant.

'Forget it, man.'

'Come on. It's only me and the orca.'

'I don't want—'

'Go on. I dare you! Sing one of them fancy-arse opera things. My mother used to love those Amici dudes. She played a CD of them all the time till Dad threw a spaz one day and broke it.'

Oh great. Nothing like playing the dead mum card. How could he refuse that? He hadn't sung in front of anyone for months. Though, maybe it was good. He had to start somewhere . . . and Min would like it, even if it made him look a dick. He walked over to the water and placed his feet squarely on the sand. Drew in a grounding breath. The light was silvering as he released the first note.

'*Che gelida manina* . . .' He sang the whole aria through, his back to Hunter as Min joined in. At the end there was total silence; even the birds were hushed.

Hunter broke the spell. 'Holy shit! Now *that* should be up on YouTube!'

Will's gut contracted as the moment crumbled. 'Forget it.' He snatched up Dean's tent and sleeping bag and threw them towards Hunter. 'I need an early night.' He clambered into the kayak and paddled out to the yacht. Boarded and shoved the kayak back towards the beach.

He folded into the gap between the seats and pulled the fly across to block out Hunter. There was no way to explain his panic. Even knowing it was a post-traumatic response compounded by the head injury didn't stop that same old shit exploding in his mind. It was etched into his brain like hate graffiti. He felt exhausted. Drained.

Min bumped around the hull while Hunter hammered in guy ropes. Will blanked it all out, humming scales to steady his breathing. Slowly the flashbacks eased. He was so sick of his brain ambushing him. Almost wished they'd give him shock treatment to wipe it all.

He knew he should go back out there and make an effort to act normal. But that would mean an explanation and he couldn't face the shame — not when Hunter was so staunch he could laugh off a beating from his dad. Right now, all Will wanted was to sleep; to switch his brain off before he blew another fuse.

He woke again to darkness, the crackle of the fire loud in the night. He stood up, holding onto the boom for balance, and stretched, trying to work the kinks out of his back and neck, and rubbed his goose-bumped arms. It was freezing. Cold and clear. Min floated at the stern, relaxed.

Beyond the embers Hunter was still hunched there, yet another can of beer in hand. His face looked ghoulish in the glow, features loose.

'Yo!' Will called.

Hunter startled, slopping his drink. 'Jeez, you nearly g'me a heart attack!' He swayed, his head drooping on his bulldog neck.

'Sorry about before. I think the sun got to me.'

'N'worries.'

'I'm freezing. Could you shove the kayak over?'

Hunter stumbled up. Dragged the kayak down to the tide and shoved it out towards the yacht. It just missed Min, who rolled and stilled again. Will clambered into it, a blanket around his shoulders, and paddled back to shore.

He fed the fire and huddled over it, willing more heat into the flames. A pile of crushed empty beer cans lay at Hunter's feet.

'You ever feel like you know what's gonna happen before it does?' Hunter asked.

Random. 'You mean like being psychic?'

'Nah. Just feel it 'cause you know someone so well that you can guess.' He chucked a log into the blaze and sparks ascended through the air like cartoon souls.

'I can tell when Mum's going to cry,' Will said. 'Though that's not hard. She cries when she's really happy — or when she's angry — as well as when she's sad!'

'I got a bad feeling about the orca. When Dad gets aggro like this . . . I don't trust him.'

'You think he'll hurt him?'

'Nah, dude. I think he'll fucking slaughter him.'

Though Dean had said the same, to hear Hunter confirm it was a shock. 'But there's a law . . .'

'You think he cares about the law?' Hunter crushed the can in one slick move. 'Our little friend has pissed him off. And if you piss Dad off, you're dust.'

'All the more reason to stay with Min.' If that's what it took then, damn it, that's what he'd do. Bruce Godsill could go to hell.

'You think you can stay with him every second of the day — and night?' There was disdain in Hunter's tone now.

'I'm not going to let anyone hurt him,' Will said. 'Not your father or anybody else.' He spat the words out past the death-squeeze pressure in his chest.

'Don't ya see? That's city talk. Down here, it's dog eat dog. The government can come up with any fancy-arse law it wants, but down here we do things the way they've always been done. Down here *Dad's* the law. He doesn't even have to get his hands dirty; there's plenty who'll do whatever he says.'

'What about you? What do *you* think?' Will could feel his hands bunching into fists. Fought to slow his breath.

'It doesn't matter what I think.' Hunter stared into the flames, listing at a drunken angle. 'Dad kills everything he can't bend to his will.'

The darkness seemed to thicken around them, conspiring, as Hunter's words tolled. 'What if he finds out you're with us? Will you be in trouble for staying out?'

'Don't care. I've had a gutsful of him. Let him try.' He punched his fist into his palm. 'But watch it: Dad'll take it out on Dean if you're not careful.'

'What? Physically?' This was like a bad movie.

'Not straight away. First he'll fire Dean's arse if you don't toe the line.'

Will shuddered out a breath, seeing its mist. Hunter clearly looked out for Dean, just as Dean looked out for him.

This was all getting far more complicated than he'd bargained for. Bad enough he had to sneak around behind Dean's back but what if he really was putting him at risk?

And as for Hunter . . . how could he keep living with such an arsehole as Bruce? Will's skin crawled just to think of it. He fought against his nausea. This was ridiculous. He had to find a way to function. If he wasn't there for Min, day in, day out, that bastard just might kill him.

He glanced over at Hunter, who stared into the flames as if they'd risen from Hell. 'Any chance you'd help me?' Will said. 'To keep Min safe?'

Hunter blinked, before a smile slowly cracked his face. 'That's what I came for, dude. I thought you'd never ask.'

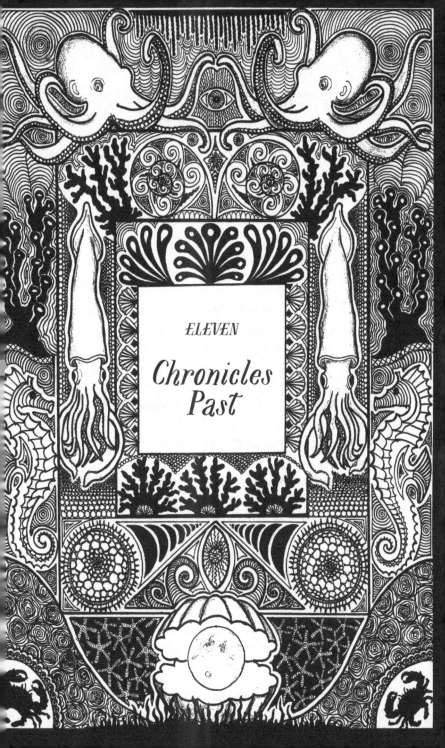

ELEVEN

Chronicles Past

When, back then, the Broad Boy came again, that thick tree-trunk of nerves, I did not shy away. I met him without fear, so sure was I. The Song Boy's singing had paled my pain, his welcome warmed, his touch brought back the tender times. Oh yes, we thirst for touch the way a bird seeks sky. Without it we are not fully formed. All I can say is that the tug towards them eased my grief. And more: without them there I surely would have died.

Know this: We, The Chronicles, have shared our lives, losses, and loves since light first lapped our skins. But in the Days of Blood, the Hungry Ones wanted to wipe us from the waves. We lost our age-old wisdoms, our sea-bound sagas that sang of seasons, stillness, souls, once passed from clan to clan, tribe to tribe, to teach the workings and the wonders of our world. These shared songs linked us to our lores and tied us all together; shaped us into who we are. They whispered warnings, pled for peace, and preached of goodness and goodwill.

But in those deadly Days all our connections crumbled, understandings loosened, stillness lost. Survivors called a great Convergence — a meeting of the only old ones left to lead each tattered tribe. And, thus, a whole new fellowship of Chronicles was founded, to save our stories — and to prod our painful pasts. We have to know the knots and knocks; must not repeat them. Nor forget. Dear friends: a Being without a story is a shapeless shell.

At first their new retellings focused on our foes, our need to understand them foremost in our mind. But as our tribes bounced back, boldness reborn, The Chronicles served up the shallows and depths of each outstanding life. Their goal? To find a pathway where we Warm-bloods and the Hungry Ones could live on, side by side. Alive.

These days, with more blighted Beings brought back from the brink, we need to take the time to weigh the lessons learnt; not only to home in on the hollow inside them, but to test the hunger in ourselves.

Deep down where water burrows into black, lone licks of light glow ghostly in the gathered gloom. Strong streamlined squid spark silver as they prey on stragglers; deep-sea shrimps spew out shining spit-clouds to warn others off. Way down, wrapped in that wintry womb, it feels like wending back through time. We learn to master our own make-up, how to tap the thoughts that truly shape our souls.

In the black Below, bubbling spouts split sulphurous seabeds, water whirling, air arising, heating tiny lives that float within its wake. This welcome warmth soothes all the senses. Mulls the mind.

The ice of White World, by the by, works otherwise. Its chill sharpens our understandings, wisdom, wit. There is a cleanness there, a spotless, stainless sanctuary from the muddy world of Men. We slide beneath thick slabs of ice, amid spiked frozen shards; anemones wave in the water's weave, jellyfish fly, and in its depths we find the thickened sea soaks up all sound. Unbridled bliss!

But do not doubt there is a darkness in the White World's wild reaches too — a blackness in the hearts of those of us who hunt with that same Human hunger. We share their stealth and strength — their blood and bones — this clan who push their prey off icy floes. They have no care for who or how they kill. Cold-bloods, Warm-bloods, young ones, old . . . It is their glee that grates, their manner much like Men whose wants, not needs, rise up to rule their every move.

All the same, I have a fondness for the good that grows, when watered, in the Humans' hearts. To hate is easy. To find a meeting place, to brave a bond, takes much more time. We Beings must surely sense the truth of that.

I fear, friends, all this drifts off course. I merely meant to say it was the snatches of these stories, first sung to soothe me off to sleep, that bolstered me back in those days. They breathed a little life in; helped to hold my mother in my mind. I dared not let her go, for fear of finding nothing, no one, no more love.

Perhaps, indeed, it was the first flutters of what would leaven into love that day — the warm wishes that flowed from their hurt Human hearts — which kept me in their cosy company, our two kinds tipping towards kinship. Song Boy and Broad Boy stayed on after shadows loomed, tucked tight in that cleft of cove. As I slept, my watchful half-mind heard the humming in and out of their two breaths, so very soothing. So like the comfort of my clan.

When the morning light came calling Song Boy swam out to sing before he left me with Broad Boy to while away the day. But as the sun made its mid-point pass, Broad Boy slipped into a sound unstirring sleep.

Left alone, with no new friend for fun, I sped away, seeking out Song Boy on my own. But when I passed another salmon swarm, balled up in their bindings, I thought to try my luck. For, though their fate — and state — was foul, I hungered for an easy fill of fish. There is a richness to their flesh, an oiliness, far too fetching to forgo. Perhaps it was my new-found friends who soothed the sickness I had felt two nights before. And so, again I bunted at the bindings; tore the webbing with my teeth. I did not stop to think past the growing grumble in my gut.

Heartless hunger, friends, in all its many shades and sizes, makes fools of all. But by the time I grasped this, it was too late to turn it back.

TWELVE

Anchors Be Weighing

As the sun rose Will awoke to the rhythmic purr of Hunter's snoring and found himself analysing how slow the tempo was. Andante? Adagio? A lazy snorting lento? The night had been a shocker. After giving up on the yacht (far too cramped) he'd bunked down in the tent with Hunter; spent the night hunched in the corner, trying to avoid Hunter's massive sprawl. Now, as he edged past his prostrate body, everything ached. Out near the yacht Min lolled in the first fingers of sun to break through the arch of rocks.

Will stripped down to his boxers and waded out, gasping as the chilly sea reached his groin. Min swam over, noisy in his greeting, and Will began to sing.

'*Come away, fellow sailors, come away, Your anchors be weighing: Time and tide will admit no delaying . . .*' The aria, from *Dido and Aeneas*, was one of the first his singing teacher, Marilyn, had chosen for him when he started. One of the few he'd learnt in English.

Min bobbed around him, filling in Will's pauses with

his unique song. Hunter stumbled from the tent and stood at the water's edge, his grin stretching as he listened to their surreal duet. At its end, Will swam back to shore and shook like a wet dog.

'That's so awesome,' Hunter said. 'My ears hear it but my eyes don't believe what they're seeing!'

Will grinned back. 'Mad, huh?' He picked up a stick and poked at the ashes of last night's fire, hoping it might rekindle. It was well and truly out. They'd sat up half the night, hunched over it, discussing Will's plan for Min. He would go back to Blythe today to see if Dean had managed to set up a meeting with his rellies. Hunter, meanwhile, had the day off. He'd offered to stay with Min till Will returned.

Once Will had dressed, Hunter punted him over to the Zeddie. He dived into the water to distract Min as Will sailed away.

'I'll be back by five,' Will called as he cleared the arch.

Hunter waved back. 'No worries! I'll see if I can catch us a feed of fish.'

There was a steady northerly out in the main Sound and Will made good time back to Blythe. He arrived just after ten to find Dean sitting on the doorstep, poring over the morning paper in a patch of sun.

'Gidday mate. Good night?'

Will slithered down beside him. 'Yeah, good thanks. Hunter Godsill turned up. Have you seen his eye?'

Dean nodded. 'Yeah. I'm waiting for the day he finally hits back. Now *that* would be something!'

'Why doesn't someone report Bruce to the cops?'

'You think I haven't tried? But it's complicated — and I have to work there.'

Will opened his mouth to push Dean further but then changed his mind. No point. He needed Dean onside. 'Did you call up your cousin?'

'Sure did. We're meeting them at the marae at noon.'

'The marae?'

Dean laughed. 'You betcha. Mike, Cathy's husband, is a bigwig there.'

Good news. 'So there'll be a proper pōwhiri?'

'Yep. Are you okay with that? I can do all the—'

'No, that's fine. We learnt all that stuff in Year Nine. I'll do my mihi.'

'Excellent. You wanna do the song too? I'm crap at that.'

A year ago he would've gagged for the chance. Now it wasn't metaphorical. He swallowed hard.

Dean studied his face. 'S'okay. I can do it if you want.'

'I—'

'See how you feel, eh? It's no biggie.' Dean folded his paper and stood up. 'I gotta do a quick check on one of the farms. I'll be back by eleven-thirty.'

'Okay. Thanks.' He hardly noticed Dean leave; jeers and taunts blared in his head.

He opened the newspaper. Scanned through the headlines to block the insults out. War, murder, assault, abuse . . . everything he read or heard these days brought him straight back to the things he wanted to forget. He tried the puzzle page. Read his weekend stars. '*Be prepared for surprises. With heart and instincts on the same page you'll know what you do and don't want and where your heart stands.*' Utter crap. His mother read hers every day — if it warned of trouble it made her tense. His father said they were a crock of shit, worded so anyone could relate to them. Mum agreed, but said she used it as a tool to help focus her thoughts. Will read his again and smiled. There was no denying the surprise part — one way or the other, today would serve up something new.

He went inside and showered away the layer of salt that crusted him. Pulled on his favourite T-shirt, black with angel wings, and his best black jeans. Tied back his hair. Shaved the wispy growth on his top lip and chin. Not that he needed to. Just nerves.

While he waited for Dean, he emailed his parents and told them about Min — not everything, but enough to let them know. He ached to talk to them in person but their usual Saturday Skype, always scheduled for six-thirty, would have to wait. Tonight he'd promised to relieve Hunter by five. It drove him nuts he couldn't just call them whenever he felt the urge; impossible with the time difference and their crazy shifts. It was ironic. He'd spent the last few years pushing his parents away — the old fight for independence, blah-de-blah — yet now he wished to god that they were here. Another of life's little jokes at his expense.

By half past eleven he was nauseous again. What if the whānau sided with Bruce Godsill and told him to piss off? And what about Dean? He probably should give him a heads-up but that risked pulling the plug. Fingers crossed the new rellies took his side.

He went outside to wait. When the car drew up, he made for the passenger door.

Dean tossed a suspiciously salmon-shaped plastic bag over onto the back seat. 'Koha,' he said, and winked.

As they drove out of town, towards Te Hora marae, Dean filled him in on who was who. 'Cathy's husband's

Mike Huriwai — him and his brothers, George and Arthur, are good sorts. For a long time the marae was screwed — all the kaumātua had pretty much died or burnt out. When Cathy and Mike moved home he stirred things up. He used to work for Māori Development. Got laid off. Since he's been back he's been a thorn in Bruce's side. About eighteen months ago he got the tribe to fight Bruce's latest expansion plans. They won.'

Will laughed. 'No love lost, then?' This was promising. If they were in Bruce's pocket, he wouldn't stand a chance.

'Whatever you might think of Bruce, he's canny. He sponsors their kapa haka group and gives them fish when they're catering a big tangi. It causes all sorts of in-fighting — some are sucked in, most aren't. Behind their backs he gives them shit.'

They turned off the highway. Ahead, a small meeting house stood in a square of perfectly mown lawn, several simple outbuildings clustered near. Pania waited at the gateway, dressed in tidy jeans and a pale blue shirt the colour of her eyes. They were so vivid Will couldn't believe he hadn't noticed the other night. They stood out against the creamy brown of her skin as though lit from behind.

'Hey, Unc. I'm leading you guys on.' She glanced at Will and nodded. His stomach rumbled so loudly she grinned. 'Don't worry. There's heaps of food.'

Dean swept her up and spun her around. 'Jeez, girl, you been eating bricks?'

She slapped his arm. 'Shut up! You're just getting old, Superman!'

'Enough of that! How's school?'

'Frustrating.' She turned to Will and rolled her eyes.

'You're lucky you do Correspondence. My school doesn't even teach the subjects I want to take.'

He was still devising an answer, and wondering how the hell she knew so much about him, when a group of about ten men and women emerged from the wharenui. They huddled under the veranda, below a tekoteko that stared out from the apex of the roof. A gaggle of kids played dodge behind the adults' backs. Pania straightened, all her focus shifting to the group ahead.

One of the women stepped forward. 'Haere mai, haere mai, e ngā iwi, haere mai. Mauria mai te aroha ki te marae e . . .' Her voice rang out across the void.

Pania nodded to Dean and all three walked slowly towards the wharenui as she called back. 'Karanga mai, karanga mai . . .' They edged closer, hands clasped, heads lowered in respect.

The two voices duelled back and forth, so primal it made Will tingle. Pania's was more melodic, more human — nervous, a shakiness in her breath — the other like an ancient birdcall.

At the door to the wharenui they paused to take off shoes then entered its cool dark interior. Tukutuku panels lined the walls while the ribs and spine, timber beams, were carved to tell the story of the people who belonged there. A couple of dozen people ranging in age from babies to very old stood to one side. One, a man somewhere in his forties, stood holding a tokotoko, its wood embellished with carvings and tiny pāua eyes. He had a tattoo, a tā moko, covering his face; gave his skin a greenish sheen. His eyes took in everything. Everyone.

He stepped forward to begin his whaikōrero as soon as the three were seated.

'Nau mai, haere mai, Ko Tutumapou te maunga, ko Te Hoiere te awa, ko Te Hoiere te waka, ko Kaikaiawaro te taniwha, ko Matua Hautere te tangata. Maranga mai, e te iwi, Pakohe, maranga mai, e te iwi, Ngāti Kuia . . .'

As Will listened, he caught a name: Mike Huriwai. Pania's father. His gaze rested on Will as he acknowledged the dead. Welcomed the living. It was a good five minutes before he repeated his mihi in English.

Now he really fixed on Will. 'Welcome, welcome, e tama. We have been waiting for you to come. You're one of us, through my wife Cathy. And you, Dean, good to have you here. We haven't seen you in a while, bro . . .' He talked about the history of the wharenui, Will straining to hold his intense gaze. He heard, enjoyed, but took nothing in. Was struggling to remember his mihi.

Finally the whole group sang their welcoming waiata.
'*E toru ngā mea,*
ngā mea nunui,
E kīia ana . . .'
Their voices blended naturally, harmonious and warm.

Now Dean gave Will the nod. He took a deep breath and stood up. Closed his eyes for a moment to rein in his nerves and summon the right words. 'Tēnā koutou, tēnā koutou. Ko Will Jackson ahau, nō Whanganui-a-Tara. Ko Tangitekeo tōku maunga, ko Heretaunga tōku awa, ko Mark Jackson tōku pāpā, ko Sally Jackson tōku whāea.' His stomach was so tense it spasmed.

He could feel all the eyes on him, friendly, welcoming. Hoped what he was about to say wouldn't piss them off. 'I'm really happy to be here and meet you all.' He felt like he was squirming under a microscope. 'I have to admit I've come for a very special reason. To meet you all, of course, but also to ask for help.'

Beside him Dean cleared his throat. Will hurried on. 'You'll have heard about the orca that's been seen around. I've come to ask your help to protect it, while I try to find out where he came from and how to help him get back to his pod.'

There was an undercurrent of murmuring. Beneath, Will heard Dean mutter, 'Fuck's sake.'

'I've researched online and we're his biggest danger — either from someone purposefully hurting him or being hit by a boat. He's lost — a baby — without a tribe. I wondered if you might adopt him into yours until he finds his own.'

He blew out a breath and launched into the expected waiata of reply. Had to close his eyes again to turn off the overwhelming scrutiny.

'*Whakaaria mai,*
Tōu rīpeka ki au,
Tīaho mai,
Rā roto i te pō . . .'

The wharenui had good acoustics and his voice flew up into the carved rafters, stronger than he'd expected. He couldn't hear if Dean and Pania were singing along. Had buzzing in his ears. At the end he collapsed back into his chair.

'Later,' Dean snarled from the corner of his mouth. He presented the salmon for the koha.

As they stepped up for the hongi, Will found himself kissed and nose-pressed with such genuine warmth he started to relax. The last, a Pākehā woman, wrapped him in her arms.

'Kia ora, Will. I'm Cathy. I can't believe it's you! Last

time I saw you, you'd just started school!' She kissed him on both cheeks. 'It's spooky how much you look like Sal!' She laughed and nudged at Dean. 'Too bad you missed out on the looks, cuz!' Around them belly laughter rumbled and the formality of the pōwhiri dissolved.

'Kai time!' someone called and they all traipsed into the wharekai.

Mike Huriwai blessed the food — a spread of bread, salads, corn on the cob, chicken and home-cured ham — then everyone dug in. Will worked his way around the table, avoiding Dean. He was loading his plate with ham when Mike slapped him on the back.

'Quite a voice you've got there. We could use you in the kapa haka group.'

'Maybe.' Mustn't get sidetracked. 'I'm sorry I blurted that stuff out back there, but I'm really keen to get some help. I've done a fair bit of research and I think what we need is a team of people who—'

From behind him Dean broke in. 'Are you out of your freaking mind? Harley's already watching out for you. Anyone who interferes will be slapped with a bloody great fine.'

'It's not the point,' Will said. 'There are experts who'll know where he came from—'

'And there'll be experts who'll chuck you in jail when you can't pay your fines.'

'Taihoa.' Mike held up a restraining hand. 'Deano, rev back, man. Nanny Merepeka reckons that little whale's something to do with Kingi. And, anyway, Will's right — you know it's doomed if Godsill gets his mitts on it.'

'Christ, Mike. It chewed through one of the farm fences — emptied the whole damn thing.'

'Ka pai! Good job!' A dreadlocked woman in paint-splattered jeans and T-shirt pushed her way forward. 'It's disgusting the way those poor fish are kept.' She turned to Dean. 'And don't give me the old *but-it's-good-for-the-community* argument. They're poisoning the seabed with their toxic shit.' She grinned at Will. 'Kia ora. I'm your mother's second cousin, Viv Reihana.' She held out a square hand and shook Will's, crushing his fingers. 'Primo lungs you've got on you, kid.'

'Thanks.' All the attention was starting to freak him out. It was the first time since he'd moved here that he'd had to cope with so many unknown people at one time. First time, in fact, since the audition.

'Viv's got contacts in Greenpeace,' Mike said. 'She's probably the best person to liaise with for now. And I'll raise it at our tribal meeting — though we don't meet till next month. But I'm fairly sure everyone will want to help . . .' He grinned at Dean. '. . . If only to stick it to Bruce!'

Dean shook his head. 'You know bloody well how many people owe their livelihoods to Bruce. Don't screw that up just because you don't like his politics.'

'*Just* because?' Viv snorted. 'Jesus, e hoa, when did you get to be such a right-wing arse-licker?'

Anger boiled behind Dean's eyes. 'When I figured out I had to pay the bills, e hoa. Remember, I don't qualify for your handouts.'

'Enough!' Cathy stepped in between them. She hooked her arm around Will. 'Leave these old buggers to fight amongst themselves, eh? Come and meet Nanny Merepeka. She wants to talk to you.' She steered Will over to a hunched old woman with a face like a sultana. Pania sat next to her. 'Nanny M, here's Will.'

'Ah, Wiremu, haere mai! Haere mai!' She took his hand between her own. Patted him with swollen fingers. 'I feel your wairua, moko. I saw you and our little māhuri tōtara in a dream. Haere mai!'

'Nice to meet you.' Will balanced his plate of food on his lap. Had yet to eat a thing. 'You dreamed about the orca?'

'Āe, moko, I did indeed. I saw you riding it, like Paikea. You seen that film?'

Will nodded. *Whale Rider.* Though, more likely, she saw him on the TV news and had forgotten where she'd seen it.

'You and him are like this, e tama.' She tried to cross her arthritic fingers. Failed. 'Two as one.' To Pania she said: 'You'll help him, eh?'

Pania glanced at Will, dipping her head when their eyes met.

'Ka pai. Ka pai.' Nanny M fished out a handkerchief and dabbed her dripping nose. 'Now, a cup of tea please, e tama. And one of them nice fancy cakes too, eh?'

Will left his plate on his chair and fetched her a cup of tea. He put two lamingtons on a plate and took them to her. Was finally settling in to eat when Viv dragged over a chair.

'I'll try to make contact with Greenpeace's whale team and get the ball rolling, eh? What's your plan?'

Will stuffed down a thick slice of ham and his stomach rumbled its appreciation. 'Well, in other cases, people found that if they spent time keeping the orca company, it didn't disturb the local businesses. When they get lonely they go looking for fun — like a toddler — so I figure if I keep him out of trouble — he's up at Gleneden now —

it gives me time to see if any orca experts recognise his markings. There are people who record them now. With any luck they can figure out his family and get him back to them.'

Viv nodded, her dreads shifting like tentacles. 'Sounds sensible. I'll get onto it. Can you take some photos of his markings and get them back to me soon as? That'd really help.'

'Sure.' *Damn.* He should've thought of that. 'I'm going to camp out there as much as possible. But when he's left alone he follows me, so what I really need is someone else to do some shifts when I'm not there. And maybe someone to deliver food. Oh, and Hunter Godsill's going to help.'

Viv's eyebrows rose. 'Good for him. Though I'd be careful what you say. He's still Bruce's son.'

Pania laughed. 'No need to worry about that. He hates Bruce even more than we do.'

'True.' Viv took a bite of bread, talking through it as she continued. 'But just be aware Bruce has his hooks in that poor kid and he's unlikely to let go.' She glanced past Will, her face lighting up. 'Taihoa, there's George! I really need to catch up with him.' She stood up, brushing crumbs from her lap. 'Later then. I'll be in touch. Keep up the good work!'

Will turned to Pania, leaning in so no one else could hear. 'He's got a black eye, Hunter has. Is it okay to let him help or will it dump him in the shit?'

'Trouble, probably. But he's pretty stubborn. Lonely too. It'd be meaner to block him out.' She pressed her finger into a pile of coconut crumbs then licked it clean. 'I could be your delivery driver if you like. I can use Dad's runabout. He won't mind.'

'You sure?'

'I'll do it after school. And Mum'll probably help with food.'

At that moment Cathy appeared at his side. 'Sorry, Will, I want to introduce you to the others.'

He had no choice but go with her, the next hour a confusion of names and faces. But everyone seemed friendly, despite the fact he was as wooden as Pinocchio. Just before two everyone began to drift away and Dean gave Will the nod. He said his goodbyes, catching Pania as she cleared dishes. They organised to meet at Gleneden the following afternoon.

Dean remained silent until they'd left the grounds and started driving back to town. 'What the hell kind of stunt was that?'

'I'm sorry. But I knew you'd stop me.'

'Damn right. Don't you realise what an impossible position this puts me in?'

'I'm really sorry, okay, but I can't desert him.' His pulse was throbbing in his throat. He was consumed by prickly heat.

'For god's sake, Will. For six bloody weeks you see no one and when you do you set the cat among the pigeons. If Bruce finds out, who do you think he's going to take it out on?'

'Tell him you've kicked me out. I'm going to camp up at Gleneden anyway.'

'Harley'll be there before you can say Fisheries Protocol.' He turned away but then swung back. 'Don't think I'm going to bail you out. I don't have that kind of cash — and your poor bloody parents certainly don't.'

'What am I doing so wrong, exactly? Isn't it *his* job to protect Min too?'

'Yeah, but your idea of protection goes against the rule book. You've lived your whole life in the city, mate. You don't understand the politics of this at all.'

'Don't I? Here's how it looks to me: there's a little lost orca who's desperate for some contact and if I don't help him no one will. Bruce might think he owns this town but he doesn't own *me*.' How could one man hold so much power? And why would people let him?

'Fine fighting words, but you have no idea.' Dean thumped the steering wheel. 'No bloody idea.' He rounded on Will. 'Can't you see what you're doing? This isn't about the orca. You're projecting your own shit onto it.'

The comment hurt like a fist in the guts. 'That's ridiculous. I—'

'You've been shat on, I get that. And I understand you feel abandoned. But you have to learn to deal with it or it'll screw the rest of your life. Trust me, I know what I'm talking about.'

Heat consumed Will's face. Could Dean be right? That this wasn't really about Min at all? It *did* make a cringey kind of sense. Except, hold on . . . it'd been Will who rescued the kittens from the sack at the river that time; Will who'd talked his mother into only buying free-range, organic chicken, eggs and pork; and what about the time he found that poor munted sea gull and took it to the SPCA? He was a rescuer from way back: geckos, bumble bees, trapped mice; his concern for Min wasn't just a figment of his own neurosis — though, he had to concede that probably didn't help — it was the obvious extension of who he'd always been.

'Ask Mum — ask Dad. I know I've been a head-case lately, but this is way bigger than me.' He tried to keep the hurt out of his voice.

'Exactly my point. Sally put me in charge of you. How the hell do you think she and Mark'll feel if I have to ring them up and say you've been arrested — or worse.'

Worse? 'I've already emailed them. I'm confident they'll back me.' *Am I?* Yes, surely they would.

'Then god help you, mate. I wash my hands of you. I'm sorry but I can't afford to piss off Bruce. I need my job.'

Will was gutted. Not only that Dean was angry, but because it made him feel like a leech. 'I understand that. I really do. And I'm sorry, okay? I'll try my best to stay out of everyone's hair. And, if it helps, I'll go somewhere else and not tell you where, in case Bruce asks.'

Dean shot him such a look of scorn Will cringed inside. 'Sometimes sorry doesn't cut it, mate.' He pulled up at the house and climbed out. Left Will to trail in his wake.

Will caught him up. Couldn't leave things like this. 'I don't understand. Why would Bruce care? As long as I keep Min away, where's the harm to him?'

Dean stopped and stared off into the distance, a muscle twitching in his jaw. Seconds stretched. Finally he sighed and turned back to Will. 'You don't know what you're dealing with. This isn't about whether the orca eats those damn fish or not any more. Everything Bruce does is a fight for power and control. You cross him, you suffer. Look at poor bloody Hunter. And Helen.'

'Who?'

'Hunter's mum.'

Will's heart clattered. Dean made it sound like Bruce had topped her.

Out of nowhere, like he'd been summoned from thin air, Hunter materialised, thundering up the drive towards them. *What the hell?* He arrived so puffed he couldn't speak. Bent double, hands to thighs.

'What's wrong?'

'You've gotta come. I fell asleep while I was fishing — just for a few minutes, I swear — but he gave me the slip. I spent the morning searching for him everywhere. Couldn't find him.'

'Don't panic, man. He'll show. He's probably lurking by the slip.' *Goddamn.* Right now he didn't need this; had to forge some kind of truce with Dean.

Hunter's distraught voice broke through his thoughts. 'He went straight to the Franklin farm. I think Bob Davers shot him.'

'What?' Will stumbled.

'I thought I'd better check the farms and, sure enough, Bob's bragging how he got Min with his .303.'

'Did you see him?' This couldn't be happening. He'd just put everything in place.

'Nope. Bob figured he'd sunk.'

Dean snorted. 'That's crap. If he'd killed it right off it would've floated. It's either scarpered, injured, or it's been bagged by Bob.'

Slaughtered whale images splattered the walls of Will's skull. 'Was he sure?' Asking hurt. These people were animals.

'Yep, reckons he saw blood in the water. I came straight here to let you know. My arms are screwed.'

Will dropped to his haunches and fought back tears. Did the breathing. Swallowed bile. He hated this place. Hated everyone. Everything.

'I'm so sorry.' Hunter was on the verge of tears as well, incongruous in such a big lump of a guy. 'It's my first day off in weeks. I couldn't stay awake.'

'Where'd you first find him?' Dean's voice was flat.

Hunter shrugged. 'I dunno. I—'

'Not you, mate. Will?' Dean nudged Will with his foot. 'Where did you find him that first day?'

'Brookes Bay.'

'Go there.'

'What?'

Dean hauled in a noisy breath. 'Fuck's sake, kid. Get off your sorry arse and go look there.'

Will stared at him, the static in his head receding as he realised Dean was trying to help. 'Yeah, maybe.' It made good sense.

He mentally shook himself and stood back up. Reached over and gave Dean a quick hug, slapping him on the back to take the girliness out of it.

'Thanks. I'm onto it.'

THIRTEEN

Close Calls, Dead Certs

What is it about death we fear, dear friends? The losing of a life we love. But do we fail to fathom there are lessons learnt as our lives leak out? For those of us whose end times edge into old age, we've danced with death too many times to falter at our final breath. We've faced it, fought it, flouted it. We've doled it out.

And though close calls pile on more pain — hobble the heart — they yield a wealth of wisdom too. We fear death yet we cannot flee it; this is why it holds such sway. Only the Great Mother, the sea and land her blood and bones, has strength enough to weather all. She will outlive us; shuck us off her back if she so chooses. Wipe out those who do her harm. It is our job to keep her well, to weigh her needs above our own. For those of us who worship her, we wish to steer a shrewder course than those who came before.

Yes, still it smarts to face the folly of my dance with death that day. I sensed the storm brewed by the Hungry Ones; should not have stalked those sickly salmon, no, not at all. Truth told, I did not have the sense to shy away from such an onslaught. I was small and hungry, had no sense to spot the snares. How unworldly. How wide-eyed. How wholly wrong to think one Human acts like all the rest.

I heard the thunder clap that took me down. Felt the stinging slug that fired into my fin. I dived straight to the seabed, shook with shock. Bright blood oozed out; fire smouldered in my flesh. In fear of further strikes I fled for open sea.

But once out in the tugging tides between the lengths of land I felt unsafe, a meaty meal. Pain pelted me, fretfulness unfolded, and the warm welcome Song Boy had worked on me was washed away. My loss lay bare.

Now I wind back with wiser eyes, there is a time in every Being's life that marks the moment our thoughts first take their tidal turn. Our youthful years are free of fret or fear; it is the old ones in our tribes, our clans, who take on all the woes. They work to shore up the ties that knit us all together. Keep us safe.

Until, that is, this first awakening — thoughts unfolding, freedoms found — when we must move from unformed to a solid state. For me, that moment met me while I quivered in the seamless sea, alone.

My heart hammered, but Song Boy's warmth rose up to soothe the tight fear trapping me. I felt his pull, as strong as any Pulse — an urge I could not, would not, fight. This was my Turning: the time to tame my urges, ailings, cross from Bait to Being. All actions call for forthrightness. All forthrightness must bring about a call to act.

I swam towards the bays where we had shared our songs, slowly, overwrought and out of breath, daring death to deal to me. The sun was slipping to the west as I slid in through the span of rocks in search of Song Boy. The beach was empty, but for birds. It's true I wailed — and could not stop — but, somehow, in my shattered state, I swam on further; found the bay where we first met.

I sheltered in the lee of that safe shingle bank, sickened by shock, mind numb, nerve endings naked, senses raw. Bloodied and bruised, I sent out one last plea to him. Waited, trying not to worry, wondering if this would be the final flick of Fortune's fickle turns.

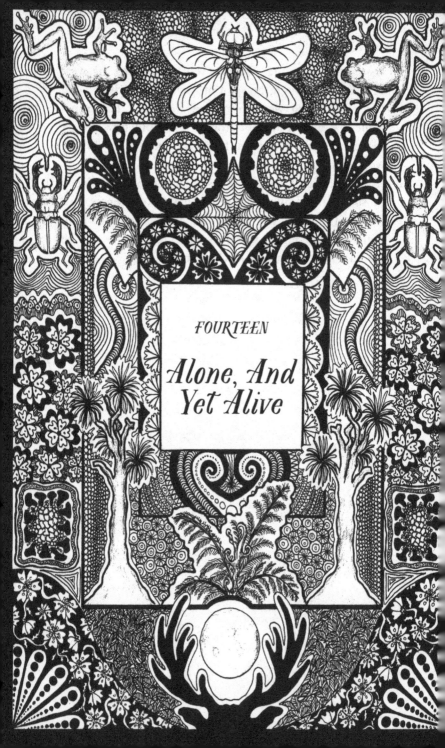

FOURTEEN

*Alone, And
Yet Alive*

As Will and Hunter ran towards the marina, Dean caught them up.

'Hold your bloody horses!' He clamped a hand on each boy's shoulder, unable to speak again until his breathing slowed.

'What?' Will didn't have time for lectures. Min needed him. Oh god, he *hoped* Min needed him. If not . . . The thought impaled him, a pitchfork through the guts.

'Take the Franklin tinny. You'll get there faster. It's not needed till tomorrow.' The first time Dean called the runabout a 'tinny', Will had cracked up. Back home the word meant something very different; he imagined Dean bouncing through the sea on a giant spliff!

'You're sure?' Hunter sounded dubious.

'Course I'm bloody sure. I'm still the farm manager, unless you know something I don't.'

Hunter grinned. 'Nope, last I heard you were the same grumpy slave-driver you've always been!'

'Watch it, sonny! Now go check it's fuelled, then get

a bloody move on.' He squeezed Will's shoulder. 'Take it easy, mate. Bob's renowned for being a crap shot.'

'Thanks.' Will tried to smile. His mouth remained as rigid as a Botoxed brow.

Down at the wharf Hunter snatched the keys from the work shed, while Will untied the mooring ropes. The aluminium runabout was roughly four metres long, its robust pontoons enough to take on any sea.

Hunter checked the tank that fed the grunty motor. 'All good to go.'

He turned the key and the outboard roared to life as Will cast them off the wharf. He leapt aboard. Hauled on a lifejacket. Sucked in a much-needed lungful of air and looked around as they motored out. The mud flats at low tide teemed with birdlife. Hunter pointed to a lanky wader at the channel's edge.

'That's a black stilt — it's rare as hell.' He powered off and scrabbled in his pocket for his mobile phone. Took a photo. Two. Three. *Wasting time.* When Hunter finally got back underway he shouted over the outboard's growl. 'We've got a lot of threatened species. Banded rails — a bit like quails but taller and more colourful — and marsh crakes too. They're hard little bastards to spot. I've seen black-fronted terns, as well, and banded dotterels. So far I've found twenty-eight different species. The local ranger says there're thirty-three.'

Though interesting, Hunter's chatter drove Will nuts. Min could be dead — and it was ridiculous how much that hurt. Like losing family. His mind flew straight to Pania. *Focus, dickhead. Concentrate.*

They swerved around the weekenders: families in their overloaded runabouts, yachts, kayaks, jet skis, launches

. . . The thought of Min having to deal with all this traffic, injured, was gutting. If he *was* still alive he'd be like a toddler trying to cross an eight-lane highway on his hands and knees.

The good news was that Hunter had now gone quiet. Will needed all his concentration. Three times he thought he saw a dorsal fin. But as they drew closer it turned into a bird, a rock, a piece of wood.

He ached as if he'd been beaten, and battled the urge to curl into a ball and howl. Instead he braced himself against the dashboard to steady his gaze as the hull slapped into the running tide.

They passed the first salmon farm, loathing bubbling up. It was so unfair. Why punish Min for such a natural urge? If that bastard *had* killed him he'd — he'd — *damn it*. He didn't know. The bottom line was he couldn't risk Dean's job.

There were so many people out enjoying the weekend sun his heart sank further. Min would've drawn a crowd by now if he was here. *Alone, and yet alive! My soul is still my body's prisoner!* Bloody *Mikado* — the lyrics haunted him, Gilbert and Sullivan heckling him from the sidelines. He switched to singing exercises to block the lyrics out. There was melodrama enough without an operatic farce as soundtrack.

When they reached Brookes Bay, two kids paddled in the creek on the southern side, their kayaks pulled up on the shore. Hunter eased off the throttle and they glided in, casting around for signs of Min. Nothing.

'Can you turn that off?' It came out surly. Will hadn't meant it to.

Once Hunter killed the motor, Will edged into the

middle of the boat. He focused on his breathing. Tried not to think how stupid he'd look. *'Meiner Liebsten schöne Wangen, Will ich froh aufs neue sehn; Bloß ihr Reiz stillt mein Verlangen . . .'* The aria wasn't one of his favourites, but the lyrics had rung in his head all morning. It was about longing and the forgoing of promised treasures to find true love. He struggled to reach the high notes. Min's absence swelled in his chest, a painful lump.

He continued to scan the bay, the pulse in his head marking time as he sang. The kids had stopped to listen, their upturned faces washed with sun. He was approaching the final chorus when Hunter suddenly waved his arms.

'There!' Hunter pointed towards the submerged shingle bank.

There was something below the surface. As Will tried to define the shadow, it moved. *Min!* He couldn't bear it: chucked off his lifejacket and dived into the sea.

Just as he reached the spot, Min bobbed to the surface. Rolled, belly up.

Was he breathing? 'Come on, little man. Talk to me. Are you okay?' He rubbed along Min's abdomen. Solid. *Warm.* His heart skipped as Min pressed back against his touch. *Thank god.*

Min clicked in no discernable pattern and righted himself. *Jesus! No!* He'd been shot, all right. A pulpy mess at the base of his dorsal fin was gouged right through, waterlogged flesh fraying at the edges.

Fury pushed aside relief. Will checked for other injuries, humming to contain his anger as he ran his hands along Min's length in firm reassuring strokes.

'Is he all right?' Hunter punted the boat towards him with an oar.

'Think so. It's through the fin but everything else seems fine.' He blew a raspberry onto Min's snout to secretly dislodge his brimming tears. Min clicked like a rusty wind-up kitten.

'What now?'

'Let's get him back to Gleneden. It's safer there.'

'You sure he'll follow us?'

Will eyed the boat. The outboard motor worried him. He'd seen the damage caused by propellers when he'd searched online. 'Are there any decent lengths of rope?'

Hunter nodded. 'Yep, but if you're thinking of towing him I can't see that working, even if he let us.'

'Not *him*. I mean, what if you towed me? Just slowly. That way I can keep him with me, well back from the prop.'

'It's nearly fifteen k's.'

'I'm not risking him further.' His heart pummelled so ridiculously fast he felt like his own life depended on this, not just Min's.

He looped the mooring rope around his chest, using his lifejacket as a buffer. Once they'd checked the knot was secure, he gave the boat a shove and Hunter fired the outboard up. The rope jerked just as he whistled to Min, shocking the air out through his puckered lips like a cartoon train whistle. As he began to bodysurf, Min kept pace a safe distance back from the prop. He was quiet and compliant, as though his batteries had run down, his hurt so obvious that Will felt it too.

Two bays short of Gleneden, a slick little cabin cruiser pulled into their path and forced them to a stop. It took a moment to register who was aboard. Will groaned. *Gabby Taylor*. The town crier.

Will ignored her, treading water as he murmured

random lyrics to hold Min's attention so he wouldn't swim away. Gabby climbed onto the cabin roof, her shorts so skimpy they bordered on obscene. At the wheel, Simone — in a red micro-bikini and matching baseball cap — had Hunter transfixed. *Poor sod*. He didn't stand a chance; above her buxom curves her smirk had 'trouble' written all over it.

'What the hell are you up to?' Gabby's built-in megaphone was in good working order.

'Nothing. Bugger off.' Hunter didn't even look at her. He was still ogling Simone.

Gabby turned and muttered something to her. Simone squared her shoulders and leaned forward, to give Hunter a good eyeful of her breasts. 'Where're you going, Hunts?'

'Gleneden.' Hunter blushed the colour of overripe plums as the girls laughed like harpies.

'Shut up!' Will yanked the rope to rouse Hunter. 'Why the hell d'you tell them?'

Hunter's blush intensified, ears aglow. 'Shit, I'm sorry, I—'

'Coming over!' Gabby leapt from their boat to Hunter's, nearly pitching him overboard. When she regained her balance she edged down the back to peer at Will. 'Oh my god! It's there!'

'Keep back!' Will blocked Min from her gaze. 'He's hurt, okay? Just leave him alone.'

'No need to get nasty. I thought you'd fallen overboard so we came to help.'

Will didn't believe a word. 'If you want to help then bugger off. He needs peace and quiet.'

'Who made you the expert?'

'Look, we've got it covered, okay?' Hunter reached

over and tugged Gabby's arm. 'Please?'

She slapped him away. 'It's not your property. I want to see it do something.'

Hunter rolled his eyes at Will behind her back, and mouthed *get it over with*. Will had to trust he knew her quirks and moods; that once she'd seen Min she'd piss off. He whistled. Felt grateful and happy when Min nudged him and squealed back in the same key.

'That all? I've seen dolphins do better.'

'He's just been shot!' *Stupid cow*. 'And, actually, orcas *are* a kind of dolphin.' She should know better. He was the townie. 'They've got the second biggest brain in the world.' *A damn sight bigger than yours.*

'So? Brain size means nothing. Elephants have big brains and that hasn't stopped them nearly dying out. How smart is that?'

Will cupped his face in both hands, afraid he'd laugh. Or cry. Could you even call a thought like that 'logic', as in 'failed logic', when it was so patently stupid and ill-informed?

Somewhere close by a phone started ringing. Gabby unearthed a mobile from her pocket. 'Hello?' As she listened she turned and eyed Simone. Nodded. Smiled. 'Yep, sure did. We'll see you soon.' She ended the call. Addressed Simone. 'He's up there now.'

With that she clambered back onto their boat and sprawled on the cabin roof. 'See you, losers.' Simone swung the boat around hard and drove the throttle forward. The launch whipped up a lather as it sped away, Will swamped by frothy wake.

'Sorry,' Hunter said. 'If she thinks she's missing out on something she gets real mean.'

'Forget it. Let's get going.' What was it with Hunter? One minute acting gullible and just plain thick, yet when he talked about the things that interested him his whole demeanour changed. And everyone walked right over him, despite the fact he looked like Rambo — well, except Dean. It must be hell to live inside a body that caused so many false assumptions. A bit like orcas. Will, meanwhile, looked like the lanky freak he was. Helpful for his ex-singing career, got him noticed, but not so good on a cold dark night. Maybe if he'd had some of Hunter's brawn they would've left him alone. A bit of extra bulk hadn't done Pavarotti any harm.

When they made it to Gleneden it was deserted, a minor miracle and a relief to see the tent and other gear still there. They anchored and Will dragged himself aboard, exhausted. He wrung out his clothes and laid them on the hot pontoon to dry, stretching along the other one to warm himself. He trailed his hand over the side, maintaining constant contact with Min.

Hunter chucked him a towel. 'What now?'

'Thanks.' Will rubbed his hair dry. 'The people in the video clips stayed with them, day and night. I think it works on the theory that touch helps to heal them.'

'That's a bit hippie.'

'Not touchy-feely psychic healing. Just staying with them for moral support. There was this poor beluga — you know, those really weird white things — got badly cut up by a boat. Jesus it looked disgusting. This woman stayed with it for days and it came right with loving vibes and constant touch. It's how they do it in their pods. Like how our mums used to kiss us better when we were little, remember? Kind of like that.'

Hunter rubbed his nose. Grunted. 'Maybe your mum.'

'Shit, sorry. I didn't mean—'

'S'all right. She didn't do that but whenever she was pissed she'd kiss me heaps. Only then she'd cry and start to throw our stuff in suitcases. That's when they'd *really* fight . . .' He stared down at his wide bare feet. Breathed noisily, a high-pitched nose flute.

Will closed his eyes. It was funny how you could look at someone and have no idea what the hell was churning around inside. He'd always thought people could be read like books if you took the time to study them, but maybe he only saw what he wanted to see, or expected to see. Maybe everyone did. Until the last couple of days he'd not have given Hunter's inner life a second thought. Yet now he felt guilty for not making any effort since he'd arrived. Dean had tried to get the two of them together. Hinted so many times that Will had blocked it out. He'd thought Hunter would be like Gabby. Or, worse, like Bruce. But it looked as though Hunter was miserable, and Will could sure as hell understand why.

'Why'd you chuck it in?'

Will dragged his thoughts back to the present. 'Chuck what in?'

'That TV thing. I bet they'd have given you another chance. You were the best singer by far.'

Defensiveness coiled around Will's throat. 'Yeah right.'

'Nah, truly, dude. Remember that show you did at school? Where you were dressed up like a chink? You were frickin' awesome in that too.'

Chink? Jesus, what century was this? What world? 'How the hell do you know about that?'

'Dean showed me the video. I laughed my arse off.'

He glanced at Will's face. 'Not 'cause you were bad, you know? But it was funny. I've never seen anything like that before.'

Heat engulfed Will. Mum must have sent a copy to Dean. She insisted on videoing everything; reckoned one day Will would want to show his kids. As if. Not that he minded Dean watching — he was proud of how he handled the role — but what had Dean been thinking? And why hadn't he said?

'It's *The Mikado*. They're Japanese.'

Surely Hunter understood the dangerous power of words? Bruce'd thrown plenty of insults at him by the sound of it. How you could damn someone's abilities, culture or beliefs in a single word or phrase? *Chink. Greenie. Townie. Killer whale. Will of the Living Dead.*

'Whatever.' Hunter scooped up a handful of seawater and splashed it onto the back of his neck. 'So, anyway, why?'

'Why what?'

'Why'd you quit? Even if you'd been rubbish, which you aren't, you would've won the sympathy vote.'

'Are you kidding?' Min let out a little squeal. Will patted him. 'Sorry mate.' He modulated his tone. 'Did Gabby show you the comments too?'

'Who cares? People just write that crap because they can. It doesn't mean it's true.'

'Easy for you to say. I'd walk down the street and total strangers would hurl insults at me and think they were being funny. It got so bad at school I quit.' It hadn't been his mates, or anyone his year. It was the younger kids who'd taunted him. They'd sniffed out his hurt like sharks do blood. Went for the jugular. The fact they were juniors only made him feel more pathetic. It was such a relief when the holidays came — until his parents told him they were buggering off to Oz.

'Didn't you want to prove them wrong?'

'I couldn't *do* anything, man. I had a munted brain. Weeks of blinding headaches. Mood swings. Insomnia. At one point I even had hallucinations.' He'd never admitted that before, not even to the shrink. It scared the crap out of him.

He slid off the pontoon and busied himself with Min, stroking him between his eyes. Min held his gaze, bringing to mind the poster on his old bedroom wall — the Hourglass Nebula — its blue nucleus like the eye of God. Both made him feel that the mind behind that staring eye was more evolved than any human being could ever imagine.

An engine broke the silence. Will looked past Hunter's worried face as a rigid inflatable cruised in through the archway. It bore the Fisheries logo. *Oh shit.*

Harley Andrews, scruffier in real life, nodded a greeting to Hunter as he pulled up alongside. Will drew away from Min.

Harley tossed Hunter a rope and they rafted the two boats together while Will climbed back aboard. He pulled on his damp T-shirt and jeans — all this before Harley said a word. The suspense was so unbearable Will went on the attack.

'He's been shot right through the dorsal fin.' Will pointed down at Min, who stared back up with trusting eyes.

'You know you're breaking all the regulations? I'm surprised at *you*, Hunter. You should know better.'

Will's heart was rapping wildly. 'Didn't you hear? Some mongrel took a pot shot at him.'

'First things first. I know your uncle passed on my warning, so what exactly do you think you're doing? Are you taking the piss?'

Hunter cleared his throat. 'Bob shot him, Harley. He's wounded.'

'Rules state you can't get any closer than fifty metres in a boat or a hundred if you're in the water. What part of that don't you understand?'

'The bit that says you'd ticket me while some old bastard gets away with attempted murder.' Will's voice shook.

'I don't write the rules, but you can guarantee they were written by people with a damn sight more authority than you.' He wiped away the sweat accumulating around the brim of his hat. 'I can't have you taking the law into your own hands. The experts say—'

'The experts,' Will said, 'would leave him to die. I've seen the stuff on the internet. If you really cared you'd be going after that crazy old prick, not hassling us.'

'How'd you know where to find us?' Hunter's face was sullen. His biceps bulged as he crossed his arms.

'I have my ways.'

'It was Gabby, wasn't it?' Hunter turned to Will. 'I bet Dad sicced her on us. It wouldn't be the first time.'

'Well, if you hadn't told her where—'

'I know, I know. I'm a dick. I get that. This whole bloody thing's my fault.' He looked so miserable that Will regretted having bitten.

'Forget it.' He turned his focus back to Harley. 'The real question is: are you going to punish *us* for trying to help Min, or the ones trying to kill him?'

'Don't take that tone with me, kid. I've been—'

He got no further. A battered cabin cruiser sped in through the arch, its fibreglass peeling. Pania was at the wheel as Viv, the dreadlocked lady, readied a rope. They rafted up to Harley's boat with practised ease.

'Is he here?' Pania asked.

'Yep. Big hole through his dorsal fin but otherwise just shocked.'

'Hey Harley!' Viv jumped across and vigorously shook Harley's hand. 'Good to see you're on the case. I hear Bob Davers has been a little trigger happy.' She looked over Harley's shoulder to Will. Winked.

'I might have known you'd show.' A frown cleft Harley's brow. He turned to Pania. 'Hey, Pans. How're you?'

'Good thanks.' She clambered over a pile of nets. Peered into the water. When she saw Min she dropped down to her knees and reached out her hand towards him. 'You poor little baby.'

Min bunted her palm and made his Donald Duck noise. She laughed and leaned right out as if to kiss him.

'Pania, don't!' Harley stamped a foot down on the side of her boat, rocking her off balance. 'What the hell is wrong with you people? It's a wild animal — not a pet. If you tame it you make it far more vulnerable.'

Viv joined Pania as she watched Min. Min sprayed them with a fine mist and gurgled, the sound uncannily like a human laugh. Viv peeled off her clothes, revealing a plain black swimsuit underneath. Her body was toned. Strong.

'Oh no you don't,' Harley said. 'You haven't the authority.'

She slid over the gunwale, ignoring him, and eased into the sea, barely raising a ripple. One hand out as if luring a timid cat, she worked her way close to Min. Once he accepted her touch, Viv inspected the wound.

Harvey's face was livid. 'Get the hell out of there, woman. You know the rules.'

'Don't give me that shit, Harley. You know I'm perfectly entitled to inspect him.'

'Only if I sanction it.'

Viv shot him a murderous glance. 'Then best you do.'

'What the hell's going on?' Will asked Hunter.

'She's a vet.'

'You're kidding? Why didn't anyone tell me?' He squatted down next to Pania and watched Viv examine the damaged flesh. 'How is it?'

'It'll be okay,' she said. 'I could debride it but I think as long as he's kept quiet and doesn't stress it'll mend itself.' She pressed her forehead between Min's eyes and gave him a hongi. 'Kei te pēhea koe? What are you doing here, little man? You're causing quite a stir.' Min rubbed up against her, clicking, and Will felt a moment's intense jealousy. Ridiculous.

Viv checked Min's teeth and gums then hauled herself back aboard. She looked like a beached mermaid, her long dreadlocks hanging down almost to her backside. How old was she? Late thirties? Early forties?

Viv pulled a towel out of a plastic supermarket bag to dry herself, then wrapped it around her waist. 'Right, time for a little kōrero.' She sat down in Harley's boat and motioned everyone to join her.

'How did you know what happened?' Will asked Pania. 'Or where we were?'

'Dean told us. We went to Brookes Bay but when you weren't there I figured you'd probably have come up here.'

'Dean did?'

Viv laughed. 'That old bugger can be a bit pōrangi but he's okay underneath.'

Pania grinned. 'I'm going to tell him you said that!'

'Don't you dare!' Viv turned to Will. 'Your uncle and I like to spar but it doesn't mean anything. I like to keep him honest — make sure he doesn't let that boss of his forget his priorities.' She laid a hand on Hunter's arm. 'No offence, e kare.'

Hunter blushed. 'No worries.'

Harley cleared his throat. 'Get to the point, Viv. If you and Mike think you're going to get your mates to kick up a fuss . . .'

'That's totally up to you, Harley.' Viv pulled a handful of dreads forward and ran her hand down to squeeze out water. 'Our little kera wēra here needs protecting. Now you can get Bruce off his case and let these kids here help the poor little bugger while I try to find his pod, or you can fight us. But I promise it'll get ugly if you go that way. Nanny M's claimed him as whānau and no one wants to see her hurt.'

'The regulations say—'

'Bullshit, Harley. You bend the regulations any time it suits you. Last year you let Bruce off for dumping all that oily bilge water down at the marina. Don't think we didn't know. Aroha's got photos.'

'So now you're blackmailing me?'

'Course not, e hoa. Just reminding you that you have a little leeway in how you interpret the rules.'

'All we're trying to do is keep him safe,' Will said. 'If Viv can help us find his family then it's a happy ending all around.'

'And when the tourists see you pulling a stunt like the one on TV the other night? I'll have my butt hauled over the coals—'

'I promise we'll keep it quiet. I'll stay with him out here. No one has to know.' He tried to look as serious and responsible as he could. 'Please.'

'Come on, Harley,' Pania added. 'Look at the poor little thing. Do you really want to see him die?'

Harley stroked his moustache tenderly, as if it was a small live animal. He stared over the side of the boat. Min hung there, whining like a puppy. Harley sighed heavily and turned to Viv. 'How long do you think it'll take to search?'

'I'll contact Ingrid when I get home. She'll know.'

Again Harley brooded as they waited. In an overhanging pōhutukawa tree a tūī sang near-perfect arpeggios. D flat followed by A major. Finally he slapped his hands down on his sunburnt knees. 'All right. Just for now. But if I get any complaints I'll have to act. And if it gets out to the press again all deals are off.'

'Ka pai!' Viv leaned over and smacked a kiss onto his sweaty brow.

'Thanks,' Will said. He swallowed hard as he shook Harley's hand. Had to get a grip on himself; needed time alone.

They shifted Pania's boat to let Harley out and waved him off like a war hero as he disappeared out through the arch.

'Thanks so much,' Will said to Viv. He scuffed a kiss

across her cheek, catching the salty taste of her.

'No worries. Harley's okay if you don't piss him off.'

'Who's Ingrid?'

'A world expert on orcas.' She pressed her hand into the small of his back. 'Stop looking so miserable, cuz. If anyone can identify our little māhuri tōtara's pod, it's her.'

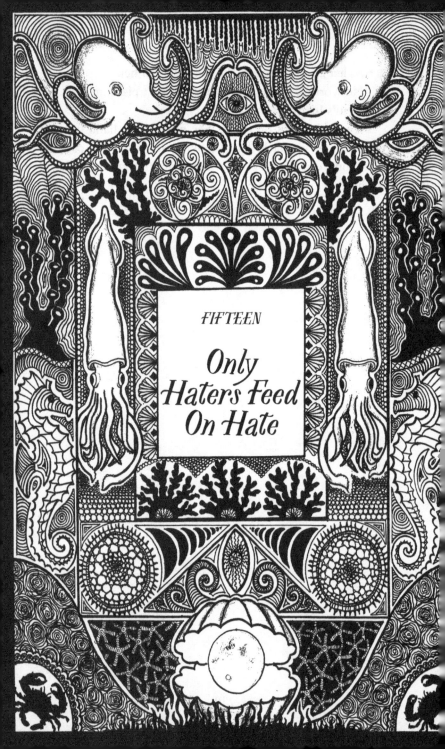

FIFTEEN

*Only
Haters Feed
On Hate*

Oh the boost when Song Boy found me floating in my shattered state. I ached, a deep dragging discomfort, but the fear that flooded through me washed away when he came forth. He stroked me, soothed me, swept me up into his heartfelt hug.

I did not know what caused my wound; the Hungry One so filled with hate had not come close. No fair warning. No fronting, face to face. A sneaky stunt. It's true we, too, can kill without kindness or care, but we mostly wish to weigh in on the side of greater good. Our old ones teach this to our young, and those who spurn such schooling are left to fret over their friendless fate.

We must reweigh, rethink, the blunders of those bygone Beings. Of course, we have all wandered into wrong, slipped on selfishness, let our lowest lusts loom large. Oh yes, it's true, me more than most. But falling is only fatal when one fails to find the strength to float back up. Believe me, all wrongs can be righted where there is a will.

In our painful past our kind made two mistakes. The

first rose from our make-up: when the Hungry Ones hunted us we failed to fight their lack of care. We truly thought that they would see our sorrows and call their bloodbath off, but we were wrong. Instead, we wound up battered, with no breather from their brutal ways.

So when they kept on carving up our clans the last limp stragglers lost their wits. This was the second sorry misstep, and it set the scene for further loss. My friends, those feeble few fought back, and who of us would blame them at the time? Mothers moved to murder; fathers fought fleets that flocked to feed upon their young. It was a hard and bitter battle with our cousins at our side, but though we spent the full force of our might we failed to drive the Hungry Ones to their doom. And though it's true our old ones' wrath was just, it neither freed us to a better future nor kept us safe. Indeed, it deepened danger; prolonged our plight.

What can we learn from such a shambles? That the wars waged on us by our foes should not be countered with our own. Only haters feed on hate. Love breeds love.

While now we try to wend the wiser path it is slow, so slow. We hope, one day, to know their minds; find meanings in shared songs. If they truly choose to listen, their hearts can hear our sameness even if their ears cannot.

It is with sadness that I sing of this, but also hope. We all have wondered why the Hungry Ones, with minds as keen and clever as our own, take not the time to understand the others of our world. Is it some weakness in their make-up? Their quenchless craving? Their take, take, take? They are the only living beings who snatch more than they need — hoarding, holding, having —

stashing wealth while others go without. Greed, my friends, is an ugly oddity. Their weakness and their wont.

What they miss, dear travellers, is the warmth and wonder of our ties to other seaborne beings. We work at building bonds and hearing hearts. I've swum the seas with manta rays, their wings as wide as I am long. In them I sensed a wealth of wit far finer than all other fish. They worked to know me and in them I found free souls. Oh, the wonder of those wings! Their slow strokes tell us all we need to know about the currents' twists and turns.

We always call on other Beings, our many cousins, when we work through weighty woes. We share a sadness; seek to salve the hurts the Hungry Ones have wrought. We work toward a world where all can win, not only one.

And my Song Boy, ah, now he is rare — though not, you understand, unique. Many move to grapple with the gap between us and the Hungry Ones, though, through all this, there was a bleakness bleeding off him then — sadness so strong his soul was sick. How could I know this still so young? Come, come. I have already made it plain! Same aches, same loneliness, same loss of love. All life swims to the sound of these rebounding beats.

So when he brought in Broad Boy and the two bewitching girls, I trusted him to pick the perfect path to keep me safe. Settled by his soothing strokes, harboured from further harm, I gave in to his goodness. Caved in to his care. He never left me, hands hot on my hide, his life force passing through his palms to bolster mine. They carried calm. Hugged hope. And in the end it was his handling that helped. The kiss of skin to skin has always been the means by which we Beings show our love. Somehow my Song Boy knew.

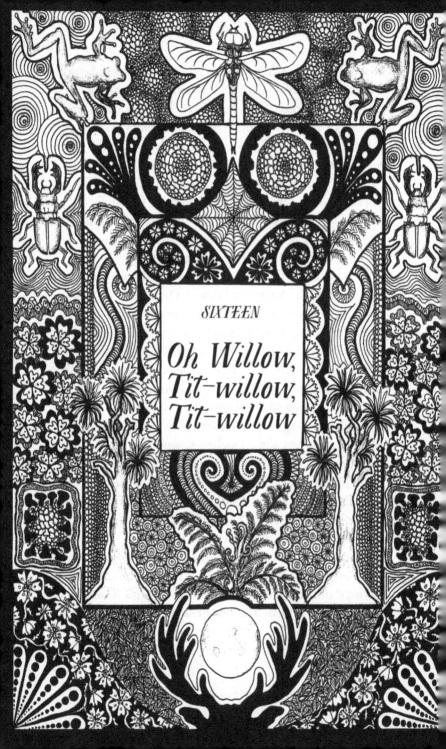

SIXTEEN

Oh Willow, Tit-willow, Tit-willow

Will floated in the water, his head cushioned by the lifejacket. Min hadn't moved, content to stay in physical contact, though it was questionable how much longer Will could stay immersed. His skin was wrinkled, waterlogged, and it was chilly. But the usual tension that pincered his skull had lessened and so he pushed away the crap that clamoured for attention in order to savour the reprieve. The peace was heavenly. Only the pop of Min's blowhole, open, shut, and the a cappella chorus of the birds.

On a tree by a river a little tom-tit, sang 'Willow, tit-willow, tit-willow!' It was driving him nuts how these stupid songs kept coming back at him. It wasn't as if *The Mikado* had a profound story or voiced some precious truth. In fact it was pretty damn silly, the words in isolation ridiculous . . . at first glance. *And I said to him, 'Dicky-bird, why do you sit singing Willow, tit-willow, tit-willow?'* It was a song about manipulation; the end a threat. Melodramatic as all hell. *And if you remain callous and obdurate, I shall perish as he did, and you will know why — though I probably shall not exclaim as I die, 'Oh, willow, tit-willow, tit-willow!'*

It was the kind of emotional blackmail his grandmother had used, eating up all his mother's spare time for the last two years before she died. His poor mum could never please her. By the time Gran's diabetes finally got her, his mum was so strung out she'd had to take five weeks off work. Little did she know that two months later they'd axe her job. When Will heard they were going to Australia he'd nearly pulled the old tit-willow trick to make them stay. But didn't. Couldn't. His mum was far too caught up in her own nightmare; it wasn't fair to drag her into his.

As for his dad . . . People could say what they liked about equality, life balance, house husbands, blah-de-blah. But the truth was his dad had no bloody clue what to do after he'd been laid off. All his self-esteem was tied up in his job — and without it he was pretty much screwed. He still got up at six and did his crossword ('*Gotta keep the brainwork up*') then pounded the streets in suit and tie, grovelling for work. But every 'No thanks' shrunk him further, until the 'go to' guy — Archives' trouble-shooter — acted like he'd forgotten his lines. Twice, Will found him sobbing in the bathroom. When he'd gone to hug him, comfort him, his dad had laughed it off. Trying to hide the tears banking in his eyes.

Will's dad went for every shitty job he could but, by the time they had to rent the house or lose it, he was fading — a cardboard cut-out of the man he used to be. His mum too, come to that. Sure, they still carted him from doctor to doctor, got their lawyer to send out the threatening letters to the pricks online. But it was all done on remote, their spark gone. If Dean hadn't given them a shove, by offering to have Will stay, they'd still be squeezed in the Suttons' spare room. It had hurt to see them so beaten. Was (almost) a relief when they took off.

Will smiled. It only now occurred to him that they were probably relieved too! They seemed much more 'together' in the last few weeks — and *together*, as if the fact they only had each other over there had brought them closer, after the stresses that had torn them all apart. Every week on Skype a little more of the old Mum and Dad broke through.

He wished he hadn't emailed now. They'd only worry, which would be a waste of all his hard work to convince them everything was fine. Hopefully Dean would stay quiet too; just leave them be.

Hunter had offered to run Viv back to Blythe while Pania fished out in the channel. Will liked the way Pania could handle a boat and was content with her own company. She made the girls back home seem trivial, self-obsessed. She was calming, not needing constant reassurance like them. He was glad to have met her. Another rellie was never a bad thing . . . unless, of course, they were like Gabby Taylor! Now *that* would really suck. His knees rose to protect his groin of their own accord, as if even the thought of her threatened his most vital parts.

As the sun lost its edge, the cold settled into his bones. He rolled over and ran his hand along Min's back, careful to avoid his fin. The wound no longer oozed but still looked painful, though Viv was far more worried about Min going into shock. 'The more you stay with him and keep him calm the better he'll be.' To have her validate his plan was reassuring — and handy ammunition should Harley reappear.

'I'm getting out now, mate. I'll just be over there.' He pointed to the beach then felt ridiculous, but Min stirred, his kaleidoscope eyes drinking Will in.

As Will made to leave Min bunted him in the ribs and fired a stream of bubbles into his armpit. Min then latched onto the neck support of the lifejacket and tugged it, emitting a rumbling gurgle, surely a laugh. The timing was too accurate. The sound too close.

He towed Will towards the shallows, his tail doing all the work. 'Thanks mate!' Will pressed his nose between Min's eyes and breathed him in. Fishy. Kelpy. Fleshy. Warm. 'Don't you go anywhere.' He held up his hand, a human stop sign. If dogs could learn such signals, then surely so could Min.

Ashore, he wrenched his T-shirt and jeans back on. Hunter had left a warm hoodie and he slipped into it like a kid playing dress-ups, rolling the sleeves damn near halfway up before he could free his hands. Hunter was the first guy he'd met who made him feel small — though only physically. He liked his company a lot.

By the time he'd lit a fire, his stomach was rampaging like a rabid dog. He cheered when Pania finally chugged in aboard her father's runabout.

'I caught three gurnard and a snapper!' She grinned as if she'd won Lotto. 'And look! I found one of Bruce's!' She pointed into the plastic bin at her feet. A good-sized salmon dwarfed the rest. 'Score!'

Will laughed. 'Jesus, we'd better get rid of *that* fast!' He hoisted it out by the tail, its eyes as opaque as an old man's cataracts.

'Yeah, I know.' Pania followed Will's dubious gaze. 'I don't really fancy eating it either — but I couldn't bear to throw it back!' She laughed. 'I thought maybe Min might like it.'

'Oh no you don't! Min's taste for salmon was how this whole fight started.'

'Pooh!' she said. 'I had a feeling you'd say that.'

Will raised an eyebrow. 'Pooh?'

She slapped at him. 'Shut up! I made a pact with Nanny M. If I don't swear for one whole year I'll get five hundred bucks!'

'How long to go?'

'Two months. It's easier now. At first I was too scared to speak at all in case I blew it!'

'Tell me about it!' For the first three months after that fateful night Will had been too shaken to sing at all. He wasn't even sure he could. But since he'd come down here and started on his daily jaunts out in the yacht he'd forced himself. During those song-free months it felt as if the only part of himself he liked had been cut off.

He threw the salmon back into the crate and hooked the snapper out. 'Let's cook this now. I'm bloody starving.'

Pania rolled her eyes. 'Hollow leg syndrome! My brother Kingi had it too.'

Would asking about him upset her? He held the snapper out. 'Should I fillet it?'

'Nah. Just gut it and scrape off the scales. It's better whole.' She checked his face. 'Have you ever done it before?'

'Yes.' He shrugged. 'In theory!'

She laughed. 'Give it here!' She produced a knife from the littered shelf below the dashboard of the runabout and carried the snapper over to a large flat rock beside the stream. With sure, deft strokes she showed him how to scrape off the scales and split the fish down the centre of its belly to free its entrails.

'How old was he?' Will asked.

'Who?'

'Kingi.' The name swelled in his mouth.

She studied him with her disconcerting eyes. 'Twenty-seven,' she said. 'Mum had him before she met Dad.'

'What was he like?'

She excised a string of gut. 'He left home to join the army when I was ten. I only saw him at Christmas after that.' She rinsed the carcase in fresh water, fingernails scraping the last clotted globules from the frame of bones. 'It really cut Mum up — and Nanny M. Seeing them so upset's the worst part of it all. Since then, all Nanny M's wairua's been seeping away.'

'Her spirit?'

'Yeah, her life force has been really knocked.' She stood up and handed him the fish, her next words less certain. 'A bit like you, Dean says.'

'I'm fine.' It burst out before humiliation throttled him. He skewered the fish onto a supple branch and hooped it over the glowing coals.

Pania looked as if he'd slapped her, her cheeks staining crimson. 'Sorry,' she said, 'I didn't mean to—'

'S'okay. Forget it.' He knew he'd gone from normal to paranoid and touchy in one second flat. He'd lost his 'keep calm and shut up' switch — his ability to filter out what was better left unsaid was shot to hell since the head injury. 'Disinhibited' his doctors called it, a fancy term that really meant 'rude moody prick'. And though they said that it would settle over time, he'd yet to see the proof of this. He offered her one of Hunter's beers.

'Here. Sorry for snapping.'

Pania shook her head. 'No thanks.' She watched as Will opened the can and took a swig. 'Do you really like the taste of that?' She screwed up her nose.

He grinned. 'Not really. But it's better than nothing.'

She jerked her head towards the stream. 'There's always water.'

'Are you a hardcore Christian or something?'

Pania laughed. 'Nah. It's just, I don't see the point. *And* I've been round too many drunks.'

She sounded like such a cranky old lady that he laughed too. 'How the hell do you put up with Gabby then?' He'd heard about Gabby's exploits from Dean. Hard drinking. Hard playing. Hard, full stop.

'She's okay sometimes. And it's better to be her friend than her enemy, that's for sure.' Pania threw a twig onto the fire. 'She doesn't have it that great either. Her dad's a real p—' She stopped herself. 'He's a creep.' She shuddered.

Will let it drop, too hungry to rustle up much sympathy for Gabby. She took too much pleasure in shooting people down. Wasn't to be trusted. 'What's the story with Dean and Viv? Not much love lost there.' The fish juices sizzled and spat from fleshy vents, smelling so good he actually drooled.

'You'd be surprised! Viv hates it how Dean lets Bruce stomp all over him.'

'Yeah, what the hell is that about? Why *does* he stay there?'

'The same reason anyone does: he needs the work.' She ran her fingers through her straggly hair and wound it into a tight coil. 'Besides, he loves the business and he promised Helen he'd look after things.'

'Hunter's mum? How come?'

Pania's eyes widened. 'You mean he hasn't told you?'

'What?'

She wrapped her arms around her legs. Rested her chin on her knees. 'It's a long story.'

'Best you start now, then!' He leaned back on his elbows, lounging dramatically.

'He was in love with her,' Pania said. 'They dated right through school. Her dad was really rich — his lot were one of the first settlers here, like the Godsills. *He* was the one who set up the first fish farm. He brought Dean in to help before he'd even finished school. Joe built the business up and Dean was going to take it over when he married Helen.'

Why hadn't Dean told him this? 'So how did she end up with Bruce?'

'She was always a big drinker, Mum said. She reckons both Helen's parents were alkies and Helen was born with the taste for it. In their last year of school their class went on a week-long trip to Wellington. Dean stayed home to help out Joe. The last night up in Welly, Helen got real coma-ed and Bruce was all over her. Three months later she was married off to him to spare them the shame of a pregnant daughter. Poor Dean lost Helen *and* the farm.'

'Then why on earth does he still work for Bruce? That's crazy.'

'I don't think he could give it up. The old boy had paid him in shares, and Dad says every year Dean tries to buy a few more on the quiet. When things got worse for Helen after Hunter was born, she begged Dean not to leave.' Pania crushed a sandfly with one deft clap of her hands.

'Worse how?'

'Bruce started beating the cra— beating her up real bad, so she drank even more. I think Dean thought she'd kill herself. Mum says that he still loved her; that she made him promise he'd watch over Hunter. When she died, she left Hunter all her father's shares, with some kind of legal thing that meant Bruce couldn't get his hands on them. Bruce was furious. He tried to fight it but didn't win. Dad reckons Dean should walk away. Dean says he won't. I think that's what Viv can't understand.' She sighed. Brushed a strand of hair away from her eyes. 'Sad, huh?'

'Maybe Hunter's really Dean's kid!'

Pania snorted. 'Get real. Just look at him!'

He pictured Bruce and Dean; placed Hunter in between them. *One tall thin man. Two burly brutes.* 'Yeah, true.' The Helen story might well explain why Dean would stay, but . . . 'Why would Bruce keep Dean on? He must've known about him and Helen. Wouldn't he want Dean out of the way?'

'He can't afford to. Dean knows the business too well and has too many links to the iwi. Bruce needs to keep them onside so he can pretend to "consult" every time he wants to build more farms.'

'It's a bloody opera!' All the double-dealing, broken hearts and tragic deaths seemed comic, crazy, on the stage. But Dean and Helen's story was sad. Painfully raw. Poor Dean. How could he work for the prick, knowing what he knew?

The snapper had started sagging off its bones, the smell of crispy skin making Will's mouth water. He flipped it onto a plastic plate and they picked at it with their fingers until only the bare carcase and head remained. It tasted sweet and buttery, peppery woodsmoke infused through the flesh.

By the time they'd rinsed their hands in the stream the sun had gone. In the bush behind, the evening chorus were tuning their voices, but out beyond the shallows Min had hardly moved. Will stripped back down and braved the water one last time. It was surprisingly warm after the chill in the air.

Min greeted him with little mews, pressing into him for contact. Will stroked him from head to tail, still in awe that a wild creature would let him do this. But he was worried that he hadn't seen Min eat since they'd arrived from Brookes Bay. Maybe Pania was right. 'Okay! I give up!' he called over to her. 'Chuck the salmon here!'

She smirked triumphantly, good-humoured sarcasm dripping from her voice. 'Good plan! It's genius!' She looked about five years old. Cheeky and shiny-eyed.

But, even when he presented the salmon right in front of Min, the orca merely nosed it back to Will. 'Come on, mate. You've got to eat.' He floated the salmon in front of Min again and jiggled it.

Carefully Min took the dead fish between his teeth and shook it, as Will had. Then he spat it back to Will. Whistled and clicked. Eyed him, a flicker of humour lurking in those remarkably complex depths.

'You're not even trying!' It wasn't as though he could load up a spoon and pretend to fly it into the 'hangar' like his mum had done when he was small. Just how long could a baby orca go without?

What the hell to do? All he could picture were mother birds regurgitating half-digested fish. He shuddered, almost gagging. *Come on, come on.* He sucked in two deep breaths and took hold of the salmon's dorsal fin with his teeth. Now he really gagged; couldn't contain it. But he presented the fish to Min, humming a high-pitched tone he hoped would sound pleading.

He could feel Min's attention sharpen, a burst of energy shooting at him through the water. Min's tail twitched. He plucked the salmon from Will's mouth so suddenly Will gasped. Bad move. He floundered backwards, choking, coughing, and scrabbled to get footing on the rocky seabed.

In the meantime Min had swallowed the fish. 'You little beauty!' Will planted a kiss on his snout, ridiculously relieved.

'Here.' Pania waved the three gurnard by their tails. 'Try these as well.'

The fish splashed down around Will and to his relief Min went for them straight away. He swallowed them without the need for further games, just as Hunter's boat manoeuvred in beneath the arch of rocks.

He drove the tinny up onto the shingle beach. 'Hey, Pans. Your mum said to head back straight away,' he said. 'She wants you home before dark.'

Pania shrugged. 'True. I guess I'd better go.' Reluctance bled off her. She called to Will, who was still treading water beside Min. 'You want me to come back tomorrow?'

'If you can. Though don't go out of your way. We—'

'Look, if you don't—'

Was she trying to get out of it or wanting a proper invitation? 'Come. Please. The more of us the better.'

A smile lit her face. 'Okay. Cool.' She packed up and headed off, waving as she manoeuvred out between the rocks.

While Hunter unloaded extra stores Will floated on his back and sang to Min until his throat grew tight with tiredness.

Finally he staggered from the water and dried himself off. Between the day's dramas and all the swimming he was so buggered his eyes kept drooping shut. As the night set in he and Hunter hunkered over the fire, talking about everything from the weather to the stupid antics of the tourists and how to keep Harley's threats at bay. But after a while Hunter's voice started going in one ear and out the other, Will too weary now to take it in. He crawled into the tent and wriggled into his sleeping bag. Beyond the tent, possums crashed through the bush; further away, he heard the expiration of Min's blowhole adding a brush-beat to the whisper of the lapping tide. He sighed, feeling all the day's stress unravel, and let the night sounds lull him off to sleep.

~

HE WOKE TO THE DRONE of an engine. Lay in the orange glow of the tent as morning light funnelled in through the front flap. He shed the sleeping bag like a snakeskin and edged past the sweaty mountain of Hunter's sleeping body. He hadn't meant to sleep so late.

Gabby smirked at him from the wheel of the little cabin cruiser as he staggered out. *Bloody hell.* A man, two women and two kids crammed along the cruiser's deck. Tourists, sporting cameras and fitted out in expensive pastel sportswear. Their accents reached him as he sprinted for the water. German?

He cast around for Min, his heart thumping. Saw a

dorsal fin camouflaged in the shade of an overhanging pōhutukawa in the cove's deepest corner. *Thank god.*

Gabby must have tracked his gaze. 'There he is!' She turned the boat and edged it over towards Min.

'Keep away from him!' Will tripped on loose stones, stubbing his middle toe. He hobbled on. Hauled off his sweatshirt and jeans and dived straight in. He pounded over to Min's side, barely registering his squeals of welcome.

Gabby brought the boat to within two metres of Min. When she throttled off she turned to her passengers, all smiles. 'You're very lucky. Not many people get to see a baby orca so close up.'

'Get out!' Will's blood was fizzing. 'He's not a bloody tourist show. He's injured and he needs to rest.'

His audience shuffled awkwardly as Gabby switched off the motor and threw an anchor over the side.

Hunter emerged from the tent, tousled and squinting. 'What are you doing here?'

Gabby turned to Will. 'We're perfectly entitled to be here — way more than you. Why don't *you* piss off.'

Will wanted to smack her so bad it hurt. He'd heard that same bullying tone too many times before. Her smirk was as irritating as jock rash. 'I'll report you to that Harley guy. This is harassment.'

Hunter was furiously punting over to Will's side, wielding an oar like a warrior. He glided in between them, a brick shithouse in a boat. 'Go home. Harley'll go nuts if he sees you've brought people out.'

Min tucked himself in behind Will, who looped his arm around Min's firm body to bolster him. Buddies. Moral support.

'How did she know where to find us?' Will shot at Hunter, too angry to think straight.

Hunter groaned and slapped his big meaty hand against his brow. 'Me. Simone. Yesterday.' He looked miserable.

Aboard Gabby's boat, one of the children started whining.

'Excuse me . . .' The man, who looked Olympic fit, leaned out and tried to push Hunter's boat aside. 'We have good money paid—'

Anger roared in Will's ears. 'You charged them?'

Gabby crossed her arms, legs astride. 'Course. It's a long way out here. Uses a lot of diesel.'

'How much did you pay her?' Will asked the man.

'Fifty dollars each for boat ride and another one hundred to swim with it.'

Will's head felt like it was going to explode. 'You exploitative bitch.' He clambered over the side, into the tinny, furious and dripping as he stood up to eyeball Gabby. 'No one's getting in the water with him, okay? He's injured and he's vulnerable. I'll report anyone who tries.'

Gabby wasn't smirking now. Her face was as pinched and mean as a scrappy Pekingese. 'Oh yeah? Well, I'll report *you* then. We'll soon see who Harley believes.'

'Back off, Gabs,' Hunter said. 'Harley knows about this, so you—'

'Shut up, Hunts. You think I care what you say? Your brain was screwed up by your boozer of a mother before you were even born.'

Hunter flushed beetroot red, his shoulders slumping at her words. The adults in her boat watched on, as if it was a sideshow for their benefit. The two kids looked scared.

Will couldn't stand to see Hunter so cowed. He turned and addressed their audience. 'What this crook hasn't told you is that if you get in the water with him you can be fined ten thousand bucks. In fact you can just be fined for coming in this close. You take one step closer — or get in the water with him — and I'll be calling up the Fisheries guy.' He glanced at Hunter. 'You got your phone on you?' Hunter nodded. 'Good. Then take their photos now. Harley might need them for evidence in court.'

Hunter's face lit up. He grinned and pulled his mobile from his pocket. Slipped it from its waterproof pouch and starting taking snapshots, one person at a time.

'Now hold on to your horses there.' The man held his hand in front of his face to prevent his photo being taken. Turned to Gabby. 'Good money we paid. I will not—'

'Chill out!' she snarled. 'This has nothing to do with you.' She elbowed the two women out of the way and leaned right out over the water, directing a lethal hiss at Hunter. 'You know I need the money, Hunts. Since when did you side with the townies?'

'I'm sorry,' he mumbled, returning his phone to his pocket. 'But Will's right. Min needs to—'

'Min? You've called it Min? What's that short for? Minuscule penises, after you and *him*?' She laughed, a cockatoo screech, and looked to her audience for applause. 'Don't you worry about a thing. These dickheads here will move now if they know what's good for them.' She, too, took her mobile from her pocket and brandished it in front of her. 'I'm sure Uncle Bruce would *love* to know what you've been up to.'

'Jesus, Gabby, don't be a bitch. If this's about money, then how much do you need?'

'Don't you dare!' Will said to Hunter. 'She's playing you, man, can't you see?' Will addressed the perplexed tourists. 'Sorry folks. The show's cancelled. I suggest you ask her for your money back and head back into town.'

One of the women shuffled nervously. 'Please, Gabrielle. We'd like for you to take us back. We don't want to make any trouble.'

'Oh, it's no trouble,' Gabby said. She dialled a number on her phone and held it up to her ear. 'Hello, Uncle Bruce? It's Gabs. I—'

Will lunged. His momentum fired the tinny backwards as he propelled himself at her. He managed to knock the phone out of her hand before he plummeted into the gap between the boats, rapping his head against the side of the cruiser as he sank below the surface. The impact was so hard it jolted right down through his spine.

For a moment he could do nothing, his brain convulsing as it crashed around inside his skull. He was sinking, unable to respond to the pull of gravity. Then he felt himself propelled upwards, vomited from the sea as Min pushed him from below and Hunter fished him up by one arm. He collapsed across the gunwale of the tinny and coughed up salty phlegm, his head pounding. Above its thump he heard the buzzing of raised voices but couldn't seem to collect his mind to decipher what they were saying.

Then, to his amazement and relief, he heard the cruiser's motor start back up. Gabby threw it into gear and powered away, leaving them tossed in its wake. Once the rocking died down Will finally raised his head. Hunter was sitting in the tinny, head in hands.

'Thanks,' Will said.

Hunter sniffed. 'No worries.' He looked like hell.

'What happened?'

'She'll dump us in the shit, no two ways about it. When she's on the rampage nothing will stop her.'

'She'll tell Bruce?'

Hunter nodded, his expression hardening.

'Jesus, man, I'm so sorry. Put all the blame on me. Don't take the rap yourself.'

Hunter shrugged. 'Forget it.' He picked up the oar and paddled them back to shore, Min nosing around the hull as if he, too, was worried for their fate.

Will dried himself and fussed around the campsite, tidying, shifting things pointlessly just to keep moving. Hunter fiddled with the motor of the tinny then threw himself into the water, seeking solace with Min. Will watched from the shore as Min worked his charm, the tension in Hunter's face retreating as he and Min played catch with driftwood. At least Min seemed livelier today, more like himself. This should've lifted Will's spirits, but the threat of Bruce and Harley hanging over him was like a brewing storm. It didn't help that the knock to his head had left him with a headache so bad his eyes watered if he moved too fast.

Hunter's phone rang in his discarded jeans but he ignored it, and when Will offered to answer, after it had rung for the third time, Hunter insisted he leave it be. It would be Bruce, he said. No point.

When Harley motored into the cove just before noon, Will felt a strange inevitability settle over him, just like it had in those last excruciating minutes before he'd been attacked that night. Then, in his drunken fog, time had slowed. He could still clearly see the scene, like he was on the outside looking in: his boot knocking a bottle over as he tried to stagger around the three hunched figures. The crazed look in their eyes as they'd taken in his state. Then came the moment when he'd felt the shift; when they clicked that he was drunk and vulnerable — and on his own. That's when he'd truly blown it — said something stupid — what was it? What *was* it? Oh god, yes, something from *Macbeth* — the three stooped figures so like the three witches in his fuddled brain, out he'd come with it: '*Fair is foul, and foul is fair: Hover through the fog and filthy air.*' Well, that was what he'd meant to say . . . God knows what they thought he'd said, but that's when the man with the rotting teeth had lunged at him; caught him by the foot and brought him down. He was far too pissed to guard himself. Fell heavily, his head hitting the concrete curb, sparks exploding in his mind. Then, through the mist of pain, the knife . . .

Will shook it off and swallowed back the aftertaste as Harley beached his boat and lumbered out.

'I warned you,' he said. 'No trouble. No publicity.' He scratched his head. Waited for Hunter to scrabble ashore. 'Your father has been on at me.'

Will felt the tension building in his gut. Watched Hunter blanch.

Harley took a notepad from his shirt pocket. Turned to Will. 'I'm sorry, mate, but now I have to act.'

SEVENTEEN

*Lusts
Looming
Large*

Sounds streak through seas in waves, my friends, some-times in a scrabbled storm, othertimes weak and wispy. But they are always overwhelming when the mood is mean. That day the air was wild with anger, calls cutting, cries clashing, unwelcome rabble ranting as they threw around unwanted weight.

Then the Human with the walrus whiskers slipped in and stole my Song Boy; plucked him from our stronghold and shipped him off. Once again, I found myself filled with that formless fear.

So when Broad Boy fled in their wake I followed too, not willing to wait in that cooped-up cove alone. I wailed, whimpered, worried, but when Song Boy tried to soothe me with a sound or touch, Walrus Whiskers halted him. I sensed such hardness hurt his heart; knew he was as soul-sick for the loss of me as I was him.

The harbour was awash with Hungry Ones and, though I hunkered at the edges of the turning tide, I felt their eyes eat into me, lusts looming large. I saw my Song

Boy break away, seeking out some sign of me, but though I ached to answer — to feel the comfort of his healing hands — I was too scared to show myself amongst those Human hordes.

Instead I watched a crowd crush in around him, Broad Boy bursting through to stand beside him, as wild words rang out. They swarmed like sardines in a shifty swell, yet in their midst my Song Boy stood quite still. I could feel his fury, sense his struggle, read his rage as those around him fought in a fog of unforgiveness and unfounded hate.

Walrus Whiskers held his ground. His song took on the tone of threats, a hateful hymn. And in the end the Hungry Ones slipped off, battle bypassed, no lives lost. But my Song Boy, too, was swept up in the wake of their leave-taking, and soon the shore was empty, as was I.

For the rest of that whole day, and well into the next, I waited just beyond the harbour yet, in all that time, not one lone look was cast at me. It was as if I'd turned to air, was as hidden as glass-octopodes who lurk down deep. This casting-off was both unnerving and unkind.

It was an awful time, spurned by all, in fear for Song Boy. To be so shunned rubbed up roughly against all my other hurt and loss.

My mind mulled the bond I had sealed with Song Boy. The sharing of our sounds tied us together; his care and kindness helped to start the healing of my broken heart. We forged a friendship in the face of all our otherness. Found ways to bridge the gaps between.

Ah, now here's the nub: we both are Warm-bloods with an inborn need to breathe fresh air; both able to open up our minds. Therein lies the gift of this. By searching out our sameness, we formed a faith to work towards the coming together of our kinds.

Though, at the time, my heart was sick with sadness. Hope is hard to hold onto when one is little and alone.

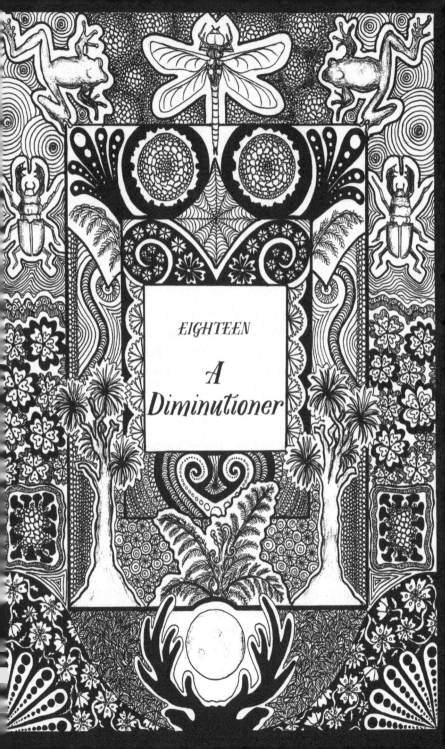

EIGHTEEN

*A
Diminutioner*

Will's head pounded so hard he felt the echoes of it pulsing through his stomach. 'You *are* joking?'

'I'm afraid not.' Harley Andrews sighed and scratched his bald spot. 'Now there's an official complaint I have to follow through.'

'You gonna fine me too?' Hunter looked ready to combust.

'Nope. Just Mr Jackson here — for now. He's the one who started this.'

'That's fucking unbelievable!' Hunter kicked out, showering the stern of Harley's boat with grit. It sounded like a spatter of machine-gun fire. 'You just saw me in the water with him.'

Harley tugged at his moustache. 'Look, Hunter. Keep out of this. We don't want things to get ugly.'

'Ugly? You think it can get any uglier than fining Will ten grand for helping save the orca's life?'

'Jesus kid, when did you get so mouthy? Loose lips sink ships.'

Hunter drew himself up to his full height. 'No offence, Harley, but Will's right and you know it. Bugger you.'

Will clapped him on the back. 'Thanks, man.' He dredged in a deep breath. He'd missed having a friend, someone to ride back-up. He was fast coming to the conclusion it was possible to be *too* alone — especially when shit went down. And this was definitely total shit. The set of Harley's shoulders made it clear there was to be no arguing. This wasn't about Min at all. It was a power play — and Bruce held all the cards.

Out past the shallows Min was spy-hopping, more animated than he'd been all day. He clearly knew something was up. *So please you, Sir, we much regret, If we have failed in etiquette, Towards a man of rank so high, We shall know better by and by* . . .

Hunter was still arguing with Harley, their voices droning over the thump of Will's headache. *Boom, b-boom, boom, b-boom. It's a hopeless case, As you may see, And in your place, Away I'd flee; But don't blame me — I'm sorry to be, Of your pleasure a diminutioner* . . . For a second the lyrics made him smile. Under threat from the Lord High Executioner. Perfect.

'. . . and paid within twenty-one days.' Harley took a sudden interest in his knuckles.

'Pardon?'

'You'll have twenty-one days to pay the fine or else you'll end up in court.' He was flushed, crimson splotches overlaying his peeled sunburn.

'And if I won't pay?' *Won't?* Who was he kidding?

'Then that's for a court to decide. But it's a big sum so it could mean, well, it could mean a short period of probation, or community service — or maybe detention.'

The lyrics thrummed in his head. *Behold the Lord High Executioner, A personage of noble rank and title. A dignified and potent officer, Whose functions are particularly vital!* It was so stupid, so totally surreal, he couldn't take it seriously. But Hunter had paled, the rims of his eyes reddening, on the verge of tears. The reality of it hit Will like a fist. He slumped. Groaned.

Hunter loomed over him. 'You okay?'

Will took in his freckles, his amber-flecked eyes. Couldn't speak. Couldn't risk sounding like a terrified little kid. He nodded but his brain screamed *No!*

'I'm going to take you back to Blythe,' Harley said. 'The orca's now officially off limits.'

There was no point fighting. All he wanted was to crawl back to bed. He'd failed Min. And worse, he could go to jail. *Ta da! Give another round of applause to Will of the Living Dead.* Ten grand or ten million, no difference. He'd never raise it. And he'd be damned if he'd ask Mum or Dad — or Dean. They'd freak.

He levered himself back up, lights shooting around the edges of his vision. A stress migraine. Utterly typical.

He turned to Hunter. 'I hate to ask, but could you sort my gear?'

Hunter nodded. 'No worries. I'll follow you guys in.' He went straight to work, packing down the tent while Harley escorted Will from the cove, then trailed them, Min dashing between the two boats and crying when he came in eye contact with Will.

The pleading tone shredded Will's heart. He reached over to comfort him, couldn't help it, fingertips brushing along the tip of his fin.

'Leave it.' Harley clamped a hand down on his shoulder.

'Don't even look. The more you tame him, the bigger the risk.'

Will hummed death metal to stop an angry tirade breaking out. Inside his skull he screamed at Harley that Bruce was Min's only danger. That he'd seen the clips on YouTube. He understood the issues. Knew that the best outcome was to get Min home. Meanwhile, Min's constant crying made him feel like he was being flayed. All he could do was transmit sorrow and regret.

They reached Blythe around five-thirty, surprised by a crowd down at the wharf. As they drew near, Will spotted Pania and Viv among them, along with others from the marae. Even Nanny M was there. And Pania's mother, Cathy, too. As Harley docked the boat, they all surged forward.

'What the hell is this, Harley?' Viv called.

'Hold your horses. He had fair warning.'

'Bullshit. Hunter phoned us. You're harassing him for Bruce.'

Harley's ears glowed pink. 'Come on. I don't write the rules. And, anyway, there's plenty of evidence. You all saw him on the news.'

Gabby stepped from the shadows with Simone, her faithful lapdog.

Pania rounded on her. 'How could you? Do you have any idea how much money it is?'

'It wasn't me.' Gabby widened her eyes, all innocent. Miss Demure. 'I never said a word to him.'

Will knitted his fingers together to stop them balling into fists. 'That's crap. I saw you—'

'You broke my phone, remember?' She eyed Cathy and Nanny M. 'He attacked me and snatched my phone. He's a psycho.'

Hunter jostled through the crowd. 'She brought out tourists. She was going to charge them to swim with Min.'

There was an explosion of asides about who 'Min' was. Will retreated into his migraine.

Harley raised his hands. 'That's enough! The law's the law.' He shooed them off like bolshie sheep. 'Go home. This sideshow's over. And from now on no one even makes eye contact with that orca, you understand? If he gets lonely enough he'll make his way home.'

'That's rot!' Viv said. 'There's absolutely no proof that showing him kindness is detrimental. In fact, quite the opposite.'

'Listen, Viv, your hippie theories are no business of mine. It's my job to uphold the law.' He raised his voice so everyone could hear. 'And I'm warning all of you that if you get close enough to look him in the eye you can expect a fine like Mr Jackson here. End of story.'

Will didn't hang around to argue, though others did. He pushed through them, startled by the friendly pats that buoyed him as he staggered up the road to Dean's. He needed a pill right now or the migraine would go on for days.

When he arrived, the house was empty. He took the pill. Fell into bed, too leaden to kick off his shoes. He dropped right into the middle of a vivid dream. Was chasing sheets of music as they flew down busy New York streets, dodging yellow taxi cabs. They eddied around corners. Fluttered. Danced. And every time he caught one the wind would snatch it back. He chased one particular sheet — *The Mikado*'s 'Young Man, Despair' — for hours. Days. Years. Finally he awoke again with a sickening jolt.

Dean stood over him, a tea towel draped across his

shoulder. 'You okay, mate? I got back from Nelson half an hour ago and you were out for the count.'

It took a moment to reorientate. His tongue felt thick. 'Migraine.'

'You taken something for it?'

'Yep.' He propped himself onto one elbow, squinting as the pressure readjusted behind his eyes. A thousand tiny men pick-axed his skull, trying to get out. 'Has Harley rung?'

'Harley Andrews? No. Why?' The light in Dean's eyes dulled to something hard.

Will swung his feet onto the floor in slow motion and pulled the infringement notice from his pocket. Handed it to Dean.

As Dean scanned it his expression soured. He screwed it up and hurled it across the room.

'This stinks of Bruce.'

'Yep.' The crumpled notice crowned a pile of dirty washing like an origami dog turd. 'Gabby sicced him onto us because we stopped her turning Min into a money-making sideshow.'

'I've gotta say up front, Will, I just don't have that kind of dough. Nor do your folks, obviously.'

'I know. I don't expect you to — or Mum and Dad.' He had no idea how he was going to fix this. 'I thought I might try fighting it.'

Dean shook his head. 'Forget it. Fisheries can afford top-shelf lawyers — and Bruce will make damn sure they do.' He rubbed his neck. 'And if you lose they'll charge you court costs. Trust me, I've been down that road. It's a shit fight.'

'Please don't tell Mum and Dad. I'll sort it.'

'If you'd listened to me in the first place . . .'

Will shrugged. If there was one thing he'd learned about lectures it was that they always stated the obvious. Though, given everything, who could blame Dean? 'I know.'

But if he'd done what he was told Min might be dead by now, so how could he regret taking a stand? It was the most amazing thing, their weird connection. Like some kind of Vulcan mind-tap. He truly felt as if Min understood him. But if he told people they'd—

Someone rapped on the front door and a burble of excited voices burst into the hallway. Hunter, definitely — and Pania too. Will hauled himself up and went to greet them.

'You've heard?' Hunter asked Dean.

'Why the hell didn't you ring me?'

'I did,' said Hunter. 'It went straight to answerphone.'

Dean slipped his hand into his pocket. Produced his mobile. 'Ah, shit. It's out of juice.'

'We've got great news,' Pania said. 'Can we come in?'

They piled around the kitchen table while Will downed another pill.

'So?' He didn't really want to know. Things had a way of compounding — and not in a good way.

Pania lit up. 'We have a cunning plan!'

He knew this game. Was impressed she liked *Blackadder* too. 'I know: so cunning you could pin a tail on it and call it a weasel — or a Bruce.'

Pania grinned. 'Exactly!'

Hunter chimed in. 'It's Cathy's idea, her and Nanny M's.'

Dean drummed his fingers on the table, the tic in his jaw working overtime. 'Out with it.'

Hunter cleared his throat. 'We thought if we could raise funds for a lawyer, they might get you off.'

Dean's lips thinned. 'That's wishful thinking. It'd take thousands.'

'What's the plan?' Will longed for bed.

'A concert!' Pania burst out. 'All the local musicians will come, Mum's already phoning around. And we thought you could sing too . . .'

'No way.' And, even if he did, his kind of singing would go down like regurgitated sick.

'Course you can.' Hunter nudged him. 'Hey, and here's the cunning part: you don't have to perform live! We'll film you singing with Min and play it at the concert. People will go nuts for it.' He turned to Dean, his eyes aglow. 'Have you heard Will and Min? It's incredible.'

Dean shook his head, eyeing Will so intently he heated up.

'And the best part is,' said Pania, 'once they've heard they'll end up wanting to help Min too!' She smiled at each of them in turn, radiating optimism. 'If the whole town gets behind it, Bruce will have to tell Harley to drop the fine.'

'There're people who'll back Bruce no matter how cute your bloody orca is,' Dean said.

'Mum said you'd say that!' Pania grinned. 'And she said to tell you they'll sort everything so you can stay right out of it. She says to make sure you give Bruce no excuse. Ka pai?'

Dean grunted. 'Ka pai. Your mother knows me far too well. But she's forgotten that Will being my nephew is all the excuse Bruce needs.'

'Then Will can stay with us, and you pretend you've

kicked him out.' She glanced at Hunter. 'You come too, if you want.'

There was an awkward silence as everyone tried not to look at the bruising around Hunter's eye. He shrugged. 'I'll see.'

Out of nowhere the flaw in their plan suddenly struck Will. 'If you film me and Min — if I agree, that is, which I'm not, okay? But, if I did, then you'd be filming more evidence I'd been with Min again. And what's the bet Harley would slap me with another fine on top of this one?'

Pania and Hunter exchanged glances, visibly deflating.

'Bugger,' Hunter said. 'We didn't think of that.'

'Shi—' Pania clamped her hand over her mouth.

Dean blocked his ears. 'I didn't hear that!' He dropped his hands and, with that, his tone grew serious. 'You know you could get around that if you said you'd already filmed it?'

'That's genius!' Pania threw her arms around him. 'I knew you'd come around.'

'Whoa there!' Dean shucked her off. 'I'm staying right out of this, remember? Not a word has passed my lips.' He pushed the chair out from the table. Stood up. 'Now if you'll excuse me, I need some kai.' He picked up a knife and headed for the vege garden.

'So?' Pania focused back on Will. 'What do you reckon?'

'I've only got twenty-one days to find the money.'

'Mum says she can pull it together for the Saturday after next. That's only two weeks. And Dad's going to the Court Registrar to see if you could pay it off. We're going to ask Greenpeace for help as well.'

The whole thing was crazy. How much could they realistically hope to raise? Maybe a couple of grand if they were really lucky. And why the hell would anyone rally around him anyway? He was an outsider. A bloody townie. And, worst of all, a joke. Most of the locals probably thought he deserved it. Especially Bruce and his big-mouthed evil niece-spawn. No way would they let him off the hook. Pit bull terriers, both of them. Which meant that, despite Harley's grandstanding, Min was still at risk. His headache squeezed his thoughts dry of hope.

'Has Viv had any luck with that orca expert?'

Pania shook her head. 'Not yet. She's out of the country.'

Nothing ever came easy any more. He yawned, the stretch shooting spears into his temples. He could hardly keep his eyes open. 'I'm really, really sorry, guys, but I've got a migraine.' He couldn't think straight. Couldn't *see* straight. He pushed up from the table. 'Thanks. I'll catch you in the morning.'

'I'll be at work,' Hunter said.

'I'll be at school.'

'Tomorrow evening, then.'

He left them staring after him. Probably thought he was a loser hypochondriac. Probably was.

~

SOMETIME AFTER MIDNIGHT HE WOKE again, starving, relieved to realise the migraine had gone. He crept out to the kitchen and raided the fridge: four chicken drumsticks, homemade potato salad, a bowl of leafy greens. He ate them in the dark, accompanied by Dean's bagpipe snores.

It was sheer relief to think again without the whole percussion section going off. Not that it clarified a lot.

Except the pull to check on Min, who must be wondering why he'd been abandoned yet again. It was unbearable. And now every time he wanted to see him, that prick would be watching. Though, hang on . . . he wasn't watching now. *No one was.* If Min had any memory of the other night, then he might be waiting near the wharf.

Will fetched the torch and snuck out to the garage for the wetsuit Dean had given him. It was too big but still would work as insulation against the cold. He stripped and pulled it on, pleased by the added bonus that it worked as camouflage.

He sprinted along the empty road, his feet tender by the time he jogged down the longest finger of the marina. Right at the end Bruce's flash twin-hulled Catamaran took pride of place, a feat of engineering and technology (according to Dean). When Will was sure he was alone he edged across its deck and whistled Min's special note.

Almost at once the water stirred and he heard the spit of Min's blowhole. 'Hey, mate.' Will lowered himself into the murky water, cold enough to make him gasp. Min bumped and nudged and whined like an overwrought puppy.

'Shhh, mate. Keep it down.' Will swam out from the wharf, beyond the scope of the security lights. He'd never swum at night before, not out in the deep like this. It freaked him not to know what else lurked below. *What the—?* There was something coming at him, strange lights tracking through the sea. What the hell?

It was Min, a sparkling iridescent trail rippling in his wake. Phosphorescence! Will swept his arm from left to right and made a trail like lit sparklers. It was beautiful, bubbly white-blue light and silver foam. Magic. And it seemed Min liked the magic too. He breached and crashed down next to Will, droplets exploding like fireworks.

They lolled in the phosphorescent glow, competing for the most brazen display. Min aced it. Swam out into the darkness and disappeared so long that tension wound up in Will's gut. Then, out of nowhere, Min shot back at him like a tracking missile. He cruised just below the surface, leaving a glowing wake, and veered off at the last minute. The trail he left looked like the Milky Way. Star bursts. Meteor showers. Solar flares.

When the novelty eventually wore off Min quietened and nestled into Will, his eye reflecting back the waning moon. Will draped an arm across him, hooked on as they gently rose and fell together in the shifting swell.

He almost dozed, right on the abyss-edge, his subconscious playing tricks. He heard voices on the breeze, but when he sharpened up all he could hear was the lap of ripples on the stationary hulls. He thought he saw things, too — a boat, canoes, and even for a moment a levitating man — but when he blinked and looked again nothing was there. Several times he must have slept, stopped from sinking by a squeal from Min, loud enough to startle him.

In the coldest, darkest hour before dawn, Will sang him lullabies and nursery rhymes from his past. '*I see the moon, the moon sees me* . . .' He could still hear the echoes of his mother's voice, the breathy way she'd scrabble for the high notes, the way she'd pat his back in time, until the act of patting became enough to soothe him on its own. And now, adrift — his buoy a living, breathing whale — the memory of her voice was soothing too. And it reminded him how lucky he was to be loved. Not like poor Hunter. Or Min. Imagine being born into a world where song was everything. Amazing. But then to find yourself alone and cut off from it all would be as mind-blowing as waking up on Mars. *Or in Blythe*.

A steely dawn was rising in the east as Will patted Min goodbye, letting the little bugger bubble-blast him back. He was still grinning as he stumbled from the water, gravity reclaiming him.

At Dean's, he stripped off in the garage and streaked back to the house. The clock was edging towards five; bed pulled him like an alien tractor-beam. But it was vital to keep Dean onside — and sleeping late would piss him off. Nothing annoyed him more than laziness. Will had learnt that the very first week, sleeping all day, trawling the internet all night. Dean had blown his top. *If you don't shift your lazy arse and stick to normal hours you're out.*

Will booted up his computer to email his parents. Needed to do a little damage control.

> Hi ya, Sorry I missed talking to you guys
> last night. It's all fine here. Things quietened
> down and guess what?

Would the fact he sounded happier be enough of a smokescreen? Didn't know. Too tired to think.

> I've met a couple of new friends — and
> get this, Mum, one of them's your cousin
> Cathy's daughter Pania! I'm going to help
> them organise a concert. I'll probably be
> tied up for the next few weekends, so don't
> panic if you don't hear from me. But I'll
> email, okay? I hope you're both happy and
> getting lots of rest. I love you guys. Will x

Lucky they couldn't see him. They always knew instantly when he was lying. *We know him well, He cannot tell, Untrue or groundless tales — He always tries, To utter lies, And every time he fails.* He snorted. Bloody Gilbert and Sullivan; they had a smart-arse answer for everything!

He heard Dean patter to the toilet and pop a fart before he peed. When he had flushed and gone into the kitchen Will wandered out. Dean was mixing porridge.

'Gidday. The head still playing up?'

'Nah, it's good now, thanks.' He had to hand it to Dean, he always sounded genuinely concerned. 'Hey, I um — look, I know I've made things hard for you — and been a pain. I'm really sorry. If you hadn't helped I mightn't have found Min again.'

'Don't rub it in. It would've been better if you hadn't.'

'Well, I appreciate it, okay? I'll sort this somehow, I promise. And I'll stay away from Bruce.' He hadn't planned to say any of this but was glad it bubbled up. He knew he tested all Dean's limits.

'It's that bloody orca you need to stay away from, mate. Though avoiding Bruce isn't dumb either.' Dean raised the porridge pot in silent offering.

Will nodded and sat down. 'Yes please.' He risked one cheeky question — a toe in the ocean to see how Dean would react. 'So . . . Pania told me about Helen.'

Dean froze for a heartbeat. Sighed. 'That's the beauty of small towns, kid. There's no such thing as private lives. It's both a blessing and a curse.'

'I'm really sorry.'

'It's a long time ago now. Old history.'

'How long did it take to feel like yourself again?'

Dean placed a bowl in front of Will and sat down with his own. 'Sorry to have to tell you this but you never feel the same again. It changes you forever. Just like what's happened to you. No going back.'

Will felt his throat constrict. Dug into the middle of the porridge and watched the milk rise up like liquefaction. 'Never?'

'Nah, mate, never.' He sprinkled on a heaped spoonful of sugar. 'Like the old saying goes, *what doesn't kill you makes you stronger.*'

Clichés were designed to gag the masses, his mother had once said. He didn't believe life really worked that way. Not for Helen. Nor his dad. Nor him. Dean's saying was the stuff of fairy tales, designed to hide the fact that life was crap. 'You really believe that?'

'I know it.' He looked up, his eyes demanding Will's attention. 'You have to leave the past behind.'

Panic rattled at Will's ribs. 'Like you? Helen's been dead for years and you're still hanging around town on her account.' Will saw Dean flinch. *Goddamn. Why am I such an arse?*

But before he could apologise Dean started laughing so hard a skinny tear took refuge in a crease below his eye. He leaned over and play-boxed Will on the arm. 'Fair cop.'

When he recovered they ate industriously for a good five minutes before Dean put down his spoon. 'I tell you what: let's make a deal. You front up for that concert and I'll man up and ask out someone I've been meaning to for ages. What d'you say?'

Will looked into his uncle's eyes and saw panic rather than piss-taking — and maybe even a little terror too. He recognised both feelings. Got them himself at the thought of singing in public again. But there was no doubt it probably would help Min . . .

'Damn it,' he said. 'You've got me.' They shook on it, man to man.

Dean wiped a bead of sweat off his top lip and smiled. 'So how come I feel like *you* somehow got *me*?'

NINETEEN

Night-time
Natterings

Night after night my Song Boy came, always when the world was still. In the dappled dark we shared our secret songs, and our lack of understanding for each other's meanings mattered not. Fine feelings fed us, kept us close. I felt the music of his mind — and like to think he heard the whisper of the wit in mine.

Amid his open outpourings I also felt the feelings that were floating there. I sensed his worry, hurts and heartbreaks, yearnings, woes — all leaked from simple shifts and slantings in his songs.

I sang my sorrows too, and let my longings linger with his own. But when the darkness grew too gloomy I sang of White World, of the wind-hewn hills and endless ice floes, fat fur seals, the green shimmer of solstice skies.

I took great comfort from our night-time natterings, nestled with my Song Boy, safe from those who hoped to do me harm. But when first light freed up the night, he had to leave, and I would slink back to that quiet cove, fretful fear always following.

At first I was alone, but soon a horde of Hungry Ones began to haunt me as I set about my day. After the tearing of my fin I did not trust them, not at all; I shied away. But, though they never came too close, they marked my every move, stares unshifting, talk untamed. It did not seem to matter how I tried to hide, they found me still. And, day on day, their fleets grew greater, freedoms gone.

It was with wonder that I watched old Walrus Whiskers see them off, time on time, anger always arising as he herded them away. Fiery feuds were fought, moods murderous. But, in the end, his warrings worked; all gazers gone.

One morning, after many moons and dragging days, my Song Boy came back to the cove, brought Broad Boy and Good Girl too. As light lapped at the tallest trees we sang, sounds swirling up around us, feelings flying fresh and free. And when the final strains were swallowed by the air, the Good Girl glided out to greet me after Song Boy bundled back into the boat.

Ah, now Good Girl, she sent forth such a sweetness, so mild and merry I was swept up in her spell — and I sensed Song Boy shared my soft spot for her warming ways.

In the end, although I loved those nights and that one dappled day, to go from Song Boy's nightly nestling to the daytime's lonely longings hit me hard. We are the same in this, both Beings and Hungry Ones; it is our clans — our close connections — that tie us to our truths. They tell us how to read our roots. Need skin on skin, mind to mind. We brush with other breathing bodies to know we are alive. To treasure it.

But alive I was, twice tricking death. Twice taken in by Song Boy and his humble Human heart.

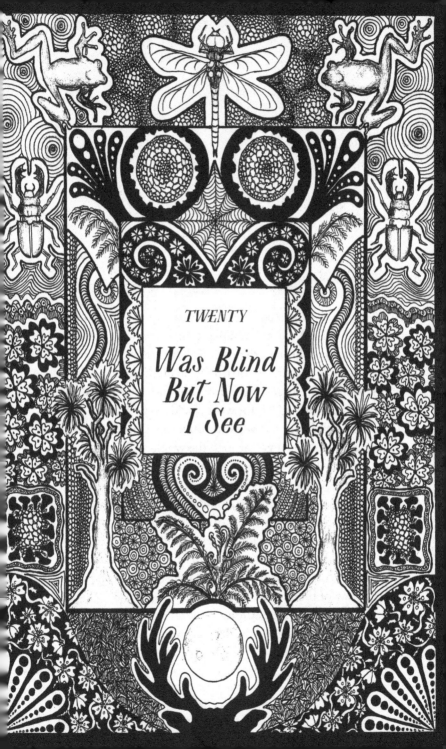

TWENTY

*Was Blind
But Now
I See*

The days passed in a blur of tiredness. Every night Will waited till midnight then trekked down to the marina. Through the darkest hours he bobbed in the water next to Min. At first light he crept home again to re-emerge for breakfast before collapsing into bed the moment Dean had left for work. He'd sleep till lunch time. Drag himself up and work through his Correspondence assignments. Then go through the whole cycle again.

Meanwhile, Blythe was awash with Min-related dramas. As word was whispered around that Min was hanging out in Gleneden, sightseers flocked in camera-clicking droves. Harley Andrews had his work cut out, buzzing around, threatening everyone he'd ticket them. Of course, he didn't. But he got the word around that Min was off-limits, and by the middle of the second week the flow of tourists had slowed.

At the same time, Cathy took charge of the concert. Tickets were flying out the door at twenty bucks a pop and bands from as far away as Wellington and Christchurch had agreed to play. She reckoned they might even make the news — Will's worst nightmare.

On the Wednesday before, Hunter knocked at his window just on midday. Will staggered out, still fugged by sleep, and let him in.

'What's up?'

Hunter thrust a digital camera in his face. 'Can you come? Dad's flown up north for a meeting so Pania's skipped school — it's okay, Cathy said she could take us in Mike's boat.'

The thought of the camera churned Will's gut. He'd tried not to think of it, and every time he did his mind sheered off, memories and anxieties kicking in. But he and Dean had shook on it and, though he wished otherwise, he had to honour it. *Had to.* Dean had backed up Will's half-truths to his parents. Sent them reassuring messages of his own. Whether for the sake of his mother's peace of mind or Will's it didn't matter. The main thing was Will's parents had no inkling of what was going on.

But things weren't smooth for Dean, with Bruce exploiting every opportunity to bait him. Dean arrived home each night with a scowl so fixed it looked like a death mask from the old Greek tragedies.

Hunter kicked the doorstep as he waited for Will to respond.

'What do I need?' He picked a speck of crusted sleep from his tear duct.

'Depends how much of that puny body you want to show!' Hunter prodded Will's long thin arm. 'Pania reckons we should film you in with Min, to prove how safe he is.'

Will bit back a groan. 'Wetsuit then.' It would make

no difference; he'd still feel naked. Look like a dick. 'Hold on a sec. I need a piss.'

He went to the loo then slapped together two cheese sandwiches, snarfing them down as they collected his wetsuit and walked down to join Pania at the boat.

As Pania manoeuvred off the wharf he asked, 'How are we going to get past Harley?'

'Mum's sorted that.' Pania steered a steady course between the channel markings. 'One of her friends phoned in a fake complaint.' She laughed. 'Maude told him tourists were bagging undersized pāua down near Blackhall's Bay. He left about half an hour ago. It'll take him hours.'

Will smiled to please her, though impending doom pressed hard. They'd all rallied around him — given him no way out — or he probably would've handed himself in by now. There was no point pretending he could pay the fine. But too many people had put themselves on the line for him, and it felt like he was toting round a hundred-kilo pack of expectations and old shit.

When they idled through the jagged arch into Gleneden, Will pointed straight towards the overhanging trees. Min lingered there, blending with the shadows. Will whistled and Min's head shot up. He spy-hopped, mouth open in a toothy grin.

Will dragged on the wetsuit. Turned his back on Pania as he hopped around in his boxer shorts. The neoprene was still damp from his midnight jaunt, a nightmare to pull on. While he wrestled, Hunter threw a buoy over the side, its rope tied to the boat.

'If you grab onto this, it'll hold you up. We'll move away a bit so it's just you and Min.'

Will froze until logic beat its way between the taunts inside his head. *Stop being paranoid.* This wasn't about him; it was a chance to show off Min.

He slipped into the water, buffeted by Min's excited greeting, keen to see his wound in daylight. It looked less raw now, cleaner. Hunter gave him no time to prepare, turning on the camera as Pania reversed off and cut the motor. *Such looks of expectation.* The trouble was he didn't have a clue what he was going to sing. Something operatic? No. They'd laugh. From *The Mikado*? No. He couldn't think. Felt wretched. Yes, that was the word, he'd had to sing it once, not sure where.

He dived under the water and Min was there, smiling back at him with his amazing all-knowing eyes. *Amazing. Wretched.* Of course! The oldies would love it. As would Min.

He bobbed back up and took hold of the buoy. Ran his hand along Min's side and cleared his throat. He closed his eyes. Blew out a few deep breaths but couldn't bring himself to open up his eyes again. Would have to do it blind or else he'd not get through.

'*Amazing Grace, how sweet the sound, that saved a wretch like me. I once was lost but now am found, was blind, but now I see . . .*' He sang it slow, focusing his breathing to sustain the notes. The lyrics made him want to cry. He fought to control himself as Min's alien harmonies rose up and wove around him.

Colours swirled behind his eyelids, reds, blues, greens, giving way to silver as he reached for the high notes. '*Through many dangers, toils and snares, I have already come; 'Tis Grace that brought me safe thus far, and Grace will lead me home.*' Tears snaked down his cheeks as a hot welling-up radiated through his chest.

When it was over, Hunter whooped. Will forced his eyes open.

'Holy crap! If that doesn't do it, nothing will!' Hunter grinned like The Joker.

Pania rubbed her nose. 'That was unbelievable.'

He felt shaky. Exhausted. Swam over to the boat and heaved himself aboard. Min edged up to the outboard motor. Started blowing bubbles and sounding off in perfect imitation of the propeller's whine. Will had to laugh. 'You go,' he said to Pania. 'It looks like he's in play mode.'

Her eyes popped wide. 'You mean *me* swim with him?'

'Go on. We'll keep watch.'

'But I don't have my togs.'

Will turned to Hunter. 'Think we can handle that?' Hunter nodded, slightly flustered. Will turned his back on her and Hunter did the same.

There was some scrabbling then a splash. He turned back in time to see her eye to eye with Min, who nosed around her, clicking.

'Hello, baby.' Soothing as warm honey. She reached over and circled his spout with the flat of her hand, in one smooth stroke. 'It's okay. I won't hurt you.' Min responded with a watery purr, clearly smitten.

Will stretched out along the vinyl seat and scraped his hair out of his eyes. Tamed it with the elastic band again. Eyed Hunter. 'So, what's been happening with you, man? Is everything okay?' The bruising around Hunter's eye had nearly faded.

Hunter shrugged. 'Dad's psycho. One of his silent partners is threatening to pull out. He's gone to Welly to see the bank.'

'Is it — safe? I mean, for you to be there?' Please god he didn't make Hunter's life any worse. 'If you want to stay home on Saturday that's fine with me.'

Hunter rubbed his nose with thumb and forefinger. 'I'm okay. He's always been like this.' He turned away and made a big deal of checking the camera.

Will dropped his head back and let the sun warm him. He really hoped Hunter wasn't going to pay for this. He must check with Dean. Behind him, Pania crooned a waiata he'd not heard before. A lilting song in a minor key — A minor, in fact — with a crisp percussive chorus. He closed his eyes to listen as the birds countered her warm caramel-sweet alto. Then he heard it: Min joining in! For a nanosecond he was jealous, but then he let the strangeness gather him up. Min sounded like one of those two-stringed Asian instruments he'd heard an old busker play in Cuba Mall back home.

Hunter scrabbled for the camera again. 'Far out!'

It was electrifying to see the two connecting — as amazing to Will as singing with Min himself. The look on Pania's face could only be described as orgasmic — or what he figured that would look like — softened, dewy, glowing from the inside out. Did he look the same when he sang? He cringed. *Soon bloody know*. But in Pania it was beautiful. He couldn't look away.

~

THAT NIGHT HE WAITED UNTIL Dean sat down for dinner. Will had cooked chicken with little spuds and beans fresh from the garden.

'Do you reckon Hunter's safe?'

Dean swallowed awkwardly. 'It's a worry. One day that kid's gonna have to whack Bruce or he'll never break free.'

'Why the hell doesn't he? He's big enough.'

'My fault I think.' Dean lined up his remaining beans, which looked to Will like gangrened fingers. 'When he hit thirteen he was so full of hormones, so bloody angry, I was scared if he took a swipe at Bruce he'd kill him. Or vice versa. I told him to control himself; made him bugger off whenever he felt the urge. Now Bruce gives him a hiding and that giant kid just takes it — but it eats him up inside. He's just like Helen.'

'Why doesn't he leave?'

'Too late. He may as well hang around now, though, in my book, he'd be better off not living in the same house. I offered to have him stay with me but he said no. It would've showed Bruce up — and Bruce doesn't like that — not at all.'

Will brushed away a hovering fly as he waded through the unsaid undercurrents. 'Why not insist?'

'Don't you think I've tried? Bruce has broken him. He doesn't have the confidence. Besides, the mighty empire's crumbling. Bruce might think Hunter's stupid but that kid's smart enough to know the end is nigh.' Dean sighed. He put down his knife and fork and spread his fingers along the edge of the table. Flexed them. 'I've kept tabs on Bruce for years and, trust me, he's had some right dodgy dealings. I'm quietly collecting evidence . . . and when he pisses someone off enough — well, then, I'll make my move.'

'Jesus. What if he catches you? He's dangerous. Crazy.'

'I gave Helen my word I'd look out for Hunter. And, anyway, I like him. In many ways he's got a lot of guts.'

'I'll pull out of the concert. I don't want to—'

'Don't you dare. I've been doing a bit of soul-searching too and you're right. I've let that bastard call the shots for far too long. He's turned me hard.' Dean picked up his cutlery again. 'Don't worry, mate. I can handle Bruce.' He stripped the meat off a chicken drumstick in one bite. Downed it just as quickly. 'Are you sure you're up to this?'

'Nope.' Will wished he hadn't asked them all for help. 'I mean, yes. I guess.'

'Well, if it gets too much, give me the nod. You look like shit.'

'Thanks,' he said, but the word stuck awkwardly. He promised himself he'd fess up about his midnight jaunts, just as soon as the concert was over.

~

SATURDAY DAWNED COOL AND OVERCAST. Will woke at midday with a headache, still knackered from his night vigil. The concert was at seven that evening in the local hall, but he'd been roped in early to help tie up balloons to make the place more 'festive'. Lipstick on a pig.

He took a shower then rummaged through the fridge for breakfast. Was frying eggs when Dean came in, looking as jittery as Will felt.

Will tried to keep his tone light. 'So, have you done the deed?'

'Eh?'

'Tonight. Who're you taking?'

Dean waggled an eyebrow. 'Wouldn't you like to know?'

'I'm gonna find out anyway.'

'Well, then, it'll be a nice surprise!'

'So the mystery woman said yes?'

Dean snorted. 'That bloody woman can't just say yes, she has to give me a full-blown lecture first.' He shook his head. 'The things I do for you, kid . . .' He slapped Will on the back. 'I've gotta go back to work this arvo — bloody Bruce insisted I do a stocktake, today of all days — but I promise I'll be back by six.'

When Dean had eaten, Will wandered out to see him off again, too restless to stay cooped up inside. He started pulling weeds out of the vege patch. Anything, to keep from freaking out. Though Hunter said the clip was fine, the boos and insults in Will's head said otherwise. He tried to Zen his mind; worked through all the vocal exercises his singing teacher had taught him to combat pre-performance nerves. But he sounded crap. And his thoughts still rampaged.

By three, Will was too wired to pull out the last few fiddly weeds. His kept listing all the reasons Min needed the kind of help he'd just been fined for — and they sounded stupid now. He retreated to his computer and watched the clips of the orca in Puget Sound again. It could've been Min. He even did the same damn trick impersonating an outboard motor! Incredible. He couldn't let Min die like Luna. It would be such a waste.

Try as he might to curb the harbingers of his panic attacks, he failed. His heart was racing, sweat pouring off. The old insults rose up and choked him. He slapped his hand over his mouth and ran, reaching the doorway of the loo just as the vomit hit. He dived for the bowl. Retched and retched. It stunk like it had been swilling in his gut for months.

After the retching stopped he slithered down the wall,

foulness on his tongue. He couldn't do it. Couldn't face a hall of small-town knockers like that Gabby Taylor. Couldn't put himself out there again, not after everything. If he went to jail, too bad. He didn't care. At least there he'd be left alone.

Except his parents would be wracked with guilt. And Dean. *Get a grip. I'm seventeen, not seven. Come on, come on, man. Think of Min.* If he didn't do it and Min died he'd hate himself. This was his best chance to convince them that Harley's way was madness — and Bruce's madder still.

He hauled himself back off the floor and flushed away the evidence. Set the shower on cold and let the water beat some sense into his pounding head.

At ten to five he jogged down to Blythe's local hall and found himself sucked into a cauldron of activity. Cathy goaded several over-excited boys into shifting chairs while Pania swept the floor around them. Up on the stage, four huge guys tuned up guitars and fiddled with amps. Pania waved Will through to the kitchen, where Nanny M was fighting with a cylinder of helium for the balloons.

'Here,' he said. 'Let me do that.'

'Ah, William! Listen to this!' She sucked on the airflow pipe and spoke, exactly like Min's Donald Duck act. 'Bet you didn't think old Nanny knew how to do that, eh boy?' She laughed in a shrill falsetto until she coughed.

When she'd recovered he reached over to take it from her and she stroked his cheek with one dry finger. 'You look too pale, moko. You coming down with something?'

Will shrugged. 'Does stage fright count?'

'Pania says she heard you sing. She said it made her cry.'

'That bad?'

She elbowed him. 'Hush boy. Learn to take the compliment.'

He nodded, too tense to go on chatting, though she seemed content to sit beside him without demanding anything back.

When, finally, he figured out how to fill the balloons, he couldn't make his fingers work to tie the knots. His hands were too sweaty and shook as if he had Parkinson's. But, in the end, the kitchen ceiling sprouted a sea of black and white balloons, strings dangling, like lethargic orca sperm.

After helping set up the data projector, he headed back to the house for food before the Big Event. Dean was home, freshly showered and dressed more tidily than Will had ever seen, in an ironed pinstriped shirt and tailored jeans that looked brand new. He even wore a tea towel tucked into his belt as he made cheese, egg and mushroom toasted sandwiches.

'You okay?'

'Yep.' Will took the offered plate and hunkered over it. Had to force the food down past the lump growing inside his throat.

They'd only just finished eating when someone knocked on the back door. In walked Viv.

'Kia ora,' she said. 'How goes it?' She wore a full-length halter dress in swirls of emerald and electric blue. Her dreads were stacked up high, freeing her sinewy neck and showing off her muscled shoulders.

'You're early,' said Dean.

Viv rolled her eyes. 'Nice to see you, too.'

Will cleared his throat. 'You look nice.'

She graced him with a blistering smile. 'Why thanks,

kind sir.' She turned to Dean. 'Now *that's* how it's done, Mr MacDonald. It's called a "compliment".'

'Yeah.' Dean grinned. 'What he said too!'

'Prick.'

'Ball-crusher.'

It was weird, the way they smiled through the insults, standing there expectantly. The air sizzled with their combined electricity. Then everything clicked into place. Will turned to Dean.

'*Viv's* your date?'

As Dean nodded, Viv cut in. 'Not so much a date as an act of kindness!' She waggled her hips and let rip with a hearty laugh.

Dean glanced up at the kitchen clock. 'You'd better get a move on, mate. We have to leave for the hall in ten.'

Will carried his plate over to the sink. Rinsed it. Dried it. Couldn't string it out any longer so he went and changed into a clean T-shirt and jeans. He brushed his hair and tied it back. Yes, Nanny M was right. He did look pale. Like a hardcore goth, without the need for make-up. He pinched his cheeks to bring some colour, something they did in movies, but it left him looking flushed.

Back in the kitchen, the air was no less charged. As Will entered, Dean sprang up.

'Best be going then.'

They walked along the middle of the road, Will somehow ending up in between them.

Viv pulled him close. 'I've had an email back from Ingrid. I sent her through a photo of Min's markings and she reckons he's one of the Southern Summer pod that migrate from the Antarctic. They hang out in the trenches off Kaikoura over the summer months. She says his handle's AS23, and she first saw him as a newborn round this time last year.'

'You're kidding me? You mean his family might be out there?'

She nodded. 'Ingrid said there've been reports of rogue whalers in the Southern Ocean. It's possible his mother was killed by one as they migrated north. They'll take anything these days. Bloody overfishing.'

Will groaned. If that was true, the poor little bugger probably saw them take his mum. 'But why would his pod desert him?'

She shrugged. 'Who knows? He could've been separated or left behind. The old ones would freak out at the sight of whalers.'

Though Will was dying to press for more info, they'd reached the hall already. People milled everywhere, many more than at the marae.

Viv looked up at Dean, who hovered at her elbow. 'Make yourself useful, man. Go find out where Cathy's stashed the wine.' Dean stalked off to the kitchen with Viv's laughter chasing him. She winked at Will. 'Enjoy this, bro. It's not often you'll see Mr Straight and Narrow dance to anyone's tune except for Bruce.'

'He's pretty nervous, you know. Maybe you should go a little easier on him.'

Viv's nostrils flared. But then, thankfully, she smiled. 'Sorry,' she said. 'Old habits die hard. Dean and I have been circling each other for years — I'm used to having to rark him up to get noticed.' She sighed. 'It's hard competing with a dead woman.'

'He told me he's been wanting to ask you out for ages, but didn't have the guts.'

Viv patted his shoulder. 'Then take this as a lesson, kid. If you fancy someone, spit it out. Life's too short for playing hide and seek.'

Cathy raced over. 'Looking good, girl,' she said to Viv, and winked. Then she turned to Will. 'Okay. We thought it best if we got the business done first. Mike's going to welcome everyone then he'll call you on to talk about Min. Okay? Oh, and after that Hunter's going to show his film.' She turned to Viv. 'It's unbelievable, doll. Wait till you hear that damned orca sing with him and Pans.'

As they kept chatting Will's brain checked out. He could see everyone moving around him, Dean handing a drink to Viv, bands shuffling gear, the hall filling to bursting point, but all he could hear was buzzing. His chest was so tight he had to consciously suck in air, which made him even more light-headed. *What the—?* He jumped a mile as someone touched his arm. Viv shoved something into his sweaty palm.

'Take a few good sprays of this. It's Recue Remedy.'

Dean snorted. 'More of your hippy shit?'

'Witch's potion.' She grinned at Will. 'It'll calm your nerves — or else turn you into a frog, I can't remember which!'

Whatever, Will wasn't going to argue. If it had even a slight chance of working he was keen. He pressed the atomiser and sprayed something into his mouth. Watery alcohol? Not a bad thing.

Mike Huriwai pushed through the crowd with Pania by his side. She was wearing jeans and a white lacey top, and was made up with eye-shadow the same blue as her eyes. She smiled at Will shyly, so unlike the straightforward girl who handled her father's boat he wanted to tow her out of there. Two fish out of water.

Are you okay? she mouthed.

He nodded. Held up Viv's bottle. Was about to ask her where Hunter was when Mike clapped him on the back.

'Right-oh, mate. We're on!' Mike pushed him through the press of people taking their seats.

He balked at standing on the stage; skulked in the wings. Beyond, a sea of faces looked up at him like hungry baby birds. He sprayed another dose of voodoo potion in his mouth. Hoped like hell it worked. If he threw up, he'd never live it down. He could see Hunter now, down by the projector. He looked unmade: his hair sticking up and a collection of ill-fitting clothes. Will saw him scan the stage, and when their eyes met Hunter nodded and gave Will a thumbs-up. Will didn't return it. Nearly ran. But it was too late now. Mike wolf-whistled for silence.

'Tēna koutou. Tēna koutou. It's good to see you all here. We've got a real choice line-up of music — thanks to all the bands who've travelled to be here tonight — but first I want to introduce a new member of our whānau, Will Jackson. He's our cousin Sally's boy from Whanganui-a-Tara and he's been keeping an eye on the little orca for us. We're here to show him some support, 'cause our good friend Harley's slapped him with a ten-grand fine.' The crowd booed, their rumble hitting Will like a freight train. 'He's going to give you a little kōrero about the orca he's called Min. Kia ora.' Mike turned to Will and beckoned him.

A cold band clamped around Will's forehead and his bowels threatened to give way right there. But the crowd was clapping and he had no choice but to walk onstage. He hurried, knowing they'd be waiting for the bands to start.

He took his notes out of his pocket and tried to read them, but his hand was shaking so hard out he stuffed them back. All the moisture had leached from his mouth and inside his head his pulse tolled doom.

'Yeah, so you all probably know about the baby orca that turned up a few weeks ago . . .' *Oh Jesus.* Gabby Taylor was sitting only two rows back with Simone, both vamped up like the Real Housewives. She held her cell phone up. Was filming him.

He scanned the rest of the crowd, a wall of strangers staring back, and started to lose it. Had all the usual flashbacks. The attack. The failed audition. The venom. Like a mantra. He was sweating as if someone had turned a tap on, drips coursing down between his shoulder blades. *Breathe.* But then he spotted Pania. She met his eye. Held it. Mouthed the words, *go on.*

He cleared the fear-ball from his throat and locked onto her face. Recalled her song, replaying it in his head until some of the horror edged back, then sucked in a deep breath. Started again. 'Look, I really want to tell you quickly what I've learned and why it's so important not to ignore Min. And why it's not safe to leave him on his own . . .'

He managed to stammer out all the points he'd swotted up, relieved to see some of the audience nodding as he made his plea on Min's behalf. For a moment he was swept by the heady exhilaration he used to get when he performed, that sense that they were hanging on his every word. But his internal critics kicked back in. *Who the hell do you think you are? You're a townie, a no one, a failure who knows nothing.* It halted him again. And this time he'd run out of steam. Had nothing left.

Mike must have sensed it. 'Thanks, Will. An excellent overview. And if he hasn't convinced you to dig deep into your pockets to bail him out — and, of course, to help protect our little friend — then wait till you see *this*!' He waved to Hunter, who turned on the projector as Cathy wheeled a screen to the centre of the stage.

Will didn't wait around. He blundered off and slunk down the crowded aisle just as the first notes of his song rose up. He ran to a toilet stall. Sat down and shook, tears threatening. He could still hear their duet, even above the tromp of boots outside. Latecomers.

When the song was over the place erupted. Stomping, clapping, cheering, voices raised. *Voices raised?* Will cracked the stall door open. Was sure he could hear an ugly undertone beneath the general noise. Nah, surely not. It had to be his paranoia. He edged out of the toilets and approached the threshold to the hall.

'. . . arrest the sleazy little shit, not help him.' *Holy crap*. Bruce had barged his way onto the stage, four muscle-bound types glowering to one side. He eyed the crowd like an angry bull. 'While he's been playing Doctor Effing Doolittle, that little bastard's had another go at my nets.'

As aggro charged the air, Will forced himself towards the fray.

'Prove it!' a man shouted from the front.

Bruce reddened. Squared his shoulders. 'Don't give me that crap, Jim. If the fish go, your jobs go too. Don't forget who pays for all your bread and butter, folks . . .'

'When?' Will lobbed it from the back. The prick was so arrogant; posturing like an opera villain. *Defer, defer, To the Lord High Executioner!* 'Just *when* exactly would

Min have had the chance? Last time he went near the place, one of your hit men shot him.'

There was a hissing like released steam as Bruce peered across the sea of heads to seek Will out. 'Last night,' he said, jaw set in a smug shark smile. 'Bob checked the nets at midnight and by five this morning there was a gash right through. No prizes for guessing which little terrorist ate your livelihood—'

'You're a liar!' Will pitched his voice through the rising din, steady, loud. He felt a hand press into the small of his back and swung around, fists ready. Dean dodged backwards.

'Whoa! Easy, kid. Calm it down.'

'But he's a liar.' He turned back to Bruce and used the full force of his voice-training to project his words towards the stage. 'I was with Min the whole time — from midnight until ten past five this morning. I've been with him every night for the past two weeks.'

Behind him Dean snarled 'Bloody hell' just as all hell broke loose. People sprang to their feet, hurling insults, pushing, shoving. Dean grabbed Will by the collar and hauled him towards the door as Bruce stormed through the melee like an arctic ice-breaker.

They all arrived outside at once, Will still collared by Dean as Bruce lunged close. 'That's it, you freaky little weirdo, you're now officially screwed. Harley was too soft on you. But when he hears what you've been up to—' He spun around, a huge grinning hyena, as his flunkies produced Hunter — and Gabby. 'You got it on your phone, sweetheart?' he said to her.

She nodded. Didn't meet Will's eye.

'Good girl. I'm sure my friend Harley will be mighty

pleased.' Bruce raised his hand, two fingers transformed to a gun. Aimed it at Will. 'Kapow.' He fired a second shot at Dean then nodded to his mates.

They closed ranks around Hunter and frogmarched him off into the night.

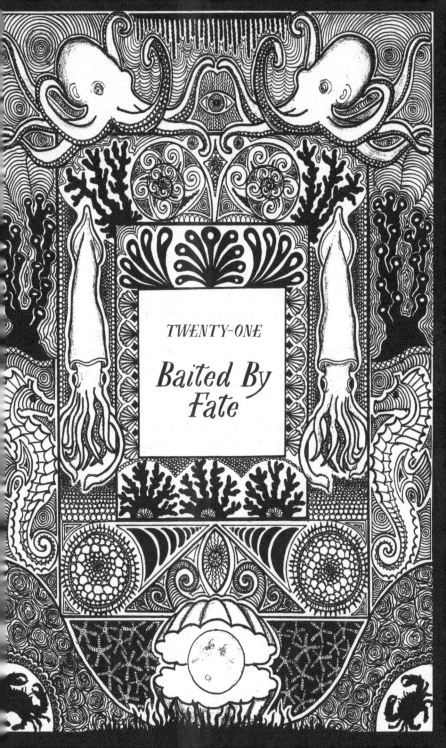

TWENTY-ONE

Baited By Fate

I wallowed in that harbour, waiting for Song Boy's brotherhood, but he did not come. Worry washed me — not for my safety, no, my thoughts were with my Boy. So strange; for many passings of the moon he held me as I slept . . . now nothing. I feared for him. Felt sure if he could come he would.

In those troubled times I had yet to learn the true nature of trust — though such teachings dawn more deeply now I ache with age. Not trust of others, no, but of the workings of the world. The secret sway that pulses through the planet pulls us to the right place at the right time, offers others up to help us on our way. Baited by fate; blessed with a moving mind that takes the scraps and shreds of tidings, good and bad, and turns them into pathways that will lead us on. My meeting with my friend was fate, forever fulfilling. Life-long. Song Boy's heart is ever bold and brave.

Such bravery is not a simple case of facing foes, beating, besting, forgoing fear. We dare death to undo us as we struggle just to stay alive. Even the greenery that grows Beneath fights for life against all odds. One stings, one strangles, still others spew out sticky seeds. All strive to snag a safe harbour, a place to thrive. Tiny fish form tight clusters to hoodwink hunters. Hagfish ooze out unctuous slime. Sea cucumbers twist inside out to dole their deadly sap. Deep-sea squids shed tips of tentacles that twitch and trick with light to fool their foe.

But bravest are the ones whose fears are to the fore; those who find a way to swallow down their fright to fight for good. They do not seek to show themselves, often aching to take flight, but still they stay. They stick it out. They last. And learn to love the long life haul.

Such strength will show itself in scores of ways. Warring walruses still open up their hearts to orphans; penguins lure off sea lions to shield their chicks. The dolphins, our dear cousins, risk death to help the Hungry Ones. They scare off sharks. Lead lost boats safe to harbour. Haul the helpless up to air.

But know this, friends: it goes both ways. The Hungry Ones have helped us too. During the Days of Blood some fought for us, thin-boned, in tiny boats, thrust between those murderers and our falling friends. It would be easy to hold onto the hate but, truth is, not all craved our killing; many ministered to our needs. And many knew how to be kind.

This back and forth, this brotherly buoying up, is like the motion of the sea, her many moods set by the moon — as are our own. And theirs. We share the same water that ebbs and flows, and all know without it we are wrecked.

Good friends, time tumbles . . . and with every turn my life force falters, death draws near. But know I will not waver. No. My life was meant for these moments; these meetings of our minds, to leave behind the lessons learnt. Send forth your strength to bolster me. Cuddle close. For soon my song takes on a different tune. The tides will turn.

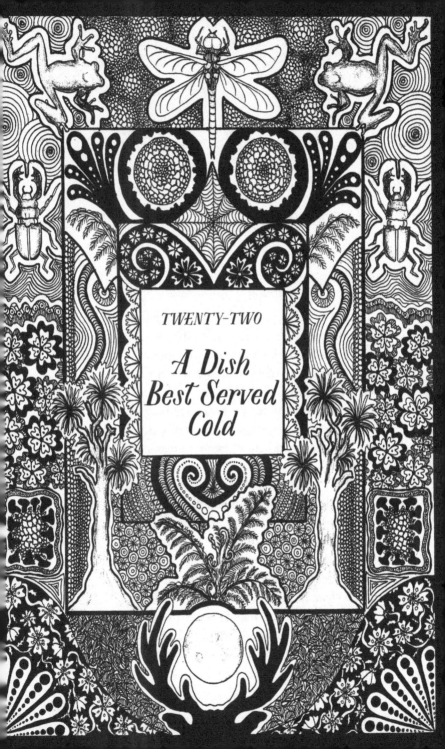

TWENTY-TWO

A Dish Best Served Cold

As Hunter disappeared into the night, flanked by Bruce and his muscle-bound mates, panic spurred Will into action. He couldn't leave him to those bastards; there was no way of knowing what they might inflict, but bets were on it would be bad.

He ran after Hunter, his heart pumping so hard it hurt. 'Wait!' Arrived breathless as they reeled around to face him. Hunter stood behind two tree-trunk men, locked in by their rigid stance.

What to say? He had to come up with something fast; could feel the moments dragging as the surprise waned. *Think.* He sought out Bruce and flinched as Bruce's scowl struck back at him, distorted to a fright mask by the shadows cast from the street light. Those three drugged crazies sprang to Will's mind; the same contempt, same ruthless lack of pity. Fear clawed his chest.

He cleared his throat and pressed his feet more squarely to the ground. Balance was everything. He'd learnt that on the stage. 'Hunter's needed back at the hall.'

'He comes with me.' Bruce's tone left no room for negotiation.

Will scrabbled for a more persuasive argument. Nearly cheered when Dean and Viv turned up and stood one each side.

Dean wrapped an arm around Will's shoulders. 'Everyone's waiting for Hunter, boss. He was picked to be MC in honour of you.'

Dean's gaze met Will's. Scuffed away. Dean's quick thinking — and his support — was such a relief. Will straightened. Pressed his shoulder into Dean's to say thank you.

Now Viv spoke up. 'If you want to keep the townsfolk on board, Bruce, I suggest you let Hunter go.' She pushed past Dean and Will, right into Bruce's personal space. She sure had guts. 'He's been invited to spend the night at the marae. You know how bad it'll look if you don't let him stay.' *Perfect!* The iwi card. Bruce couldn't afford to piss them off, especially with so many whānau at the hall.

Bruce drew himself up to his intimidating best and loomed right over her. Beside him, Gabby shrank back from the light. 'I suggest you tread very carefully, Vivian. Don't go poking your nose into family business.' Anger seethed behind the words, his lips bloodless and stiff.

Viv laughed, to Will's astonishment. How could she sound so relaxed? 'Come on now, bud. You know when Nanny M gets something in her head nothing will stop her. It's her who asked Hunter to stay — she's all for good public relations.'

One of the men glanced at Bruce. 'What d'you want us to do?'

'Fuck's sake. Let him go — *for now*.' Will had never

heard two words spoken with such chill, even *that* night. As Bruce continued, the threat extended to encase them all, freeze-drying them. 'Like salmon, revenge is a dish best served cold.'

Viv somehow managed to force out a laugh again. 'Damned right, cookie boy! You can count on it.'

Bruce snorted. Jerked his head to sanction Hunter's release. Hunter stumbled as he ran for Dean. Meanwhile Bruce, with his men and that little toady Gabby Taylor, turned on his heel and left. They slid into the night like Tolkien's Ringwraiths.

Viv sagged at the knees. 'Fu-u-u-u-ck.' She looked shattered, shadows gouging her face.

Dean tucked his arm around her waist. 'You bloody psycho. He could've hurt you. Still could.'

'Piss off! I was spectacular!' She winked at Will and Hunter. 'Of course it takes a woman to sort things out.'

'Oh, it ain't sorted.' Dean's words tolled like one of Shakespeare's prophecies. A really bad one. He play-punched Hunter's arm. 'That was far too close, kid. You stay with me tonight and tomorrow you wait till Bruce goes out, then high-tail it home and pack your gear. You're not spending another night with him. It's not safe.'

Hunter swayed. Dean caught him by the elbow and propped him up until he steadied. 'Thanks guys. I was— it was—' His voice caught as if his vocal chords were tied. Went husky. 'I thought I was a goner.'

Viv pressed her cheek to his. 'Never fear, e hoa. We're on your side.'

The poor bastard was struggling to hold back tears. Will turned away to give him some dignity, aware for the first time since they stepped outside that music was pumping from the hall. So the concert had gone ahead, no doubt thanks to Cathy. But he couldn't face going back. Felt way too exposed. Why the hell had he agreed to being filmed?

'I'm going to hit the sack,' he said. 'I need some sleep.'

'Are you okay, matey?' Dean asked.

'Yeah.' *Hello headache. Short time no feel.*

'We'll talk about your little night-time expeditions later then.' Dean eyeballed him. 'But don't you bloody dare go out tonight — Bruce will be on the prowl and you *really* don't want to know what he'll do if he finds you in the dark alone.'

Viv elbowed Dean. 'Leave it.' She beamed at Will. 'That song, it was frickin' awesome! I had tears running down my face.' She cupped his chin and pressed her nose to his, their two breaths melding. 'You're pretty damn special, kid.'

'Thanks.' Her words made him want to cry as well. He wiped his nose on his sleeve, feeling Hunter's gaze on him. 'You okay, man?'

Hunter nodded. 'Yeah. And thanks.'

'No probs.'

Will watched them walk towards the hall, Dean draping one arm around Viv and the other around Hunter. He'd have made a great dad, Dean. Beneath that gruff Blythe exterior, he had a heart the size of a country. A giant warm landmass. *Australia.* Will's mind flew to his parents. Thank god they didn't know what was going on. All he could hope was that, by the time they twigged, he'd found a way to sort his shit. Yet he ached to speak with Mum. Just the sound of her voice was usually enough to calm him.

He sprinted back to Dean's, nerves so shot he jumped at every unexpected sound and shadow like a skittish colt. Once home, he rang his mother's mobile. Really needed to. It clicked through to answerphone on the first ring.

'Sally Jackson speaking. Sorry not to take your call. Please leave a message.'

'Mum? It's me. I just wanted to say hello' — *Where are you?* — 'and to say I love you. And Dad.' *No, no. Too much like a hostage tape.* He conjured up Viv, all bright and breezy. 'All's good here. The concert went really well. I'll ring back soon.'

As he hung up he had a sudden flash, right back to the first time he sang alone on stage. It was his Year Five Christmas concert and he'd been chosen as a soloist. When he'd stepped forward, he'd frozen, just like tonight; each second expanding as Mrs Jenks started to count him in. But then he'd seen his mother's face, shining as she mouthed for him to start — just like Pania tonight. He'd scooped in breath and held her gaze. '*Not on a snowy night, By star or candlelight . . .*' The rest of the class joined him for the chorus, harmonies a little jagged but executed with great gusto. '*Te Harinui, Te Harinui . . .*' Life had seemed so full of promise then.

Exhaustion swamped him. He swallowed two Panadol and crawled into bed, worried that Min was waiting, expectant and alone.

~

WILL WOKE TO A SUNNY morning, the birds outside singing disorderly operatic trills. One tūī stood out as more melodic than the rest. He'd love to find it; teach it how to sing an aria. Back home one aped the way their neighbour called the cat, '*here, puss-puss-puss*', with exactly the same intonation. Like that kindergarten teacher on the news who'd taught a starling how to talk: '*We must learn to love each other, no matter what our colour.*' It was the most surreal thing, hearing that statement coming from a bird. The really freaky part was that the damn thing sounded like it really meant what it said.

He stretched out in the finger of sunlight that probed between the curtains. What if the whole animal kingdom could talk! What if they'd hidden it all these centuries. Had grown so sick of humans screwing everything they decided to speak up. Min could be part of the whole plan, a messenger from the deep! He laughed aloud, a rare event. His thoughts bounced back to Viv. Amazing she could stay so calm when, really, she was terrified. Like his voice on the film, no hint of the barbed nerves that clamped his throat. And they'd clapped. They'd cheered. Some even cried. *A wandering minstrel I — A thing of shreds and patches, Of ballads, songs and snatches . . .*

He could hear Dean clattering dishes in the kitchen. By the time Will appeared Dean was sitting down with his porridge and cup of tea. Will helped himself to a cuppa then sat down opposite as usual.

'Thanks for last night. I hope it didn't stuff things up with Viv.'

Dean spluttered in his tea. 'Nothing like a little argy-bargy to pep an evening up!'

'She really likes you, you know?'

'That's your expert opinion is it, Dr Phil?'

'Nope. She told me.' Hell, why not? Dean needed to know. 'She said something about finding it hard to compete with a dead woman.'

Dean slopped his tea. 'Did she just?' He sighed and put down his cup. 'I dare say she's right.'

'Look, about Min—'

'What the hell would've happened if something went wrong and I didn't know where you were? You could've bloody drowned. Not to mention if Bruce or Harley caught you.'

'I didn't want him on his own — all the stuff online says it helps to stay with them while they're injured. And it keeps him out of trouble.'

'Not if he was at the nets again.'

'I don't believe Bruce. He's either lying altogether or he's sliced the nets himself. God knows why.'

'Actually, I can think of several reasons. I'm gonna go out and check for myself, though it wouldn't be the first time Bruce sabotaged something to claim insurance.' He was silent for a moment then slammed his fist down on the table. 'I bet that's why I got stuck doing stocktaking yesterday — all he really wanted was to keep me busy. Out of the way.'

'Can I come? I want to see if Min's okay.'

'Sure. Hey, that wasn't a trick, was it? You know, him singing and all?'

Will shook his head. 'You're kidding? Ask Pania — he sang with her too and Hunter videoed it all.'

'No offence, eh? I've just never seen or heard anything like that before.'

Will grinned. 'Yeah. It's pretty insane.'

There was a knock on the back door and Viv popped her head around the corner. 'Can I come in?'

Dean started to rise. 'You want a cuppa?'

'Stay there. I'll help myself.' Viv poured herself a cup and joined them at the table. She and Dean looked as coy as hell, glances scuffing off each other, little shy smiles.

'Well, the total's in: after everything's paid for there's a grand total of two thousand, eight hundred and forty bucks! Not a bad start.'

Will's heart sank. Nearly seven grand short. There was no way he'd be able to scrape up the rest before the fine was due. 'Cool. Thanks so much.' He tried to inject enthusiasm into his voice.

'Everyone's buzzing about your song, kid. Cathy reckons we should stick it up on YouTube and ask for don—'

Will shot to his feet. 'No!' The familiar tightness ring-barked his chest. 'You have to promise me that won't happen.'

'Whoa! Calm down. It's just a suggestion.' Dean raised an eyebrow at Viv. 'Sorry. Old history. Tell Cathy thanks but no.' He drummed his fingers on the tabletop in a regular 4-4 beat until it faltered. 'If needs be I'll sell down some shares.'

Will shook his head, dizzying himself. 'Like hell you will.'

'Will what?' Hunter emerged from the small bedroom that doubled as Dean's office. He looked as if he hadn't slept a wink, deep purple slicks under his eyes.

'Nothing,' Will said. 'You sleep all right?'

Hunter shrugged. 'Crazy dreams. I was a salmon, can you believe it? And it was horrible, I was choking on PCBs and dioxins. Woke up at four a.m. Couldn't get back to sleep.'

'Those poor fish,' Viv said. 'Say what you like but it's damn near impossible to farm them sustainably.'

'Course there are ways,' said Dean. 'It just takes money. Mega money. And the will.'

'Dad spends it in the wrong places,' Hunter said. 'I've been checking out closed containment tanks and new types of feed, but he won't listen.'

Dean stood up and addressed Hunter. 'Grab some food, bucko, I want to check those nets before Bruce gets to them. I could use your eyes.' He carried his bowl to the sink, pausing to tuck the label into Viv's T-shirt, his finger lingering on the back of her neck. 'You wanna come and eat with us tonight? My friend the orca-whisperer here fancies his cooking skills — how about we make him walk the talk!' He smirked at Will.

Humour warmed Viv's eyes as she turned to him. 'You any good in the kitchen, maestro?'

Was he? He'd gone through a phase of experimenting when TV cooking shows were all the rage. Thought it would go down well with the girls. So wrong. All it did was further feed the rumour he was a raging poof. Singing, acting, cooking — hell, he didn't have one so-called manly skill. *Hang on.* Actually, he could sail now — and deal to fish.

'Good,' Dean said. 'That's settled then. We'll check the fish farm this morning and then we'll collect Hunter's gear. Shall we say dinner at six?'

Viv grinned. 'Sounds good.'

'Okay then, it's a date.' As he pronounced the 'd' word he reddened. 'Oh, shut up!'

He stormed out the back door, followed by their teasing laughter.

~

THEY REACHED FRANKLIN'S COVE BY ten. Min was nowhere to be seen along the way, though the upside was no sign of Bruce, either. Dean moored the tinny to the pontoon and they stepped up onto the walkway as Bob Davers sauntered from the shed to greet them.

Dean met him halfway. 'What's all this about the nets?'

'See for yourself,' Bob said. 'That little bugger bit clean through.'

Will caught his gaze. 'You saw him?'

'Don't have to see it to know what happened. There's nothing makes more sense.'

They followed Bob to the sea cage on the eastern side. Dozens of salmon still wallowed inside but nothing near the seething mass that filled the others.

'There.' Bob pointed down to the outer corner. Someone had tacked the netting back together where the metal wires were sheered clean through, the cut about a metre long.

'That's nothing like the other one — it was all jagged and pulled out of shape,' Hunter said.

Bob grunted. 'Maybe it learnt from last time.'

'Bullshit,' Dean said. 'Who was working yesterday?'

'No one. Bruce said he'd fed them. Said we could all take the day off.'

Dean's expression soured even further. He opened his mouth to speak again but was interrupted by the rumble of Bruce's big Cat as it sped into the bay. 'Damn.' He turned to Will and Hunter. 'Go wait in the shed. Now. This's between Bruce and me.'

Will's gut contracted. 'But—'

'No buts. Just get your arses in there now and don't come out.'

It was a crap idea, but if he didn't hide neither would Hunter. 'Come on, man. Let's beat it.'

Hunter wavered a moment, then growled from deep in his belly as Will tugged him by the arm.

They disappeared into the shed just as Bruce pulled up. They huddled by the door, trying to catch what was being said as Bruce stepped up onto the walkway. His tone was angry but controlled, making it impossible for Will to decipher any words.

He glanced at Hunter. 'What do you think? You reckon it was Min?'

Hunter snorted. 'Doubt it. I saw the net Min got at — it looked nothing like that. Dean's right. It had to be Dad.'

Outside, the volume had risen now. Dean was in full flight. '. . . some bullshit excuse. You think they won't take one look at that—'

'Keep your bloody nose out of it. I own this business and what I say goes.'

'Yeah? Well, I've put over twenty years of my life into it and—'

'Then you can piss off. I'm sick of your interfering and your pansy—'

There was a grunt, and then another, different, like the forced exhalation of air. Will shot into the doorway as Dean staggered backwards, Bruce all wound up, fists raised.

'You stay here,' Will said to Hunter, pushing him further back into the shed. He sprinted down the walkway. 'Leave him!' He slid to a halt beside Dean.

Bob Davers and a real munter of a man called Rick hovered nearby. Bob put a restraining hand on Will's shoulder. He shrugged it off.

Bruce turned on him. 'This is all your fault, you poncy little git. Get the hell off my farm — you and your bloody uncle — and if I ever see either of you here again—'

Dean was back in the game, fists bunched. 'You leave Will out of this. It's nothing to do with him. And if you dare try it on with the insurance companies I'll dob you in, you lying prick—'

He got no further as Bruce slammed him with his meaty fist. Dean reeled back, stumbling in a terrible flailing scrabble of slow motion, his head hitting the deck with one horrendous thump. Will flew to him, shook him, panicked, but Dean was out cold. Will wasn't sure if he should put him in the recovery position, throw water on to wake him, or just wait for him to come around. *Oh Jesus.* Staring down at him — pale-faced, out cold, swelling already puffing up his eye — was almost like having an out-of-body experience, only this time the poor sucker on the ground was Dean, not him.

Will heard a roar behind him and the walkway rocked as Hunter thundered down.

'You bastard!' Hunter launched at his father, ramming his head into Bruce's chest.

Bruce staggered but didn't fall. Threw himself back at Hunter, fists pounding, boots in. Hunter fought back with abandon; the air filled with the sound of grunting, flesh thwacking, knuckles striking bone. Will tried to get between them, but Rick grabbed him by the neck and choked him as he tried to batter free.

Hunter was on the ground now, still struggling, still cursing the old prick through bloodied lips, but Bruce didn't let up. As Hunter tried to curl into a defensive ball, Bruce booted him. Over and over. Steel-caps into Hunter's kidneys.

'Stop him!' Will struggled but Rick held firm. *How the hell could they stand back?* He was hyperventilating now, caught between the horror of old memories and this real-life nightmare.

When he'd kicked the last skerrick of fight out of Hunter, Bruce spat on him. 'You're as pathetic as your mother.' Blood dripped from his nose, smearing across his cheek as he swiped at it. He didn't even glance at Dean, just stormed back to his boat, threw off the mooring rope, and powered the Cat away so fast the whole structure heaved in its wake.

Will turned on Bob and Rick, who huddled nearby. Just standing there, not doing a goddamned thing to help. 'You bastards. Get your arses over here and do something!' Dean stirred. *Thank god.* Though now Will had to make a call: help Dean, who looked as if he would survive, or Hunter, who might not.

He squatted next to Hunter's inert body and cushioned his bleeding head with his outstretched hands. 'It's okay, mate, he's gone.' He wiped blood out of Hunter's eyes, pinching together the split in his friend's eyebrow to try to stem the flow. He shuddered as the aftershocks of Bruce's attack now hit full force.

Dean groaned. He raised himself to hands and knees, stopped and closed his eyes, swaying, and then crawled over to Hunter's side. His face was ashen, one eye a pulpy swelling mess. 'Whadhappened?'

'He took on Bruce,' Will said, worried by Hunter's shallow breathing. He pressed his fingers to his pulse: fast and weak. 'I think we need to get him to the hospital right away.'

Dean pulled out his mobile phone, fingers fumbling,

unable to make it work. He shoved it at Will. 'Call one-one-one.'

Will transferred Hunter's head to his knee and took the phone. Dialled. His tongue felt thick and clumsy as he struggled to describe Hunter's injuries.

'Can you get him back to Blythe?' the operator asked.

'Not sure. Should we even move him?' He glanced at Dean, who was checking Hunter's limbs for breaks.

'The problem is, the chopper's out already and it'll take us nearly half an hour to get an ambulance crew to Blythe, and then they'll have to find a boat — if you can get him back there, it'll speed the whole process up.'

'Okay. I'll do my best.'

'Do you want me to stay on the line and talk you through anything?'

How many hands did she think he had? 'No, though can I call back if I need to?'

'Of course. We'll keep an eye out for your number. And ring me when you're there — if the ambulance hasn't arrived I can give you an update.'

Will ended the call and turned to Dean. 'We have to get him back to Blythe. They'll meet us there.' He scouted around for Bob and Rick; spotted them back by the shed. 'Help me carry him to the tinny,' he called, surprised by the steel in his voice. How *could* those pricks have just stood there, doing nothing? It was inconceivable.

By some miracle they didn't argue. Hurried over and took the bulk of Hunter's weight surprisingly carefully as Will supported his head and neck. Dean staggered along beside them, still wobbly on his feet. They folded Hunter's inert body into the boat and cushioned him against Dean's chest.

Will fired up the motor, mashing the boat on the pontoon in his hurry to pull away. Even above the roar of the outboard he heard Hunter moan. *Please god, let him live.*

The trip back was a blur; Will pushing the boat to its limits while Dean remained unnaturally silent as he supported Hunter's bleeding head. It felt like hours before the channel markers finally came into view. When Will saw the flashing lights of the ambulance waiting at the wharf his eyes fogged with tears.

The paramedics were in the boat before he'd even turned the motor off. They stabilised Hunter's neck with a brace then slid him onto a board-like stretcher, lifting him out with expert ease to lie him gently on the ground. Checked all his vital signs then hauled him up onto a gurney; plugged him into oxygen and a saline drip. Hunter's brow still oozed, and this they sealed with tape and bandaged before loading him aboard.

'Take Dean,' Will said as they made to leave. 'He was knocked out too.'

'Nah, I'm right,' Dean said.

One of the medics approached him. Prised open his golf-ball-sized eye and flashed a light into it. 'You'd better come. No arguments.' He turned to Will. 'And you, mate? Are you okay?'

'Yeah.' His pounding head and heart were nothing new.

The medic looked unconvinced. 'Maybe you should come too, eh?'

Will glanced at Dean. 'It's fine, man. I'd better sort the boat properly or he'll kill me.'

'You sure?'

'Please, just get going. I'll be fine.'

'Don't underestimate shock, kid. Get some support before you do anything else. We'll take them both to Wairau Hospital.'

Will shrugged. Like he needed a lesson on shock. He was an expert on it.

He watched them load Dean into the back of the ambulance with Hunter, then speed off, sirens blaring.

As soon as he'd secured the boat and returned the keys, he slumped. He held his pounding head together as the retching started, wave on wave of painful purging until his knees gave out. He dropped down hard onto his butt. This is all his fault.

He wished he'd gone in the ambulance now; hated that he didn't know what was going on. He had to get to the hospital. Couldn't just sit here like a blubbing kid.

As he rose, sniffing away a ball of teary snot, Pania came pelting down the wharf.

'What's happened? We heard an ambulance go past.'

'Bruce went psycho and beat up Hunter real bad. Dean too.'

'Oh my god!' She reached out and gripped his arm. 'Are you okay?'

'Yeah, yeah, I'm fine.'

'You're bleeding.'

Will stared at her, confused. Impossible. *He* was the wimp who hadn't even had the strength to fight off Rick. Then he looked down. He was covered in Hunter's blood. 'Not mine.'

'Good. And bad. Oh god, poor Hunter.' She wrapped her arms around him for a moment. Smelt of green Fruit Bursts. He had the overwhelming urge to sink his face into her thick loose hair, close his eyes, never pull back.

Instead, a sigh stuttered out of him. 'I gotta go.'

'How are you going to get there?'

'Dean's car.'

'You got a licence?'

'My Restricted.'

'Me too. Come on,' she said. 'I'll take you. You don't look like you should be driving.'

'But if you get caught with a passenger—'

She shrugged. 'So? It's an emergency.'

He knew he shouldn't involve her; that if Dean found out he'd go mental. But she was right: he wasn't in the best of states. Could hardly think. Every time he closed his eyes he heard the thwack of Bruce's fists; saw blood arcing through the air from Hunter's mangled brow.

'Okay. Let's go.'

TWENTY-THREE

Wanton Wildness

I saw Song Boy that day; watched from the water as he heaved against the Hungry One who held him back, fists flying, face awash with anger, flooded with fear — and fight. I felt his fury, his body-ache for Broad Boy's plight. And marked the madness of the man who struck at Broad Boy, eyes crazed, coarse sounds cutting cold as ice.

His onslaught lacked a level head — snapping, snarling, splitting skin — as mean and mindless as any Being gone bad. Not even sharks slay from spite, only need; never had I seen such wanton wildness meted out, Man on Man, in such a ruthless rage.

I never understood the Hungry Ones in this: we all have hankerings, both bad and good, must choose kindness or cold killing — or float forever in between, falling short on every front. We have to pick a path, mull meanings, live a life given over to the goal of good — or ride the wretched waves of wrongs. Why choose to foul our fate, when we can welcome wisdom, goodwill, sweet and soulful songs?

This day that wayward Human hungered for poor

Broad Boy's blood. Left him broken; bolted in his booming boat as I nosed nearer in. Song Boy never noticed; bundled Broad Boy up and hurtled for the harbour, blind to me. Deaf to my song.

And how I ached when I was left, fear tumbling back when the one who hurt me fixed me with his evil eyes. I knew it was not safe to stay. Had no support, with Song Boy's thoughts so tuned on Broad Boy, bothered, harried, hurt.

What lesson can be learnt from this, my trusty fellow travellers? This, oh this: that we are bent towards the comfort found in clans — no love lost for lone lives — and yet to truly test the mind we all must seek some time alone, delve deeper, find freedom in the fallow times and swim with our most secret selves.

Oh Broad Boy, how my heart did ache for you — and for my worried, white-faced friend. We were too young to know that facing our worst fears full on will set us free.

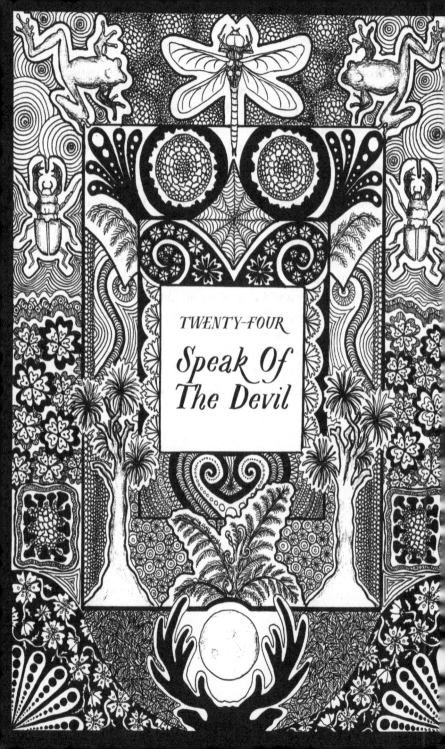

TWENTY-FOUR

Speak Of
The Devil

Pania drove with the same confidence as she steered a boat, calm and steady as they sped through the parched countryside towards Wairau Hospital. Will slumped in the seat beside her, humming scales to calm his mind and exorcise the sound-bites of Hunter's beating. They mingled with his memories; he felt every blow as if the pain was his own.

'Surely the police will charge Bruce now?'

Pania glanced over. 'You'd hope. Dad says the only reason Bruce gets away with it is that he catches Hunter when they're alone.'

'Why the hell hasn't Hunter said something? I still don't get it.'

She shrugged. 'Dunno, but Bruce is a real control freak. Dean says Hunter's like those beaten women who never leave their husbands, terrified and kind of brainwashed.'

'Yeah, he told me that. But that doesn't explain why no one's spoken up for him.'

'Come on. Don't you think everyone's tried? But the

local cop is Bruce's mate and when anyone goes higher it's been ignored. Mum even called Child, Youth and Family but all they did was put him on a list. And when he *is* asked questions he won't say a word. It's horrible.' She approached an ambling tractor, tooting thanks when it pulled over to let them past. 'With any luck, now you and Dean have witnessed it the cops will have to act.'

'It's all my fault. If I hadn't stirred things up, encouraged Min, this never would've happened.'

She backslapped him. 'Don't be daft. Things've been building for a long time now. If it wasn't over Min it'd be over something else.'

'You think so?'

'I know so. That's how Bruce works.'

They approached the outskirts of Blenheim through acre upon acre of neatly cultivated vines. A hawk soared on the up-breeze just above them and Will pictured the land as it must look from above: dark plaited cornrows on the dry scalp of the earth. He tried to still his jiggling foot, a new joke played on him by his nerves. What if Hunter didn't make it? Or Bruce went after Min again?

They found the hospital and then a parking spot after two circuits and made their way to A&E. The spike-haired nurse did a double-take when she looked up.

'Oh, hello! I know you! I was at the concert last night. You were incredible, the way you sang with that little orca.'

Will felt heat rising. 'Thanks.'

'So what can I do for you?'

'They've just brought in my uncle and my friend from Blythe. Can we see them?'

She glanced back at her screen. 'Dean MacDonald, right?'

'Yeah. And Hunter Godsill.'

'Oh yes.' Her gaze bit into the blood stains on his jeans and T-shirt. 'Your uncle's under observation — but you can see him if you want.'

'And Hunter?'

'They're still assessing him.' She rose and pointed to a security door. 'Go over there and I'll buzz you in.'

When they'd entered she ushered them to a curtained cubicle. Dean was on his back, a light cotton blanket pulled over him. His eye was now so swollen it had closed right up.

'Hey.' Will hovered near the foot of the bed while Pania hugged Dean gingerly.

'Bloody hell, Unc, you look like you've stepped out of a zombie movie.'

He raised an eyebrow. 'I thought you weren't swearing.'

'Damn.' Her hand flew to her mouth. 'Oh shit, I did it again. Oh *shit*.'

Will laughed, relieved to see Dean's mouth twitch too. 'Five in a row! Bravo!' He grinned at Dean. 'We could make a pile of hush money out of this!'

Pania rolled her eyes. Will edged forward and offered her the only chair while he perched on the corner of the bed. 'How're you feeling?'

'Stupid. I told them I was okay but they insist I hang around.'

'Hunter?'

'Not sure. He's still pretty much out to it. I think they're worried about internal bleeding. He's being scanned.'

'I'm so sorry. I really am. All I've done is cause you trouble.'

'It's not your fault. This's been brewing for a long time.'

Pania grinned. 'I told you so.'

Will's pocket started to vibrate. He had forgotten he still had Dean's phone. Handed it to him.

'Yo?' Dean closed his eyes as he listened, fingering the swelling around his eye. 'That's great. I'll let him know.' He looked over at Will and gave him a thumbs-up. 'Hey, about dinner tonight. I'm gonna have to bail. Something's come up.' Nodded his head. Frowned. 'Don't be daft, woman. We're at Wairau Hospital. Bruce beat the crap out of Hunter, really bad . . . yeah, okay, will do. But hey, the good news is the cops are onto it . . . yeah, I will. Thanks.' He kneaded his forehead as he ended the call.

'Everything okay?' Will asked. The raw reds and deep bruised purples stood out starkly against Dean's pallid skin. He looked older, and terminally tired.

'Viv says the boys at Whale Watch in Kaikoura think they spotted Min's pod about ten k's offshore.'

Will's heart clashed like cymbals. 'You're kidding? His family's out there?'

'She's going to try to get hold of Ingrid. See what she suggests.'

'That's brilliant!'

A nurse slipped through the curtains. 'Sorry, but the police are here. They'd like to have a word — but only if you're up to it.'

'Send them in.' Dean tried to wriggle up in the bed.

She stopped him with an outstretched hand. 'You stay flat for now, okay? The less you move around, the better.' She looked at Will and Pania. 'You'd best wait outside.'

'No, Will, you stay. He was there too,' he added, to the nurse.

'I've got to call Mum anyway,' Pania said. 'She'll be

wondering where I am.'

She left just as the two policemen entered, one grey-haired, the other with acne-pocked skin. They got straight down to business, first grilling Dean on what had taken place with Bruce. Will cringed. Dean made him sound far more heroic than he'd been. When it was his turn he 'fessed up and put them straight: he'd been useless, powerless, no help at all. Shame swilled inside.

'You'll lay charges?' Dean asked, after all the questioning was done.

'I imagine so,' said the older of the two, Detective Sergeant Gilroy. 'It's a serious assault.'

'And not the first one. That poor kid's been on the receiving end of Bruce's fists for a long time now. You should speak with Ron Toogood over at Blythe. He's been turning a blind eye to complaints for years.'

'That's a very serious charge, Mr MacDonald. You're sure about this?'

Dean nodded so vigorously he bit back a groan and clutched his head. Cradled it between his hands for a moment before he carried on. 'And while you're on the case you'd better check out Harley Andrews. He ignored the fact Bob Davers shot the orca — and I've got a file on Bruce's business dealings, too. Insurance scams, you name it. Someone should take a long hard look at them as well.'

The nurse, who'd nosied in and out, fussed with Dean's pillows. 'That's enough for now, gentlemen.'

'We'll be in touch,' DS Gilroy said.

It was strangely anticlimactic, given everything that had happened. Will felt like crying. Poor bloody Hunter. 'Wow. I'm really glad I went over *that* again. Are you okay?'

'Yeah, mate. Painkillers deaden everything. What about you?'

'Okay, I guess. I'll go find Pania.'

She was sitting in a corner of the waiting room, flicking through a tattered women's magazine whose cover screamed '*How I Lost Twenty Kilos in Two Weeks*'.

'How'd it go? Are they going to do something?'

'Looks like it.' Will squatted on the floor beside her. Leaned against the wall. 'You get through to your mum?'

'She's sending someone to pick me up — that way you can drive Dean home.'

'Cool.' He rose and pecked her on the cheek before he could chicken out. 'Thanks so much. You were right, by the way, I wasn't up to driving.'

Where he'd kissed her he swore her cheek glowed pink. 'Will you ring me when you know how Hunter is?'

'Sure. But I don't have a phone. Got pissed off with it one day and threw it in the drink.' He shrugged. 'Has Dean got your number?'

'Probably not my mobile but he'll have our home one.'

'Okay, I'll check.' He smiled at her, trying to decide what shade of blue her eyes were. Sky or sea? Maybe a bit of both, kind of flecked. He shook himself. 'I'd better head back. You wanna see Dean before you go?'

'No, just give him my love. He needs to rest.' She tucked a tendril of hair behind her ear, which was long and slightly pointed at its tip, almost elfin. He liked it; made him think of Arwen in *The Lord of the Rings*. 'I'll go out and check on Min for you, if you want? Let you know he's safe.'

'Thanks — that would be great.' He stood up, reluctant to leave. Being around her made him feel better in a way he couldn't define; he felt a simmering warmth and the same light-headedness as when he sang.

Back in the cubicle Dean was snoring. Will tiptoed out to find the friendly spike-haired nurse.

'Is it okay if he's sleeping? I thought that was bad.'

'It's fine. These days the doctors think sleep is helpful — so long as someone keeps an eye on him. That's why he's here.' She patted his arm. 'Looks like you could do with a rest yourself.'

'Yeah, it's been quite a day. Is there any news on Hunter?'

'They've taken him to surgery. There's some concern about one of his kidneys and his spleen.'

'He will be okay, won't he?' The dread was back, pressing at the pit of his stomach.

She nodded. 'So long as everything else is fine. But it's just going to take a while before we know for sure.' She studied his face. 'There's a staff kitchen through those doors over there — go make yourself a cuppa and help yourself to the biscuits — a little sugar right now wouldn't do any harm.'

She was right. Once he'd settled in the chair next to Dean and downed a sugary cup of instant coffee and four chocolate chip biscuits the awful gnawing in his gut started to ease. He closed his eyes. Should he phone his parents? But what could they do? Nothing, bar worry, and he was already doing enough for both of them.

His mind kept returning to Pania, how being with her was like drinking cool water, quenching, calming. How he wanted to kiss her properly. How he'd never dare. Wasn't even sure it was allowed with second cousins — Jesus, was it incest? Though what about Dean and Viv? *Let me make*

*it clear to you, This is what I'll never do! This, oh, this,
[kiss] Oh, this, [kiss] Oh, this, — [kiss] This is what I'll
never, never do!* When he'd sung this in the show he'd had
to kiss poor Carmel Ritchie, much to the delight of the
Year 8s and 9s at the dress rehearsal. At first he'd enjoyed
it, the chance to snog her in the name of art, but then her
meat-head of a boyfriend got all weird and came to every
rehearsal *and* performance just to glare at him. It was
impossible to enjoy it after that, with him breathing down
her neck — and Will's.

Not that the stupid prick had to worry. Unlike most
of his old friends, the closest Will had ever come to real
sex was serious fumbling at the *Mikado* after-party. One
of the Three Little Maids had let him slide his hand into
her knickers. It was all on then, until she'd had to run
for it, spewed on the floor before she made it to the door.
That killed it dead for him but she insisted she was still
keen. The trouble was his mum had lectured him about
informed consent (*Sober consent, Will. If she's drunk, it's
rape*) so in the end he didn't dare. But he often thought
of it, that soft damp velvety flesh. It still had the power
to induce a hard on. He felt guilty now, as if Pania would
know and think he was a sleazy jerk. She wasn't the
kind of girl who'd allow a random grope. And this was
something different, anyway. He didn't want to stuff it
up. She was far too nice.

He glanced over at the bed, startling when he realised
Dean was awake and watching him.

'You were deep in thought there, matey. You okay?'

Will felt a blush erupting. Dug his fingernails into his
palm. 'I was thinking about you and Viv. Isn't she your
second cousin?'

'Yeah. Why?'

'So it's okay then? You know, being related and all?'

'What are you, the gene police?'

'Shut up! I was just wondering.'

'Yeah, yeah, all good mate. It's only first cousins getting it off that's dodgy, so they say.' He shifted slightly on the bed, wincing. 'Thanks for your concern, though!' His gaze seemed to penetrate Will's feeble excuse and recognise him for the horny jerk he was. Dean grinned. 'It always pays to check!' There was a rummaging in the curtains and Viv poked her head through. 'Well, well . . . speak of the devil!'

'That'd be Bruce you're referring to?' She edged around the side of the bed and examined his battered eye. 'Ouch, that looks nasty. How're you feeling, pretty boy?'

'Ready to go home. Why'd you come?'

'To find out what the hell is going on.' She swept her lips across his forehead. 'And to collect Pania for Cathy.'

'Is it really true?' Will said. 'About Min's pod?'

Viv settled by Dean's shoulder. 'Those guys should know. They help keep track of things for Ingrid.'

'Do they know how to get him over there?'

'I'm sorry, I didn't have time to ask. But I'll get hold of Ingrid tonight if I can.' She glanced down at Dean. 'Cora says if you want I can take you home, so long as I keep an eye on you for the next twelve hours.'

'Cora?'

'The nurse, dipstick. Didn't you recognise her? We went to school together.'

'These women forget nothing, kid,' Dean said. 'Be warned!'

Viv snorted. 'You wanna go home or not, smart-arse?'

'You okay to bring my car back?' he said to Will.

'Yeah — though maybe Pania could, after all? I'd like to wait for news of Hunter, then stay with him a while if that's okay.'

'Nice,' Viv said. 'Good plan.' She eyeballed Dean as if to say *don't you dare argue*. He didn't. Still looked wiped out.

By the time the nurse coached Viv on warning signs (which she already clearly knew) and signed Dean out, Will was relieved to wave them off. His nerves were shot, and the effort to speak, to maintain cheerfulness, was exhausting. His head pounded like a funeral dirge.

With still no word on Hunter he took the forty bucks Viv had slipped into his pocket and went in search of the café. Ate two stale ham and egg sandwiches and ordered a double espresso to wake himself up.

Stomach full, though hardly satisfied, he camped out in the waiting room and watched the ebb and flow of patients as he tried to guess what brought them in. Some were easy picks, like the kid whose arm was jutting at a crazy angle, or the idiot who'd shot a nail through his foot. Others came in tearful, some hunched over, nauseous, and a few in pathetic states from too much sun and booze.

For three and a half hours he hunkered there, dozing, reliving the fight, trying to figure out what he could've done to stop Bruce, hating that he failed. Finally the nurse, Cora, came to find him.

'He's in post-op now. They had to take out most of one kidney. On top of that he's got a badly bruised spleen and five broken ribs — but the good news is it looks as though his head's okay. Poor kid. It's just as well he's so fit.'

'Can I see him?'

'It'll take another couple of hours before the anaesthetic really wears off and we're sure he's going to come around.'

'He *will* be okay, right?'

'Should be. But he'll be here for a couple of weeks at least — until we're sure his spleen has healed and the remaining kidney's functioning okay — and then another couple of months to fully recover after that.'

It felt wrong that something so terrible could somehow sound like an improvement. 'Thanks.'

He found a pay phone to let Dean know, and when Viv answered she reassured him all was well. He told her what he could of Hunter's progress and then phoned through to Pania's. No answer. To kill some time he left the hospital and walked to clear his head. After two blocks he found a fish and chip shop. Oiled his jiggling nerves with greasy chips.

By the time he was taken to the room where Hunter lay, it had grown dark outside. Hunter was strung up to machines and drips, so pale his freckles stood out like stars in a photo negative. Will pulled an armchair closer to the bed, grinning with relief when Hunter's eyelids flickered open.

'Hey.' Hunter tried to smile. Couldn't quite. But tried, and that was good.

'Gidday.' Will leaned in close. 'How're you feeling?'

'Sweet.' He spoke as if his tongue was twice its normal size. 'Good drugs.'

'Shit, man, if that's all you wanted there are easier ways!'

'Yeah.' Hunter drew in a shallow breath. 'How's Dean?'

'He's fine. He's got a really thick skull — like you, apparently. Viv's around there fussing — she reckons it's perfect, that he doesn't have the strength to argue!'

'Choice.'

'Don't bother speaking, eh? I'll stay right here and have a doze myself.'

'Thanks.' His eyes drooped shut.

It was enough for Hunter to know he wasn't alone. Like Min. The need for moral support as the body did its thing. Like Will's parents had done for him, once he'd fled home after his humiliation at the audition.

The possibility that Min's family was out there — maybe only a couple of hundred k's or so away at most — was so infuriating. Totally frustrating. In the clips he'd seen from overseas, most times they used a sea cage to catch the orcas then shipped them overland. But that kind of expenditure sure as hell wasn't likely to happen here in any hurry — if at all. The only other real alternative was for Min to follow a boat out of Pelorus Sound, right around the top of the island, through Cook Strait, and then along the coast to Kaikoura on the other side. *Yeah right.* In Puget Sound, they'd trained Luna to follow by turning it into a game, towing a buoy strung out the back of a boat. Not hard, but the little bugger only had the attention span of a toddler, same as Min, and was just as likely to swim off after a logging boat, canoe or stick. What kind of boat could Will even get his hands on to make the trip? The Zeddie sure as hell couldn't manage it, even if he *did* feel confident enough to try. The Strait was far too rough and unpredictable. It would be madness. Suicide. Probably take days, even if the boat could handle the waves.

And then, of course, there was the fine. It was due next week and Will still had no idea how he was going to sort it. But he had to admit the concert takings *were* impressive. In fact, the more he thought about it, the more he was astounded by the town's support. For a place he'd scoffed at, thought he'd never fit in, they'd rallied round like he was one of them. Amazing. Bizarre. A tiny ray of sunshine, like when Hunter tried to smile. Goddamn, they'd better arrest Bruce.

See how the Fates their gifts allot, For A is happy — B is not. Yet B is worthy, I dare say, Of more prosperity than A! Yet A is happy! Oh, so happy! Laughing, Ha! ha! Chaffing, Ha! ha! Nectar quaffing, Ha! ha! ha! Ever joyous, ever gay, Happy, undeserving A!

It was clever, really, the way old Sir William Gilbert slipped things in like that, about how tricky fate can be; that switch from happiness to misery in a heartbeat. So bloody true. *If I were Fortune — which I'm not — B should enjoy A's happy lot, And A should die in misery — That is, assuming I am B. But should A perish? That should be — Of course, assuming I am B! So B should be happy! Oh, so happy! Laughing, Ha! ha! Chaffing, Ha! ha! Nectar quaffing, Ha! ha! ha! But condemned to die is he, Wretched meritorious B!* Not that he knew what meritorious meant. Something to do with merit, he supposed. But he did know the song was all about perspective, like now. Here he was, he should be chuffed Min's pod was theoretically in reach — and that Hunter had survived. But there was Hunter, half his bloody insides stitched, Will possibly going to jail for not paying a stupid fine — and Min out there unprotected and alone.

~

HE WAS WOKEN BY THE sound of whispering. Looked up, bleary-eyed, to find Gabby Taylor and her friend Simone huddled in the doorway.

'What the hell are you doing here?'

'Pania told me what happened.' Her gaze was fixed on Hunter as he slept. 'How is he?'

'Apart from losing half a kidney and screwing his spleen — oh, yeah, and a whole lot of broken ribs — he's fine. No thanks to your arsehole uncle.'

'Oh my god.' She shuffled into the room, her eyes puffy from crying. 'I didn't know he'd do this, okay? I mean, I knew he gave him the bash sometimes — my dad's the same — but never this bad. Oh my god.'

'Is he going to be all right?' Simone asked.

She edged up to the bed at the moment Hunter opened his eyes. As it dawned on him that Simone was there, a smile blossomed. 'You came.'

'Hi.' She dug into her bag and produced a chocolate bar. 'Here. Sorry, it's not much.' She laid it on the bedside table.

Gabby sidled around Will and perched next to Hunter. She brushed a kiss onto his ear. 'God, Hunter. I'm so sorry.' A tear leaked down her cheek. 'The police have taken Uncle Bruce for questioning. They stopped him on his way in to see you.'

'Good fucking job,' Will said.

She flinched. 'He's only ever been nice to me. I had no idea he'd go this far.'

'Really? Everyone in the whole town knew, apparently,

yet you were too busy taking his handouts and—'

'Don't,' Hunter said. 'Just don't.' He smiled up at Simone. 'Did you enjoy the concert?'

'I'm sorry I didn't talk to you. I was— it was—'

'Doesn't matter.' His gaze never left her face.

She turned to Will. 'That was awesome, what you did. That little orca — Min, is it? — man, it was awesome.'

'Yeah, well, lucky he survived Bruce's attempt to have him shot.'

'I want to talk to you about that,' Gabby said. 'And something else.' She jerked her head towards the door.

If Hunter wasn't lying there all loved-up he'd have said no. But it wouldn't hurt to give the poor bastard a little time alone with Simone. It'd probably help him more than any amount of drugs.

He followed Gabby out into the corridor. 'What?'

She scuffed her sandal on the lino. 'Look, I'm sorry, okay, so stop giving me the evil eye for a minute and listen.'

'Why should I trust anything you say? If you've brought some kind of message from that prick, I'll—'

'He's going to kill Min!' Tears boiled in her eyes. 'When I heard you sing with him I couldn't believe it. I had no idea they were so smart — or cute. But straight after we left Hunter with you, Uncle Bruce told his mates he was going to shoot Min himself. He's going to do it in a storm so no one notices until a few days later.'

It sounded all too plausible. 'Why are you telling me? What's in it for you?'

She stamped her foot. 'Fuck you. I thought you'd want to know.'

'Why now? Ever since I arrived, you've been an utter bitch — and now you come over all helpful?'

'How many bloody times do I have to say I'm sorry? Hunter's my cousin, okay? And what Uncle Bruce did was bad. Real bad. I never thought things would come to this. Pania says he hit Dean too. That's really shit.' She swallowed hard. 'It's all total shit.'

'Well, at least we agree on that.' Will could feel his anger abating. She genuinely seemed upset. 'Look, are you sure he really meant it?'

She nodded empathically. 'There's a big southerly due round Wednesday and he told them he's doing it then. Do it "properly" he said. It made me sick. Min was so awesome, the way he sang.'

Awesome? God he hated that word, it was so overused. 'Bruce can't, if he's been arrested.'

'But you don't understand. If he can't do it, he'll get someone else to. And, anyway, Mum says he'll get bail.' She wiped her nose with the back of her hand. 'Please do something. But don't say I told you. My dad and Uncle Bruce are real close — and Dad's, well, they're really alike.'

'He hits you?'

She shrugged. 'It's just how they are.'

Jesus. His mum had always told him to look behind the bully, to see who was bullying *them*. He'd never really taken it in. 'Look,' he said. 'This whole thing with Hunter never would've happened if he'd spoken up sooner. You have to do the same. It's a good time, with everything out in the open like this.'

She shook her head. 'You don't understand. Mum'll take his side. She always does. I'm out of this hole as soon as I leave school, anyway. I can tough it out till then.'

'You sure? Cause I reckon people like Cathy and Dean

and Viv would support you. And me, if you want.' Irony or hypocrisy? He wasn't sure.

Another tear snaked down her cheek. 'Nah, I'm sweet. But thanks.' She swiped it away. 'Is he going to be okay?'

'Hope so. Look, thanks for telling me about Min.'

'You sing real well — nothing like that dumb YouTube clip.'

He nearly laughed, hearing this from her, number one on his harasser list since he'd been here. 'Thanks.'

As they walked back into the room, Simone sprang away from Hunter. Had she been kissing him? Judging by the goofy grin on Hunter's mushed-up face, she had. *Well, whaddaya know?* Gotta be keen, to kiss that pulpy mess.

A new nurse popped her head around the corner of the door. 'Visiting time's up, folks.'

'Can we come back tomorrow?' Simone asked.

'Sure. Visiting hours are eleven-thirty until seven-thirty. It's ten past nine now.'

Gabby shrugged petulantly. 'Sorry.'

'We'll see you then,' Simone said to Hunter.

'Love you, Hunts,' Gabby said.

'See ya.' Hunter's gaze limped after Simone.

Will walked the girls to the lift, then went in search of the nurse. 'Can I stay with him? Please? Sleep in the chair?'

'It's not usually allowed.'

'Please? He doesn't have anyone. His mum is dead and his father did this to him. I hate the thought of him waking up alone.'

She tapped a pen to her lips as she considered this. Nodded. 'Okay. Sure. But let him sleep. He needs all the healing he can get.'

She rustled him up a pillow and two blankets. By the

time he got back to the room Hunter was out again, so Will settled in the armchair, extending the footrest out, but knew he'd never sleep. How could he protect Min? It was all very well going out and staying with him when the weather was fine, but if a storm blew up he'd have to head for home. Gabby was right. The cunning of Bruce's plan was sickening.

~

HE WOKE WITH A START. Hunter was crying out. Something desperate. Indecipherable. He scrabbled over, catching his little toe on the bed leg.

'What is it?' He switched on the light above Hunter's head, his toe in agony.

Hunter was dreaming, eyeballs rolling beneath their lids. Will shook him gently, not wanting to startle him.

Slowly Hunter surfaced and opened his eyes. 'Where?'

'You're in the hospital. You had a bad dream.'

'Will? Shit, I thought Dad was here.'

'Nah, you're safe, man. He can't get at you here.'

'Has he been to see me yet?'

'Can't. The cops have him.'

'Damn. They shouldn't.'

'Damn right they should. He nearly killed you.'

'He doesn't mean it. Sometimes I just set him off.' He spoke as if on automatic, as if Bruce had drilled it into him.

'Bullshit, man. He's a mental pig. No — shark. Pigs are too nice!' *Get a grip.* 'You've gotta stand up for yourself. When the cops ask questions, tell them everything.'

'You don't understand.'

'So tell me.'

'Can't.' Hunter scrunched his eyes. Blinked away tears. 'Was Simone really here?'

Okay. Still a no-go zone. He'd have to work on it. 'Sure was! There's the chocolate on the table.'

'She kissed me. Told me to ask her out when I get home.'

'Score! Maybe she has a thing for sick people. A nurse fantasy!'

He grinned. 'Suits me.' He tried to move but winced. Stayed put. 'Can you turn that light off?'

Will flicked the switch and eased back into the chair. 'You need anything?'

'No. What did Gabby want?'

'Forget it, man, you don't need any more complications.'

'Tell me. Please. I need distracting — don't want to think about that dream.'

'Fair enough.' He sure knew how *that* felt. 'She overheard Bruce say he's going to shoot Min during a storm that's coming in.'

'No!'

'Yeah. The really sucky part is that Viv reckons Min's pod is in the trench just off Kaikoura. If I could somehow get him there . . .'

The problem hung between them as Will thought again about the yacht. He hated to admit defeat. But it would be far too dangerous, especially with bad weather due. Maybe he could try Harley? But he might tip off Bruce. The cops? Maybe. But would they take it seriously? Or care? He truly didn't know. What about Viv? Her contacts in Greenpeace might help. The trouble was they'd have to source a boat and get it here and blah, blah, blah — chances were, the whole thing would end up like Luna, everybody pissing around so long the poor thing died.

'Take the Cat.'

'What?'

'Dad's big PowerCat would make it round there in about nine or ten hours, no sweat. Get Min to follow you . . .'

'You're out of your freaking mind if you think I'm gonna ask to use his boat. Anyway, I don't know how to operate it. And how the hell would I get Min to follow all that way? You know what he's like. He'll be off in a flash if he sees something more interesting.'

'Don't ask, just take it. I know where the keys are and Pania knows the boat — it's a piece of piss. There's a GPS to tell you where to go. And Min will follow if you sing.'

'What, sing non-stop for ten hours?'

'You wanna save him?'

'Course I do. But you're talking about stealing a boat probably worth hundreds of thousands of dollars and taking it through one of the roughest stretches of water on the planet in a frickin' southerly! Your head must be way more munted than they thought.'

'Yeah, maybe.' Hunter closed his eyes.

Bugger. Why the hell had he said that? It sounded just the kind of put-down Bruce would use. 'Sorry, man. I didn't mean for it to sound that way.'

Hunter's eyes flicked open for just a second. 'I know. It's cool.'

Hunter was probably right about Min following if he sang, though whether he'd be able to hear him over the engine was another story. And as for stealing Bruce's boat, well . . . Though, actually, what the hell, he was already in the crap. If he could somehow pull it off — get Min back with his family — it'd be worth whatever they threw at him. And it wasn't like he had a life to ruin. But it would have to be tomorrow night, if Gabby heard Bruce right. Could he trust her, though? Possibly. She wasn't the type to say sorry if she didn't have to.

His heart was thumping, emotions shooting everywhere. *There is beauty in the bellow of the blast, There is grandeur in the growling of the gale, There is eloquent outpouring, When the lion is a-roaring, And the tiger is a-lashing of his tail!* Oh, for god's sake, bloody *Mikado*. Now its lyrics weren't just haunting him, they were trying to tell him what to do!

Through the darkness Hunter's voice broke in. 'Tell you what: if you've got the balls to nick Dad's boat I'll press charges against him. Do it, Will. You'd save Min's life.'

Holy hell. Talk about bargaining with the Devil. But what Hunter offered up was as dangerous to him — both physically and mentally — as any illegal orca rescue. More so. At least if Will pulled it off he'd have something to cheer about. What would Hunter have? A hollow victory and no father, just a psychopathic prick in jail . . . with any luck. But speaking up *had* to be the right thing to do. The only thing to do. And if it meant him doing something crazy to spur Hunter on, then it was worth it.

He reached over and carefully shook Hunter's hand. 'All right, you crazy bastard. I know I'm gonna regret this, but you're on.'

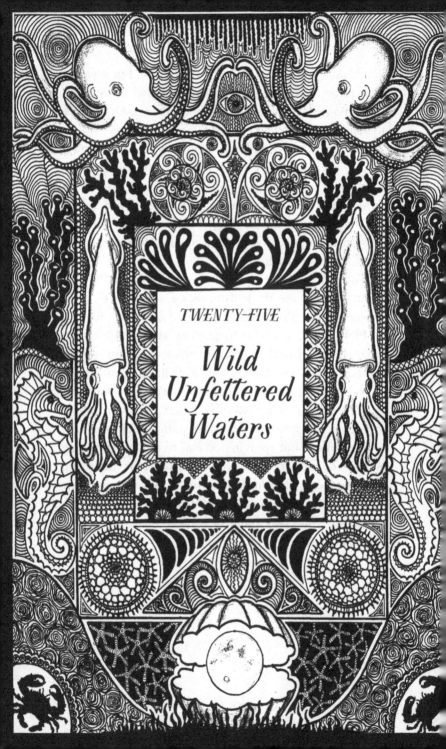

TWENTY-FIVE

Wild
Unfettered
Waters

You may wonder why we old ones always sing around in circles. To remember, to remember, and to spread our songs so all will hear. When we were young we took our elders' kindness as a token of the truth that life was fair. But, we, dear friends, know otherwise. Fairness only forms from willingness to open up the heart — and from fairness freedom comes. I'm sure my Song Boy felt this too, for in that time of total trust and touch, we heard each other's heart. And, heed me, friends: once heard, only a fool forgets.

He came to me at midnight, the moon licking the lips of waves, and called for me to meet him at the harbour's edge. I waited two long nights and days to hear his soaring song alight again; was filled with hope and happiness; had feared he'd lost his way. Though the Good Girl came and gave me comfort, how I missed the company of my one and only Boy.

There was a whisper on the wind that night, a whine, which told of wild weather brewing down in White World's skies. After he held me, drew me near so I could feel his friendship flow, he boarded a big booming boat, eyes ever on me, and started singing sweetly; somehow sent it down beneath the surface as he egged me out to sea.

I followed as the night grew darker, led on by his lulling song. Out past the squalls of salmon, further than the comfort of that tiny cove, until we reached the wild unfettered waters that linked the two long lengths of land. And still he sang, tunes tumbling out, and though I longed to linger, pined for play, I could not spurn his call. It had me, held me, hungered for me. Spurred me on.

Ever onwards Song Boy led me, heading towards dawn's new day. As sunlight swamped the dark I sensed a tightening, a tingling, a reawakening deep inside. I knew, yes truly knew, that many of my kin, my kind, once passed this way. Like The Pulse, and our most long-lived songs, the paths we ply are known deep within us; we Beings have wended them since our first seaborne souls were birthed.

A feathered wind whipped up the waves, seabirds shot skyward, clouds speeding ever faster from the freezing south. But still he sang, his throat so torn and tattered his sound was tossed up by the waves and whisked away. And so, to help, I added in my own — could not hold back — hoping against hope my cosy clan would pass and hear my plea to seek me, save me, take me back.

Fate is a fickle friend: one moment giving, the next whipping it all away. One wins, lots lose. Back then I thought I played no part, washed this way, that, tumbled by each turning tide. Now I know otherwise. We each make of our own lives what we will. Wish Fate farewell. Find grit inside. Find gall. Try trust and thankfulness.

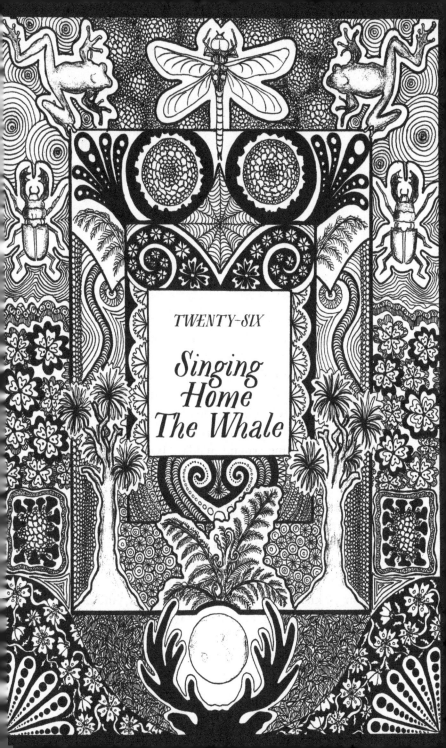

TWENTY-SIX

Singing
Home
The Whale

Will wrote a note to Dean and left it on his rumpled bed. He tiptoed out, accompanied by Dean's purring snores; a bag of food, the wetsuit and a change of clothes clutched tightly as he sprinted to the wharf. By twenty past eleven it was nippy, the first stirrings of wind dancing around his head. The forecast had confirmed the worst: a storm was marching from the south, due to hit tomorrow, sometime around midday. Twelve hours was roughly all he had. Enough, Hunter assured him, to get there . . . so long as everything went right. Will planned to leave the boat moored safely at Kaikoura when Min was sorted. If . . .

Will slipped the wetsuit on and swam to where Min lurked beyond the wharf. He squealed as Will approached and rubbed against him like a hungry cat. It was good to see him, to know that so far Bruce had failed. And now, tonight, all going well, he'd never have the chance again. *This* was what mattered, despite the stern parental voice inside his head that claimed he'd either kill himself or get locked up. Not like he didn't bloody know. He was shit-scared. Had to hold Min up front and centre, or else he'd chicken out.

As he swam, he replayed the last twenty-four hours. Total rubbish — except for Pania. While he'd stayed with Hunter she'd kept Min company till nearly one a.m., as late as Cathy would allow. Mid-morning, when he'd cadged a lift home from the hospital with Viv, he'd nearly blabbed the plan, but she was tired. Stressed. Had cried when they'd left Hunter. He couldn't risk her arguing. All afternoon he'd fretted, worried Pania would think the whole thing crazy, finally meeting up with her when she came home from school.

He sat on Dean's doorstep with her, watching the clouds, and told her what he planned. For a moment she said nothing, staring off into the greying sky. Finally, after Will had nearly burst, she spoke.

'It's kind of crazy but I think you're right. I'd offer Dad's boat but it's not really up to it — it would take you too long, especially with that storm.' Again she stopped, deep in thought, and he bit back the desire to rush her. Any offer of help had to come freely or it wasn't fair. 'Okay, I'll do it. I'll show you how, on one condition: if the forecast gets any worse you pull the plug.'

'Fair enough.' He didn't say he'd probably be on his way, no turning back. It was best she didn't know.

Now, after ten minutes singing quietly to Min, he heard her whistle. He swam back to the ramp and clambered out.

'Hiya.' She wore a long black coat that blended with the shadows. 'Are we still on?'

'I reckon.' He towelled his hair but kept the wetsuit

on to wear against the cold — and for flotation should he end up in the drink. He might be stealing a boat the size of Africa but it was quite another thing to go out *totally* unprepared. Dean would kill him . . . hell, Dean was going to kill him anyway — and wouldn't be the only one. *Don't think of it.*

'Okay,' Pania said. 'Let's do it.' She pulled a torch out of her pocket and they stepped aboard; went straight to the locker by the engine. Will opened its hatch and found a set of keys hooked to a nail. *Step One.*

'Listen,' Pania said. 'Are you sure you want to go ahead alone? Maybe I should come to help?'

'No way. It's mad enough, without involving you any further.'

She frowned. 'You sure? I'd never forgive myself if you—'

'Forget it. I've got nothing to lose; you have.' Pania opened her mouth to argue further, but he placed a finger over her lips. So soft. 'Full stop.'

They locked eyes as Will dropped his hand. He could read her. Her pluck. Her frustration as it hit her that he had to do this on his own. She was one hell of a girl.

She sighed and held out her hand for the keys. Unlocked the cabin door and ushered him inside. With toneless efficiency, she proceeded to explain what each thing was and what it did, step by step, like an impromptu memory test he knew he'd fail.

'How the hell do you know all this?'

'I've been on boats since I was born — and Bruce used to take us to the Hopai sports day every Christmas in this. He let me drive it if I asked. That's the weird thing about him, sometimes he's really nice.'

'Not that I've ever seen.'

'Yeah, well, he's definitely been worse since the down-turn. Everyone says he's on the verge of going under.'

'Good job.' Will pointed to a screen beside the dash. 'What's that?'

'The GPS — your butt-saver! I'll programme it so all you have to do is stay on course. It'll take you right around, no problems, just *don't* fiddle with it.' She handed him the torch. 'Hold this.'

He provided extra light as she programmed in longi-tudes and latitudes, set waypoints and compass bearings. *Amazing.* He may as well have been on the bridge of the Enterprise for all he understood. Fifteen minutes of intense concentration later, she nodded to herself.

'Okay. So, these are your waypoints, here, and see that there? That shows the distance to the next waypoint and your speed. And see that one? It tells you how long until you reach it at your current rate of knots. It'll let you know if you're off course — you'll hear an awful alarm — and it'll tell you how to correct it and when you've reached each point.'

'It uses satellites?'

'Yeah. Pretty cool, huh?'

'Sure beats the hell out of trying to read a chart — or the stars.'

She laughed. 'Don't knock them. If all this fancy gear breaks down and you don't know that stuff you're really screwed.'

'I *don't* know that stuff! What the hell would I do?'

She pointed to a radio. 'Use the VHF. See the hand piece there? Pick it up and call on Channel 16 — that sticker tells you how and what you need to say. Just repeat everything three times and remember to say "over" when you've finished speaking — it's actually quite fun.'

'Yeah? Well, it won't be fun if I have to use it.'

'True. Sorry . . . but there's always someone listening, so it's your best bet.' She leaned over and turned the knob. 'Keep it on. They give good weather updates.' She took the torch back off him and shone it through the cabin window; lit up a bulky container on the forward deck. 'Ah, good. See that? That there's the life raft. If all else fails, pull the big red cord and it'll open up.' She turned to him, the whites of her eyes gleaming in the torchlight. 'Promise if anything goes wrong you'll radio for help. It's really unpredictable out there.'

'Don't tell the forecasters that. They'd lose their jobs!'

'Shut up! You know what I mean.' She hit out at him and he caught her hand. Pulled it to his chest. Tugged her close.

'Do you think you could give a doomed sailor one last kiss?' His heart was going absolutely mental.

She smiled. 'S'pose.' Switched off the torch and stepped into him. Raised her head. By the yellow glow of the marina lights he bent down and found her lips, gently at first, then hungry, like she was his only means of rescue.

When they pulled apart he ached to start again. It was as good as he'd imagined. Better. Had never felt so giddy or stupidly happy. Wanted to sweep her up right there, forget this shit and kiss her till their lips wore out. He couldn't help himself, sang: '*Were you not to Ko-Ko plighted I would say in tender tone, "Loved one, let us be united — Let us be each other's own!"*'

Pania snorted. 'Crazy nit!' She switched the torch back on, and they blinked as its beam revealed them. She put the key into the ignition and turned it just enough to light the console. Pointed to the diesel gauge. 'That's good.' It was nearly full, thanks to Hunter, who said he'd made it his job to keep the boats topped up. Maybe his subconscious planning a quick get-away? Whatever the reason, one tank would get Will there, he'd said, but not both ways. 'It wouldn't be good to run out of juice with a storm in the Strait.' A classic Blythe understatement. He hoped he lived to quote it at a suitably unsuitable time.

'Okay,' Pania said. 'Anything else you need to know?'

'Yeah. How'd you get to be so smart?'

She stared down at her feet. 'Shut up!'

'No, really, thank you. As Simone would say, you're awesome.'

She smiled, head at a coy angle, her fringe veiling her eyes. 'You too.'

This should have elated him. But a doomsday clock had started ticking down inside his head. If she wasn't here, he knew he wouldn't have the guts to follow through. 'One more kiss before I go to war, Ma'am?'

'Not funny,' she said, stiffening.

Stupid, stupid. 'Oh god, I'm sorry. I didn't think.' How could he forget her brother?

She turned the key and pressed the ignition button to fire the engine. It roared to life, so loud he cringed. They waited several tense minutes, half expecting a security guard or nosy neighbour to appear, but no one showed. Now Pania ran through the basics one more time: how to accelerate, how to power off, how to reverse and to weigh anchor. Then she showed him one last switch.

'Only use this big spotlight once you're past the channel markers. Someone might see. Don't worry though, there're navigation lights up on the aerial so other boats can see you, but this'll help you keep an eye on Min. Okay?'

'Got that. Thank you.' He liked that she thought of Min. But the noise, on the other hand, was bugging him. 'Do you think he'll be able to hear above that racket?'

'Yeah, it's pretty loud. But I may have a cunning plan!'

'Another one?'

She poked out her tongue. Disappeared down into the cabin and brought back a coil of tube, the kind he'd seen Dean lug out to the farms. 'You're in luck,' she said.

'I don't get it.'

She held one end of the tube to her mouth and roared down it, sound trumpeting out the other end.

'Damn, you're smart.'

She grinned. 'Like Viv says, woman power!'

'I bow to your greater superiority, oh breasted one.' Why the hell did he say *that*? Thank god she laughed.

They secured the tubing to the handrail and fed it through the cabin window so he could steer at the same time. He sang a couple of lines of 'Nessun Dorma' in the sonorous voice of God while Pania watched for Min's response.

'He's nosing round it, all confused.'

Will leaned out the wheelhouse door and sang another couple of lines, straight this time. Min looked up, spied him there, his mouth gaping open in his toothy grin. 'Cool. Good thinking, Catgirl!' He laughed to spin out time but couldn't sustain it. 'Okay . . . that's it then.'

'Good luck — and be careful, eh?' She stretched up and he caught her. Kissed her. Too short but infinitely sweet.

'See ya,' he said. 'Post me a file and bolt cutters care of Rimutaka Prison!'

'Very funny.' She jumped off and untied the mooring ropes. Threw them onto the deck, waving as he wrestled the big Cat away from the wharf. The accelerator, or thruster, or whatever the hell she'd called it, was sticky, and it took him a moment to get a feel for how it worked. He cleared the wharf with only minor scrapes, not daring to think about the cost. Felt like a fool as he sang down the tube. But Min's belly was flashing through the water next to him so, for now at least, the plan was working.

He steered between the channel markers, keeping the speed right down. Away from the town the sea was lit by half a moon but he turned on the spotlight anyway — it was reassuring — and watched Min surf the wake up by the bow. He looked so small next to this bruiser of a boat. It had the same implacable hardness as Bruce.

Will knew this patch of water well from sailing it and, even though the boat was unfamiliar, it was okay — he knew where every dangerous rock or headland was. After the drama of the last few days, it was peaceful, chugging past the first of the salmon farms with its well-lit markers, watching how the lights played on the rippled sea.

He ditched the tube, hated it. Instead, he opened doors and windows wide and sang at full volume, enjoying the freedom and anonymity of the night. The song was one of his mum's favourites, another G & S, and it was frickin' perfect. He puffed out his chest, going for pomposity, and sang all the parts, including orchestration.

'*I am the Captain of the Pinafore! And a right good captain, too!* . . .' It was so good to sing, to hurl it out there into the night, that he went through every song. Though he loved straight opera, it was these comic ones, thanks to Mum, that brought the biggest grin. There was a joy to them, a total piss-take of the English nobs. Subversion via laughter, such a powerful weapon — and he should know; had been the butt of way too many jokes.

It was the kind of humour Dean and Hunter used to survive Bruce. It came naturally, that national need to rib the shit out of anyone who dared stand out. Some of the comments aimed at him had been real rippers. He should've laughed them off, he knew that now. But it had been all tangled up with the attack, his parents leaving, being sent down here. Until Min, he'd hardly laughed for weeks, months, and now look what he does: makes a lame joke that upsets Pania. *Dick.*

'. . . *I thought so little, they rewarded me by making me the Ruler of the Queen's Navy . . .*' Comic timing was everything. Min bounced along, swimming parallel, watching Will, his eye reflecting back the moon. He embodied the freedom Will desired: two crazies racing through the night, seeking something bigger than themselves.

He increased speed, amazed how much grunt the boat had, lifting and lunging forwards until it planed at sixteen knots. It felt ludicrously fast, but he'd need to average this to make it to Kaikoura before the southerly struck. The acceleration stirred Min into a series of slapping breaches as he flung himself through its bow wake. But with added speed came the fear of losing control, of the boat bolting into the darkness at a full gallop, no time to think where he was, what was underneath, either side, or coming up ahead.

He'd passed most of the settled bays now, not a single light confirming life elsewhere. Headlands loomed up way too quickly, huge black shapes lurched from the dark — undefined monsters — and the fear of unseen rocks sent Morse-code panic signals from his heart. He flew through space, singing but not feeling it, head full of carnage, mayhem, prison. Too fast, too dark, far too powerful. Terrifying. The only thing he had to reassure him was the GPS. He watched it with manic distrust, still waiting for the crunch to come; Pelorus Sound slipped off behind them and they entered Cook Strait.

Immediately the seascape changed. A choppy swell slapped at the boat, making it even harder to hold the course. He peered into the void beyond the pool of light to check for other boats. Nothing stirred besides Min's darting presence. Will was in awe of the first people who headed off in wooden rafts with only the stars to guide them and, later, the waka paddlers who sat so low in the choppy seas. He felt as vulnerable right now: lost in time and space, except he had to trust a gadget that could break down at any moment and he'd be stuck in a stretch of water known as one of the roughest in the world, so many lives lost in its depths. He changed to singing Wagner now, more fitting for this brooding sea: tongue-twisting German to take his mind off all the things that could go wrong. It didn't work. He sweated as if he'd run a marathon, head pounding, his throat closing up.

Four hours out from Blythe he was exhausted; he powered back and let the boat rock in the slop as he went out on deck and edged along the handrail to check on Min. When his little shadow bobbed up Will reached over and scratched his rostrum, trying not to transmit his own jangly nerves.

'How're you going, matey?' Min made his bubbly propeller noise and nudged against Will's hand. 'Hang in there, eh? We're still a long way off.' The fine mist of Min's exhalation spritzed him. 'Thanks mate, I needed that!'

He grabbed a couple of sandwiches and wolfed them down as he urged the boat back up to speed. They'd passed the halfway point according to the GPS and, sure enough, there was the faint aura of Wellington's lights in the northeast. It was surreal; the night now inky black, the moon having deserted him, and the stars, through a web of cloud, dull and weak. His eyes were playing tricks again, shapes looming out of nowhere then fading back. He felt confused, disorientated.

When a screeching started up he jumped about a metre in the air. *Jesus Christ!* The GPS alarm! He stared at it, trying to decipher what it said. *Come on, come on.* Realised he'd strayed off course. He spun the wheel hard and powered the juice on, the back sliding out sideways. *Fuck!* His mind went blank. He pushed wrong buttons, pulled wrong levers. *Had to calm down.* Talk himself through it. Take a few deep breaths then set things back on the right course. *Dumb, dumb, dumb. Now concentrate.* It was only thanks to Pania's calm voice ringing in his head that finally he brought the big Cat back on course.

By five a.m. he was leaden. He'd tried to keep the singing up but his vocal chords had seized up by the time dawn scuffed the horizon. Its silvery tinge turned from dark to light as quickly as a flaring match — and it was such a relief to orientate himself again: the hills of the North Island's rugged coast to his left, the long spine of the Kaikouras and the Southern Alps pitching straight up to his right. And, sure enough, a threatening cloud bank rolled up the Alps to greet him, a looming prophecy, and the wind was rising, tops blown off the swell, gulls hurtling past like arrows. But there was still a ferry tracking down the coast and a couple of small fishing boats off Island Bay . . . the water was safe, for now.

Two times more in the laborious, numbing sixth hour he brought the boat back to a halt, worried Min might disappear now Will couldn't sing. Yet, both times the little trouper popped up like a piebald cork and called back, urging Will on as if he knew where they were heading, eager to arrive. Tiredness so weighed Will down that the worries he'd tried to bury were resurrected. What the hell would happen when the authorities caught on? And what would happen if he didn't find Min's pod? He couldn't risk returning with him; would have to leave him in Kaikoura's waters and hope the Whale Watch guys would help. A gutting thought.

Seven long hours after he'd left Pania waving at the wharf, his body packed up good and proper. The constant seesawing was murder as the hull slapped into the rising swell; he was as sore as if he'd been pedalling all the way from Blythe. Now squally raindrops punched the windscreen so he turned the VHF up to catch another forecast. Not that the weather would change anything; he was far too close to give up now, well past Cape Campbell, heading down towards Kaikoura on the other side. The seas were even bigger here, rolling straight in from Antarctica, sick-making. He couldn't focus, was hot one minute, cold the next, with gritty, watering eyes and constant tension in his stomach as he fought to keep the Cat on course.

'This is the Cook coastal forecast for the next twenty-four hours. Southerlies rising early Monday to forty-five knots . . .' As the forecast continued Will eyed the front.

It smothered the Alps like a malevolent spirit, and he could almost hear it hissing: *I'm going to get you, boy, tip you out . . .*

Five minutes later, while he was still panicking over the thought of forty-five knots, the radio burst back to life again. 'This is Marlborough Marine Radio. We have an alert out for a stolen vessel — believed to have been taken from Blythe Marina sometime last night. Be on the lookout for a twelve-metre aluminium PowerCat with Pelorus Salmon signage, sides and back. Contact us on any channel if you spot it and we'll pass the info on to the police. Over.'

Holy crap. He checked the GPS. Was nearly there — another hour at most, though as the seas rose his speed had dropped, the boat bashing straight into the teeth of the rising gale. He upped the revs and pushed it to its limits. *Screw it.* Too late trying to sing now, even if he could. Instead he willed Min on. *Hang in there, little man.*

When the GPS started to beep, he freaked again. Scanned the screen, laughing out loud when he realised it was telling him they'd reached the final waypoint. Below him lay a submarine canyon over a thousand metres deep, tectonic plates alive and cranky, currents clashing, sperm whales, dolphins, orcas . . . *Min's orcas.* He cut the revs and left the boat to idle as he summoned up the nerve to walk the deck. It was awash with spray, bucking like a rodeo bronco. He grabbed one of the mooring ropes and tied it around his waist. Edged out to the stern. Dropped down to his haunches and slapped the water to call Min.

'Min?' Nothing. 'Min?' He wolf-whistled. Still no sign. *Jesus Christ.* All this way only to lose him now? What sort of bullshit was *that*? 'Min! Where the hell are you? Get your fat little orca arse here right now!' It hurt to shout.

His nose was itching. *Don't cry, damn it.* He was so bloody tired. Shattered. Seasick. Frightened. 'Min, please, where are you?' No more than a froggy croak, burning deep.

He stumbled to his feet and fetched the tube. Thrust it down into the wild water and called again. Forced out a song. Cajoled. Pleaded. All hopeless. He couldn't hear above the idling engine or the wind, and the sea was so choppy it was impossible to spot Min's fin in its midst. He sagged onto the deck. Pressed his mouth up to the tube, fighting to keep it submerged, and called again; tried scraps of every song he'd ever learnt. Still nothing. Zero. Zip. It was too much. Unfair. *Stupid.* Should've kept his eye on Min. He rested his head onto the deck as rain pecked at him, fat drops turning to sleety drizzle. Closed his eyes. Felt bile swilling in his gut. *All this for nothing.* Pathetic. Useless. Lame. *Will of the Living Dead.*

Strange echoes taunted him, so real he glanced around; was he going nuts? He really *could* hear something. *There!* Coming from the tube's mouth. He thrust it to his ear and held his breath. Listened with every fibre of his being.

Holy hell! He could hear them: a whole damn choir of whale song, right there, below. A great cacophony of welcome — and he could hear Min in amongst them, that unique little waver at the end of every phrase. A sob broke deep inside him. He hauled in three shuddering breaths and called down again, trying the first harmonic he'd recognised as Min's. Should've used it straight away.

Below, a chorus burst back. And then — suddenly — there they were: rising from the sudsy sea like missiles, a whole host of orcas, seven, ten, no, at least twelve, spy-hopping above the swell in front of him, strong glossy bodies, white throats and bellies gleaming through the rain. And, yes, there was Min, weaving in and out, leaping, breaching, full of joy.

Will scrabbled to his feet, wanted to throw his arms up and boogie with them but he didn't dare let go of the handrail as they celebrated in a jubilant mass of tangled bodies, crashing tails, bellies slapping, huge seaborne creatures dancing in the furious sea right before his eyes.

He didn't care the rain was icy now. He clapped his hands, croaked out his favourite bit from *The Mikado*'s first finale. '. . . *There's lots of good fish in the sea, In the sea, in the sea, in the sea, in the sea!*' The perfect ending to this comic opera.

Then, like a dream, one by one they came, rolled over on their side and stared into his eyes as their powerful tails threshed to anchor them in the swell. Love and gratitude poured off them, he could feel it, truly could, such a sense of warmth despite the filthy weather. Huge orcas, some nearly as big as the boat, all eyeing him. And when the last one filed past, Min remained. He came right up, squealing as Will leaned over, hoping like hell the rope would hold him steady, spume slapping at him as he grasped Min's head between his hands. He kissed between Min's eyes as they rocked together, bridging the sloppy sea. Breathed him in: that fishy kelpy scent. Gave him one last loving hongi of farewell.

'You'll be okay now, mate. For god's sake don't get lost again.'

Min clicked and mewled, then hooked Will's gaze one final time, holding the connection as he slowly sank below the surface of the agitated sea. And, like that, he was gone. *They* were gone. And Will was left staring out at wind-tossed waves, alone.

He tried to stand, conscious again of how rough it was, and scanned the sea in hope of sighting one final glimpse of them resurfacing. Instead, a boat materialised between the sheets of rain, clearly emblazoned with the word 'Police'.

TWENTY-SEVEN

Boisterous Bliss!

What can I tell you of that time you do not already know? My heart was weary, hopes so stretched, while Song Boy's sullen thoughts grew grimmer still. Together we had crossed a world of wild water, fled his home, but we were still without shelter from the stormy seas.

Right as the day reached its most dismal peak all my pleading calls were answered! Passed from unknown Being to Being until they found my family further out, the first I knew that they were there was when I heard the happy heart-cry of my aunt. She sped beneath the wind-swept sea — wailing, weeping, full of wonder — calling for me and my mother, heart humming hope.

But when they found me so forlorn, my mother gone, they were as wounded hearing of her death as I was telling them that terrible truth. I knew my aunt, my mother's fondest friend, would mourn most deeply; could feel her loss as sharply as my own. I nestled in against her heaving heart and told the story of my mother's fearsome — fearless — fight.

Such woe washed out. Such seething sadness. But from above, through their great grief, came the comfort of my Song Boy's caring call. It somehow dug down deep to see if I was safe. My family feared at first, until they heard how he helped me, showed me kindness, led me here — and how, for this, I owed him life-long loving thanks.

They rose right from the swollen sea to scan him; watched him with their weathered, wary eyes. But they could feel the goodwill washing off him; saw the sweetness; heard the love that lit his limping song. And then it was, oh, most moving; still holds the sway to send a shiver through my brittle bones. Such merriment, breaching, bodies brushing past, minds mingling, love let loose to lift me from my depths and wrap me in the comfort of both my Song Boy and my clan. Much tail slapping, boisterous bliss!

One by one they berthed beside him in that squally sea, sent him such a force of feeling I sensed he felt it too. Once all were past then I swam up, swept by sorrow as I bid him my most fond farewell. I was so torn, heart hauled between the pull of my dear family and the friendship I had fostered with this brave bewitching Boy. Of course, my underwater family won. But, dear friends, do not doubt me, Song Boy still holds the weight of my most weary heart.

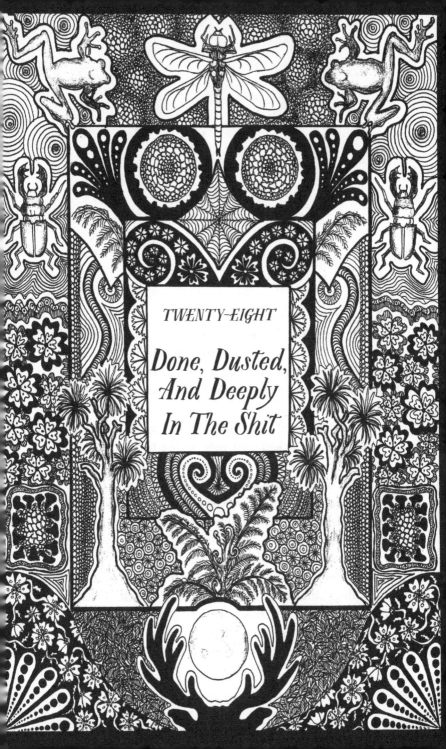

TWENTY-EIGHT

Done, Dusted,
And Deeply
In The Shit

Will braced himself on the bucking deck, watching the two policemen struggle in the wild sea to raft their boat to his. No point in running. His job was done and this was always bound to be the outcome of his stunt. The first to stagger aboard the Cat was none other than DS Gilroy.

'What the hell do you think you're doing?'

Will's gaze flicked past him, trying to spot the pod between the upright swells. Thought he did. *Thank god.* Min was safe now, back together with his family, and that was all that mattered. 'A rescue mission,' he said. 'It was life or death.' He pointed to the orca cluster but couldn't stop his hand shaking, the wetsuit no match for the sleety rain that wormed inside to chill his spine.

'For god's sake, son, you're going to get hypothermia.' DS Gilroy turned to his partner. 'Let's switch.' He had to shout. 'You bring this beast into Kaikoura and get it moored. I'll take the boy with me in ours.'

It was terrifying trying to time the step from one

bucking bronco to the next. When he finally negotiated it, Will hunkered down and wrapped up in the silver thermal blanket the cop had thrust at him. They bashed through swell, spray crashing in. It was impossible to speak. Not that he could; his throat felt like he'd swallowed a roll of razor wire.

When they made it back to land Gilroy took him straight to the Kaikoura Police Station. Gave him a towel. Then a boiler suit and woollen jersey. Then he was bundled into a patrol car for the long drive back to Blenheim. Of course the heater didn't work. Gilroy stopped on the main road out for fuel, returning with two coffees and hot chips for Will. Not what he'd expected; he'd imagined a paddy wagon and handcuffs. He sipped the coffee slowly as it burned down to the pit of his stomach. It gradually thawed him from the inside out.

Gilroy didn't push. He waited for Will to finish eating before he started in. 'Okay, now you're warmer, start from the beginning. This isn't on the record yet, just a chat, so fill me in. I hope you understand how serious this is.'

Will nodded. Began with finding Min, then unpicked every thread that led up to Bruce threatening Min's life. In retrospect, he should've seen the pattern of Bruce's violence from the start. Dean had warned him.

'Why didn't you tell somebody?'

'You heard Dean: Harley's in Bruce's pocket — and the local cop's. And, anyway, there wasn't time.'

'But stealing a boat? You must've known you'd get caught. You could've killed yourself.'

Like he didn't know? Will's mouth gave an ironic twitch. 'Min had already been shot once, and everyone just talked, no one actually *did* anything. Now he's safe.

You should've seen him when he found his pod.' The memory was so overwhelming he couldn't go on. He swallowed thorny tears. Jesus, he was knackered.

Gilroy continued with his lecture but Will switched off now; just sat there watching the windscreen wipers flick back and forth, breathing in the stink of damp wool. He thought of Min surrounded by his family. Was his mother there? He'd seemed to circle one big orca in particular. Maybe that was her? God, he hoped so.

The wind was even fiercer now, buffeting the car. It took them just under two hours to reach Blenheim. They drove straight to the police station and Will was led into a room for more official questioning. At the end, he signed his statement and was charged with theft, photographed, fingerprinted and locked into a cell. It was cold, no natural light, the bed no more than a narrow bench with a mean squab. He curled up under two blankets and tried to blank his mind. It didn't work. He shivered as if electricity was shocking through him. Felt numb.

They'd offered him a phone call, but he couldn't face speaking to Dean. No way. Dean would think he had to solve it. Same with his parents. He'd known what he was getting into; he would take the blame and stick it out. Had even told the cops he couldn't pay all of Harley's fine in time, so he was on the hook for that as well. He may as well go down in one big fiery heap.

He dozed, dipping in and out of dream-infested sleep, waking disorientated and frozen to the core. He had no idea what time it was; whether it was still even day or had slipped into night. All he could hold onto was Min's pure joy at being reunited with his kind — and that kiss with Pania. He'd kept her out of his confession. Hunter, too.

No point in dumping either of them in the shit when he could take it all. He owed them everything.

He sat up quickly as the lock rattled. The cop who'd processed him leaned into the cell. 'You've got visitors. The boss says you can come and see them.'

'Thanks.' Will collected one of the blankets around him like a cape. *Them?* He half expected Dean — of course the cops would've rung him — but who else? Maybe a lawyer?

In another small room, Dean and Viv sat holding hands, faces anxious as he stepped inside.

Dean rose and hugged him, slapping his back. 'Jesus, mate, you look terrible.'

Viv nudged Dean aside and threw her arms around him. Pressed her lips to his cheek. 'Yeah, you even look too cold for death warmed up.'

Will shuffled around, sat opposite them at the table and waited until the officer left the room. 'I'm sorry,' he said to Dean with a rusty croak. He sounded ninety. 'I know it was a crazy idea. But I found them! You should've seen it. All these huge orcas — so excited to have him back.' He couldn't think of it without a lump swelling up; felt tears rise.

'You're a legend, kid,' Viv said, scowling at Dean. 'Don't pay any attention to old Mr Grumpy here. Everyone's so proud of you — well, now we know you're still alive, that is.'

Dean's lips thinned. 'For god's sake, woman, don't encourage him. Apart from the fact you're condoning theft, how the hell am I going to explain this to his parents? I'm supposed to keep him safe.' He glared at Will. 'Did you think how they'd feel if you'd carked it out there? For fuck's sake, Will, why don't you use your bloody—'

'Don't ever call me stupid,' Viv interrupted. 'That's *such* a male put-down.'

'Well, excuse me for having some balls.'

'Don't flatter yourself. Now this kid here? *He's* got balls.'

'Goddamn you're a difficult wo—'

'Guys!' Will shook his head; he had enough crap in there already, didn't need theirs. 'I said it was dumb, okay? I'll take whatever they throw at me. But don't ask me to regret it, because I can't.' He held Dean's simmering gaze. 'Sorry.'

'Don't you worry, hon, I told Greenpeace. Now that it's a big news story—'

'*What?*' His guts nearly emptied on the floor. *No, please god, no.*

Dean's voice oozed anger. 'Yeah, seems you've got Gabby to thank for that.'

'Gabby? Why?' *Oh shit. Shit!*

'She uploaded the clips of you and Pania with Min to this crowdfunding site last night. She's asking for donations to help you pay the fine.' Viv smiled. 'I know it freaks you out but, Will, she's nearly raised the eight grand already — from people all around the world! And then the press turned up this morning, looking for you.'

They'd dragged Pania into this? No wonder Dean looked so pissed off.

'Yeah, sorry mate,' he said.

No, not pissed off. Miserable. 'How the hell could you let them set Pania up like that?' Heat flooded his face.

Dean thought Will meant *him*. 'You think I didn't try once I knew? But she insisted — said if it would help you pay the fine then she'd agree. You know what women are like once they've set their minds on something.'

'It's called action,' Viv said. 'Good for her.'

But what if Harley decided to fine Pania as well? He wished he had the energy to shout. 'How the hell did Gabby even get them?'

'They were still on Cathy's laptop from Saturday's show. Gabby conned them out of her.' Viv seemed oblivious to the disaster here.

'Yeah, and I started getting calls at work,' Dean said. 'That's when I went home to look for you and found your note.'

'*You* told the police?'

'What the hell did you expect me to do? You were out in a bloody gale, in a boat you couldn't handle.'

Will's heart was pumping way too fast. He felt dizzy. 'But I made it there okay.'

'Yeah, well, you fluked it.'

It would be so easy to reassure Dean, admit that Pania had shown him how to set the course. 'You didn't notice the boat was missing?'

'I didn't get down to the marina till late. Thought Bruce had taken it out.'

'But he's—'

'Bailed, mate. Got out last night. He didn't show his face this morning or you can bet *he'd* have called the cops. The joke is that at first I thought he'd scuttled it for insurance.' Only half his face smiled. 'Anyway, now, somehow, the press all seem to know. They're everywhere.'

A silence built in the room, as if they'd all run out of steam. How could it be fair that Bruce was walking free while Hunter lay in hospital? And how the hell was Will going to face the press? It was one big mother of a nightmare. All the joy he'd had from seeing Min back with his pod evaporated. Thank god he was here, locked away from the media, those invasive pricks.

'What happens now?' he finally said.

Dean sighed. 'You'll have to stay tonight and go to court sometime tomorrow. The cops reckon they'll grant you bail.'

'How much?'

'Dunno. They'll probably just set down some conditions, but I can fork out for it if I have to, so long as you don't do a runner.'

'Course I won't.'

'Yeah, well, you'd better be telling the bloody truth this time. Are there any other bombshells you'd like to drop?'

He shook his head. 'Nah, man. I'm done.' Done, dusted, and deeply in the shit. 'Please don't ring Mum and Dad. I'll sort it on my own.'

'Too late. I called and left a message as soon as I found your note. You could've been bloody dead out there for all I knew. I thought they had a right to know.'

Will groaned and buried his face in his hands. They'd freak. Would get all stressed and miserable like they were before.

'Don't worry, we've left another message telling them you're safe.' Viv patted his back. 'Is there anything you need?' she asked. 'Besides some clothes for court?'

'And take those frickin' piercings out,' Dean said. 'From here on in, you'd better play it really straight.'

He knew they were doing their best but he was so tired he just wished they'd go away. He had to think. Figure out how the hell he was going to handle this. Bloody Gabby. Sure, it was remotely possible she was trying to help — be nice even — but she had no idea how much the thought of more attention made him want to puke. And poor Pania had no idea what she was getting into. That shit had the potential to go global. *Will of the World Wide Web.*

'How's Hunter?'

'Good, mate. Doing okay.' Dean stared hard at him. 'How'd you know where to find the keys for the Cat?'

No flies on Dean. 'A lucky guess.'

'Yeah, right.' He scratched his scalp; truly did look miserable. 'You do know Bruce'll be gunning for you? If he can make you out to be the scapegoat for his charge, he will. You may as well have handed him a "get out of jail free" card.'

'Can you make Gabby take the clips down?' He had to try, though knew full well it was impossible. It only took one person to download them and post them again.

'That would be crazy,' Viv said. 'It's your best defence. Anyone who sees that clip will understand your motives — and if it comes to trial you should let them play the thing in court.'

'For god's sake,' Dean said. 'This isn't some Yankee courtroom drama. They'll just read the charges then sentence him. No dramatic speeches.'

It was as if Viv wasn't listening. She reached over and took Will's hand, her fingers so much warmer than his. 'I want you to think about allowing Greenpeace to use that footage for their anti-whaling campaign. I know you don't like the publicity, but think about the wider picture. You could really make a difference, Will. Those clips could change the way people think about orcas and, by default, other whales as well. It's really important. No one's seen anything like it, anywhere in the world.'

'Leave the poor kid alone, for chrissake,' said Dean. His voice was abrupt, though his gaze had lost its sting. He patted Will's shoulder. 'Hang in there, mate. I know it's a lot to take in right now.' He stood up. 'We'd better go. We'll look in on Hunter while we're here. See you tomorrow, eh?'

'You'll come? What about work?'

'Of course I'll bloody come. Someone has to be here until we can drum up a decent lawyer. Anyway, I can take time off if I want and if Bruce has a problem with it, let me at him.'

'Whoa, big boy!' Viv laughed as she kissed Will goodbye, then whispered in his ear. 'What you did was amazing, Will. Thank you. You saved Min's life.'

It made him want to howl. He was so damned tired and the cold wouldn't shift from his bones. But he *was* proud of himself. Would never regret what he'd done. *Never*.

When they'd gone he went back to the cell, where a meal of some indefinable stew, potatoes, boiled carrots and bread awaited him. It needed salt but he scoffed it down anyway, hungry as hell; grateful.

Later, the cop on duty told Will he was due at the District Court first thing in the morning. Will asked him to let Dean know, then curled up and tried to sleep. Even now, the squab rocked under him like he was still aboard the boat. He thought about his parents, how angry they would be, and hoped they wouldn't rush over. Tomorrow he would ask if he could call them; try to reassure them he could manage on his own. Hoped he could.

It was impossible to settle, the squab too hard, blankets too thin, and far too many worries buzzing around inside his head. The charge, the state of Bruce's boat, Hunter, the clip doing the rounds, Pania, Gabby. *Jesus.* The media too. *And* the fine, and his mum and dad. The only thing that brought him any comfort was the thought of Min. He pushed the other crap away. Nothing he could do about any of it tonight. Instead, he relived the moment when the crowd of orcas had risen from the sea. It made his heart thud. Nothing else would top that, for the rest of his life.

~

THE DISTRICT COURT WAS BUSY, full of cases from the night before. Will sat in a waiting room with Dean, uncomfortable in one of Dean's good shirts and tie. Tried to ignore the others who were called before him: a couple of drunks, a drug dealer, one pretty tragic homeless guy, and an old lady (who was clearly not all there) nabbed for shoplifting one miserable tin of cat food.

He'd seen the duty solicitor first thing this morning and asked about his chances of getting bail. She'd seemed confident. Said all he had to do was plead guilty, she'd do the rest. She assured him she'd try to get an order for Diversion if she could, though said it would depend on the details of the case. But, once he'd given her an honest account, she wasn't willing to commit. Now she said it depended how much pressure Bruce brought to bear. So here he was, still dependent on that prick.

When he was led into the courtroom the crowd in the public seats unnerved him. Cathy was there — winked at him — and Viv. He met her eye, raised an eyebrow newly stripped of its piercings, shrugged, warmed by her grin.

There were a few other familiar local faces, and several journalists, he guessed, notebooks out, gimlet eyes trained on him. He looked away.

As the registrar was reading out the charge sheet, in walked Bruce with another man. They found seats up front, ignoring Dean. Bruce was well turned out in a fancy suit and florid tie. He scrubbed up well for such an arsehole. His angry stare burnt into Will, who turned away, hating that he blushed. He coughed, his throat on fire.

The court officials ground through all the formalities: Will pleading guilty, the lawyer explaining there were extenuating circumstances — that his friend had just been brutally beaten (everyone glanced at Bruce who didn't even flinch, the bastard), and how Will was concerned Min was in immediate danger of being killed. She said he came from a good home, had no previous convictions, and his uncle would post bail if need be and guarantee his good behaviour.

The police said they wouldn't oppose bail, and the judge looked like she'd go for it; she was checking through her papers when the man beside Bruce spoke up.

'Your Honour, please excuse my interruption, but on behalf of my client Mr Godsill here, I'd like to oppose bail.'

The judge looked over the rim of her glasses, assessing him. 'Mr Godsill? I thought we dealt with him yesterday. This is most unusual, but since the boat is his I'll allow you to quickly say your piece.'

His lawyer deferred to Bruce, who stood and puffed himself out. 'Well, apart from stealing my boat, Mr Jackson here has been the source of trouble since he came to town. He's blatantly ignored Fisheries regulations, is an accessory to the destruction of my commercial enterprise, and he had no experience in my boat — has damaged it significantly — and now I hear he's planning illegal actions with Greenpeace, threatening my farms.'

'That's bullshit!' Viv yelled. Around her, the journos perked up like wilted flowers given water.

'Silence, madam. No more now.' The judge stalled for time, shuffling her papers, then addressed the officer who'd detailed the police case. 'Sergeant Morrison? Your thoughts?'

'This is news to me. But there certainly has been a heap of interest in the case — and it's got a lot of locals really riled up.'

What? Will glanced over his shoulder at Cathy, who shook her fist in a show of solidarity. He felt stupid and naive — not only that he hadn't predicted all the interest from the press but, worse, he never thought Bruce would have the nerve to stand up in a court of law and spout such lies. *To sit in solemn silence in a dull, dark dock, In a pestilential prison, with a life-long lock, Awaiting the sensation of a short, sharp shock, From a cheap and chippy chopper on a big black block!*

Will's lawyer stood again. 'Your Honour, I think Mr Godsill is over-egging the potential dangers. Mr Jackson merely wanted to prevent the illegal killing of the orca. Now that's been achieved I'm sure he'd like to reassure the court he'll cause no further trouble.'

Bruce broke in again. 'I disagree. Just this morning I had a group of greenies protesting down at the wharf. He's the ring-leader — look at him.' Will felt every eye in the courtroom turn to him. Was relieved he'd taken Dean's advice and stripped his face of rings and studs.

'He came down from the city with this plan in mind.'

How ridiculous. As if he'd organised for Min to be abandoned right on cue. Will glanced at Dean, whose anger was set in concrete on his face, fists shackled by his armpits.

'Mr Jackson? Is this true?'

'No. None of it. Well, except for the boat — it may have a few scratches, but—'

Bruce snorted. 'A few? The insurance company has looked it over this morning and they say there's nearly fifty grand of damage.' Gasps came from the stalls like a matinee pantomime.

Now Dean was on his feet. 'That's utter rot! How you can stand there and—'

'Enough! I've been more than lenient.' The judge looked heartily pissed off. 'All right, I can see this needs further investigation. I will grant bail, but am prepared to revoke it should more information — solid information, Mr Godsill — come to light. A bond of two thousand dollars, given the serious nature of these new allegations.' She stood, and the game was over.

Will rose to his feet, stunned. Another two grand? Did Dean even have that much? He stood there as Bruce marched out, a trail of reporters hot-footing it after him. Will had to be moved on by the cop, who took him by the elbow to guide him out.

'Can he do that?' he asked. 'Just make stuff up and get away with it?'

The cop shrugged. 'That's up to the judge to decide. But you're lucky it's Judge Harris. If you'd had any of the others you'd probably be staying put.'

He had to wait while Dean signed on the dotted line,

promising to deliver Will to a probation officer next week and then back to court again for sentencing the following month. Clearly they didn't trust him to get there on his own. They both had to swallow a stern warning about staying away from Bruce as well, before they finally let Will go. He walked out with Dean's arm tight around his shoulders, straight into a milling crowd. Cameras zoomed on him; reporters threw out stupid questions: was the clip for real? Had he trained Min? What had happened out at sea? He said nothing; let Dean bustle him into the Commodore, past a pushy TV crew.

'I'm so sorry,' Will said. Always apologising. 'Is it possible to go see Hunter?'

'Yeah, no worries.' Despite a face like a brewing storm, to Will's surprise Dean didn't say another word until they reached the hospital. 'I've gotta go and do a pick-up. You okay here for an hour? I'll come and find you when I'm done.'

'That's cool.' He climbed out of the car but poked his head back through the open window. 'Thanks. I promise not to cause you any more grief.'

'Good. See you don't.' He drove off at speed, the old Commodore spewing fumes.

Hunter was dozing when he reached the room, only a slightly healthier colour than last time Will had seen him, still hooked up to all the machines and drips. Will sat down beside the bed and closed his eyes. Summoned up Pania; replayed their kiss. He was sprung grinning stupidly by a nurse, who'd come to rouse Hunter for his medication.

'Oh, hey! You made it!' He gave Will a weak thumbs-up.

'Oh, mate, you won't believe it . . .' Will turned the

trip into a rollicking story for Hunter's entertainment, stalling on the courtroom drama until the nurse had left the room.

'Don't worry. I'll fix it,' Hunter said.

'Yeah, good one, man.'

'I mean it. I'm gonna talk to Dad.'

'Don't be mental! And, anyway, if the cops have any sense they'll have slapped a restraining order on him.'

'But I can make the whole thing go away. I've had all night to think about it.'

A tiny germ of hope started to grow in Will until he stomped it dead. 'Forget it, man. I can sort it. It'll be okay.'

Hunter tried to shift. 'Gimme a hand up, will you?' Will helped him slide up the bed and jammed the pillows in behind him. Straightened out the covers and tubes while Hunter started up again. 'Listen. I'm gonna tell you something — a secret — but you can never tell anyone, okay? Never.'

Will hated this. But Hunter's gaze fixed on him, pleading, the look so hurt and fragile it made him think of Min. 'But what if it's—'

'Never. That's my one condition. Okay?'

What was it with these people and their conditions? Secrets ended badly. Fact. 'Okay. But if it—'

'Just listen. I've never told *anyone* this before.'

'So why me? Why now?'

'It's time. Hell, you're the one who told me to let it out. Please, Will. Just promise.'

How could he refuse? It was true he'd badgered Hunter to open up. Now he'd been hoist on his own — with his own — pet-something, damn what the hell was it? Ah, yes. A petard. They'd discussed it when they studied *Hamlet*. A kind of ancient bomb. Appropriate, when everything was blowing up around him.

'Will! Answer me, you dick.'

'Okay, I promise.' He had a strong feeling he'd regret this.

'Shut the door.'

'But—'

'Dude, just shut the effing door.'

'Okay, okay.' He did as he was told. Sat back down and struck the pose his counsellor used for 'active listening'. The joke was lost on Hunter.

'You know when you had to wake me from that intense dream?' Will nodded, his dread returning. 'It's like Dad rattled something loose in my head. I've always remembered bits of what happened to Mum, but there were gaps — and if I tried to force them all together I'd get all panicky and stop.' He rubbed his nose and Will recognised the signs of battling tears. Felt sick. Had a horrible feeling he knew what was coming. 'Mum was a big drinker — I remember *that,* clear as anything — and before she died it got real bad. That night she was really pissed — two or three bottles of wine and then straight on to spirits. I've got this really strong memory of her burning something on the stove — a terrible smell — and when Dad had a go at her she threw the pan at him — and got him too. He went completely nuts, started yelling, then they were both at it. I hid behind the curtains — Dad never thought to look there — and he grabbed her, shook her real hard. That's all I ever could remember. Until the other night.'

Will's heart was beating a hundred k's an hour. 'You sure you want to tell me this?' *Please say no.*

'Look, this is really hard, okay? I need to say it out loud. Just once.' Hunter flinched. *Oh god.* 'So, yeah . . . he held her down and poured a whole bottle of whisky down her throat — I could hear her trying to swallow, but she kept choking. By the time Dad stopped she was pretty much out of it — I saw him pick her up and throw her on their bed, face down. He stormed out, left me terrified. I went to check but couldn't wake her up.' He stopped, his chin crumpling. Sniffed back tears. 'I gave up after a while and went into my room. Closed the door. Thought she'd wake up grumpy. The next morning she was dead. Suffocated in the duvet. Dad told me it was my fault for not checking her.'

'Jesus Christ! He killed her, then blamed you?'

Hunter nodded. 'I think so. And I think *he* thinks so. He used to threaten me to keep my mouth shut and I never knew why. But now I'm having flashbacks, all mixed up with when he came at me the other day.'

'Shit, man, I'm so sorry. I know how *that* feels.'

'Yeah, figured you might.'

'You know, they must have done an autopsy?'

'All it showed was that she was totally tanked. And everyone knew what a boozer she was. In those days, Dad was the poor bastard whose drunk of a wife had died. They're all anti the smacking ban down here, mate — it's how they deal with shit. Old school. My grandad put Dad in hospital when he got Mum pregnant. Munted his head so bad he still loses it whenever he's under too much stress. Poor Mum never stood a chance. Gabby's dad's a real prick as well.'

'Come on, man. You have to tell someone.'

'Just did.'

'Not me! You have to tell the cops.'

'What for? I've thought about this all night and today. I've got something concrete over the old prick now. I'm going to get him here, threaten to tell the cops unless he makes them drop the charges against you — Harley's too. And I'm going to make him hand over all his shares of the business. He's already in the shit, so I reckon right now's good timing — he hasn't got a lot to lose except more debt.' He moved. Winced. 'He's nearly screwed it, but if me and Dean get hold of it, then Mike might partner up, bring in some iwi money, and we might really make a go of it. Make it sustainable. Make it the best bloody fish farm in the country.' His face was flushed, the circles under his eyes nearly as bruised as Dean's shiner.

Will blew out a breath he hadn't noticed he was holding. Hunter's plan had a scary kind of logic. Damn smart, in fact. As cunning as Bruce, but without the rotten core. Anyone who thought Hunter was thick was seriously mistaken. If he did nothing and Bruce went down for assault and fraud, then the whole business would go under — all Hunter's hard work . . . and Dean's. They both deserved a break. If it meant him keeping quiet it was worth it. Blabbing wouldn't bring back Hunter's mum — and Hunter's plan would screw Bruce over nicely.

He looked him in the eye. 'Do it,' he said. 'But not for me. Do it to get the farms, then go for it. But here's *my* condition: he never contacts you again unless you want it. And never want it, okay? He's never going to change.'

'I know.' Now Hunter did cry, hiding his face behind his baseball-mitt hands, shoulders shaking like an earthquake going off. Will got up and patted his shoulder, couldn't not.

'It's all right, man. Let it out.' Poor Hunter, holding onto this since he was a little grieving kid, living with it festering away, blaming himself, not knowing, while that murderous prick threatened him and beat him up. His own life was a dawdle in the park compared to this. *Nectar quaffing, Ha! ha! ha!* . . .

He clapped Hunter on the back. 'Listen, will you at least promise that when you talk to him you have a cop right outside?'

'Fair enough. It's not like I expect him to be sorry.'

There was a knock on the door. They looked at each other. Will nodded and mimed buttoning his lips just as Dean walked in.

'Gidday, mate,' he said to Hunter. Turned to Will. 'There's someone who wants to see you.' He jerked his head towards the corridor.

Pania, with any luck. He hadn't had a chance to speak with her yet. Hoped to whisk her off somewhere quiet. Private. He walked out with a half smile — and looked up into the eyes of his dad.

'Hey, buddy.' His father spread his arms out wide.

It did Will in, the shock and the comfort of his father's embrace. His familiar smell. His quiet show of love. Will cried into his shoulder, his father crying too.

'Oh, matey, what a mess.'

'How'd you get here so fast?' Will said.

'You don't think I'd have sat around and waited, do you? Mum sends her love. She wanted to come, but, to be honest, I wanted you to myself. It feels so long since it's been you and me. I've missed you, mate. We never should've left you here. I'm so sorry.'

'*I'm* sorry. I've stuffed things up. I've been a real dick.'

'Mum and I watched those videos on the internet last night — you and that little orca. My god, Will, what an amazing thing. It was incredible.'

'He was so lonely, Dad, I couldn't just leave him on his own.'

'Course not, matey, course not. What you did was right — crazy, dangerous, and totally illegal, but your heart was in the right place and that's all that matters. We're just relieved you're alive. You could've told us, you know. We would've helped.'

'I love you, Dad.'

'Love you too. And I'm proud of you. Never think otherwise, okay? That's one incredible gift you've got, though god knows it didn't come from me!'

'I've missed you guys so much.' He couldn't remember when he'd last had such a real conversation with him. Liked it. Missed it. 'Hey, come in and meet my friend Hunter. Poor bugger has a real dad from hell.' He made a move but his father stopped him.

'You know, I've kind of worried that's how you felt about me. I'm sorry, mate. But my head's clearer now, and things are looking up over there. When we've sorted out this business I want you to come back over with me.'

'That'd be great! I miss Mum too.' He realised he was still clutching tight to his dad like a four-year-old. He let go, but didn't want to break the physical bond entirely, so put his arm around his father's shoulders. He'd grown since the last time he'd done this, and was now just as tall as him. 'A couple of weeks in Aussie could be just what the doctor ordered!'

'No, mate. Not a holiday. We want you to move over, join us there. You can finish your Correspondence off with us and Mum's already sussed out a uni with a really good music degree you can apply for.'

Will dropped his arm. 'But I can't.' He didn't know what to say; how to translate what was shouting in his head. Didn't even know he felt like this till now: he belonged here, and didn't want to leave. Everyone in Blythe had stood by him — well, nearly everyone — made him feel part of them. 'I want to see the year out with Dean, Dad. He's been so cool about all this, I want to have some time to pay him back.' *This*, at least, his father would understand.

Even so, his dad looked gutted. 'Let's talk about it later, eh? I promised Mum as soon as we got back to Dean's we'd Skype.'

'Yeah, sure.'

He led his father in to meet Hunter. Put one arm around Dean's shoulders and pulled Dad in with the other. Was so damn lucky to have them. And Hunter too. And Pania . . . Who the hell was he kidding? There was no way he was moving away from her.

TWENTY-NINE

*Fondled
With Such
Fawning*

What a wonder it was, back in the bosom of my first family. We swam down to the depths that fell from shingle shelves; saw spoonworms spreading, crabs creeping, squids shimmer in their silver sheaths. The ocean's skin was thick there, took on the changing hues of clouds, sky meeting sea, stacked with simple tiny teeming souls we turned to meaty meals.

Our friends the Sperm whales sheltered there, as did the humming Humpbacks, the Blues, the Beaked; dusky dolphins, fur seals — a wondrous world of air-breathers, fat full-bodied Beings — all gathered to gorge upon the riches rumbled by the tide in this, our summer store. I still recall this mellow mixing of our many kinds, a chummy crowd of cousins keen to hear my story, swapping tales of close calls with the Hungry Ones — though some had heard of other Beings and Boys, none could match the love I lucked onto with mine.

They fussed until my mind, again, filled up with foolish pride. To be fondled with such fawning stroked my simple make-up, made me smug — and I showed off, sought nods when no notice was due. In the end it was my aunt who slapped me down. She saw my plight, the pitfall I had tumbled into; took me well away from all the rest and turned my wrongs to rights.

We Beings can only live like this, she sang, so long as none nose higher than the rest. The Hungry Ones have never heeded this; is why they wage such bitter wars. Each heart must undermine its meanness, not seek to steal another's song. Wanting more, moving to out-match, is for the small of mind; the weak. We Beings are better than that; she settled in my mind, a fair foresightful lesson I did not forget — although, from time to time, in truth, the whispers of wanting test me still.

When summer waned we set off back to White World, to spend the winter under our Mother's most southern skies. A great gaggle of us set forth, flukes flicking, fins, flippers and flanks flying as shearwaters warned of windborne storms and albatrosses sniffed the briny breeze. Songs shimmered through the frosty sea so far, so fast, I shook off my fears and wandered. Wondered.

But as the days dragged on I missed my Boy, thoughts ever on him, heart heavy, a hole where once his songs had filled me up.

All winter long I watched and waited for the thaw, and when at last it came I took my aunt's tidings with much merriment and mirth. My wait was over. We were going back.

THIRTY

Awesome Singing Baby Orca

As they walked towards the exit of the hospital Harley blew into the foyer on a squally gust of wind, hunched over a basket of oranges and grapes.

'Oh, good,' he said. He blocked them so they had to stop. 'Can I have a word?'

Will tensed. Didn't have the energy to face him now.

'Give it a break, Harley,' Dean said. 'You've done enough.'

Harley's wet moustache drooped like a dead lizard. 'Please. Just listen. I'm so sorry. When I heard about this it made me do some major soul-searching.' He shuddered, knocking an orange from the basket. Scrabbled to pick it up. 'Forget the fine, okay? I'll tell the boss we've reinvestigated the, ah, circumstances, and on balance . . .' He ground to a halt. Shuffled his feet. Sighed. 'The honest truth is, I was under pressure. I owed Bruce quite a bit of money. It's my own fault. I lost everything when Southern Finance went under. Bruce said he'd help and I was dumb enough to take him up. I've handed in my resignation.

Can't believe I let myself get so sucked in.'

All Will could do was stare; couldn't quite take it in.

Dean slapped him on the back. 'No worries, eh? So long as Will is off the hook, no harm done then.'

'How's Hunter? Mike told me he was really bad.'

'He'll be okay. Don't worry about him, we've got him covered. You just sort your shit.'

'Yeah, yeah, I will. Thanks.' He juggled the basket to offer an outstretched hand to Will. 'No hard feelings? I hear you got the orca back to its pod. Good on you. Though next time, try to work within the law, eh?'

Will shook his hand. Wanted to laugh. Gabby had raised all that money, hung him and Pania out to dry, for nothing. *B should be happy, oh so happy . . .*

Back at Dean's, they Skyped his mother, who'd taken the day off work to wait. It was so good to see her, had been too long. She looked stressed. Older. He was glad he was too knackered to cry; it would've upset her more than she already was. He tried to explain why he wanted to stay, couching it in terms he knew they couldn't argue with: that he should repay Dean for his support; that he wanted to be there when Hunter came out. He promised he'd apply to the Music School back home — he could reconnect with Marilyn, his old voice teacher, who taught at the university too. They knew she always got the best out of his voice. Couldn't really argue.

'Are you sure, love? We've really been missing you.' His mother looked so sad it wrenched his guts.

'I know, Mum. Me too. But can I at least stay until the end of the year and then see how I feel? I have a feeling Dean's going to be really busy with the business soon — I'd really like to help him out.' An understatement, if

Hunter played his trump card.

'Can you at least come over next holidays?' She laughed. 'It's a mother thing. I won't know how you really are until I see you in the flesh.'

'Yeah, that'd be great, so long as you can afford it.'

She reassured him and this seemed to satisfy them both for now. And if things didn't pan out in Blythe, at least he had another option, although he hoped he wouldn't need it.

After they ended the call he ran a bath. Washed his hair and soaked until his fingers went wrinkly. Pania would be home from school by now. He had to convince her to get Gabby to delete everything. She didn't understand the risks.

He dressed again, still bone weary, and went back out to join his dad. Explained he needed to pop over to Pania's house. Wouldn't be long.

'Excellent! I'll come as well. It's years since I've seen Cathy. Mum'd kill me if I didn't make the effort while I'm here.'

If they were such good mates, how come Will hadn't remembered them? Or was it that they didn't trust Will now? His dad insisted they take Dean's car. On the way, wind and rain hurled at the windscreen like toddlers in a tantrum.

Cathy answered the door. 'Mark! How lovely to see you! Come in!' She hugged him, smiling broadly.

Okay, so he *did* know her. Cathy pointed Will towards Pania's room; said she was doing homework. He felt weird, invading her space. Knocked on the door but only cracked it open a bit.

'Hiya.'

'Will!' She was sitting at a desk, its top littered with books. 'Come in!' She flushed as she scooped clothes off her floor and chucked them in one corner.

He edged in. Closed the door. Perched on the edge of her bed. All he could think about was that kiss. 'How goes it?'

'Tell me about Min!'

Her face lit up as he described the moment when he'd realised Min had found his pod. His whānau. Loved how tears welled up in her eyes as he described the way they'd surfaced to check him out. He told her about meeting Harley; about the fine being dropped. He'd hoped he might be able to broach Gabby and the clips, but when she said nothing he worried he'd piss her off if he just blurted it out. He didn't trust his anger at Gabby not to boil over. He stood and roamed her room, glancing at the books in front of her. Maths. Physics. Genetics. Computer coding.

'Intense. You do all this at school?'

She laughed. 'Doubt it. I want to study biotech down at Canterbury next year. Dad's got some contacts there — thinks he can get me a job over next summer in their lab.'

'Wow. You really *are* as brainy as you seem. No wonder you knew all about the GPS.'

'Shut up!'

'What's wrong with being brainy? You should be proud of it.'

She smiled up at him and he couldn't help it: bent over and kissed her. Not too hard or needy, just long enough not to torture himself when he had to pull away. He leaned against the side of the desk, his leg a hair-breadth from her knee. 'Listen, I know what Gabby did.' *Keep control, remember Gabby is her friend.*

Her smile dropped. 'I'm sorry. I know you hate that kind of thing, but she was really trying to help — make up for being awful — and I didn't stop her 'cause I couldn't think of a better way to help. And it worked. She just didn't tell me she'd edited us in together and posted it on YouTube too. I heard at school.'

No! 'She has to take it down — right now! You've no idea how sick people are. They'll hound you — share it everywhere; write stupid comments—'

'You haven't seen the comments then?'

He felt sick. Furious. Betrayed. 'I know the kind of things people write. I've spent the last few months trying to forget them.'

She pulled her phone out of her pocket. 'You have to see them, Will. This is different.' He really wanted to snatch it off her; chuck it out the window. Felt dizzy. But she went ahead and accessed the site. Handed him her phone. 'Sit down,' she said. 'Take your time. Read them all.'

He glanced at it, dread blurring his vision. Groaned. She'd called it *'Awesome Singing Baby Orca!'* If that wasn't being set up, what was? He hated her. Was gutted Pania didn't understand.

What? She must be joking. It showed a hundred and sixty-three thousand views — and looked like nearly everyone who watched it had made a comment too. He really had to get a grip; could feel bile rising.

It was hard to take this in; accept such an altered reality. Only four 'thumbs down' amongst over a hundred thousand 'likes'. Could that be right? Person after person, praising Min, Pania . . . and him. No negative comments he could see, except a few who thought it must've been jacked up, but they were shouted down by others, all talking about how clever, how precious, how amazing Min was, *all* whales were. He let the phone drop in his lap.

'O—kay.' Couldn't believe it. *Just like Viv said.* 'There has to be a catch.'

'If there is, I haven't found it yet.' She sat down on the bed beside him. Picked his hand up and wove it into hers. 'Please don't freak out. It's an amazing thing you've done.'

He felt exhausted again. Confused. 'Have you been hassled by the media yet?'

'Mum has. She took their names and fobbed them off. I said it should be you who talks.'

'Not going to happen.'

'You *have* to, Will. Viv said this could really change the way that people think. It's going viral. Imagine, they'll see it in Japan and Iceland — and that other place—'

'Norway.' On automatic. 'You think it'll actually change their policies? Come on. It's all about the money. Jobs. And the media are no better — they take things and they twist them round.'

'Then let's agree only if we're interviewed together. We can look out for each other — and if they're being jerks we'll just walk out.'

She was so damn practical. Sensible. 'Maybe.' He flopped backwards, sprawled across her bed. Reached up and brushed his fingers through the wispy tips of her hair. 'Come here.'

She dropped down beside him, her face against his chest as he curled around her. His heart was beating so hard she surely felt it through his shirt. He held her, pressed his nose into her hair. Closed his eyes. Wished the world would leave them be. *See how the Fates . . .* Yeah, yeah. He could run, hide away, but jerks like Bruce would go on killing for the sake of it, convince others it was okay, and those incredible creatures — who'd looked into his eyes, his soul — would be even more at risk.

He'd have to tough it out. Pania was right. He'd be a fool to blow it now. He sighed and kissed the crown of her head. 'Okay. Let's do it. Screw the haters. Let's kick some ass!'

She lifted her head and kissed him on lips. What else mattered?

~

HIS DAD STAYED ANOTHER THREE days — he couldn't take more time off — but was there when Will and Pania were interviewed for the TV news, three newspapers, and a chat show in the States that Will had balked at before Pania talked him around. Each hour, hits multiplied; they reached a million within days. Gabby cancelled the pledge site for his fine, but set a new one up to help fund anti-whaling campaigns. Already nearly forty grand. Will hated it. The effort to maintain his cool, to not freak out, left him permanently knackered.

Pania was such a natural on camera that he steered as many questions as possible her way. Should've realised she'd handle it: she'd been doing karangas and speaking on the marae all her life. Her shyness came across as humble — *was* humble. Her answers were always technically precise. Her eyes were so intensely blue onscreen, they were practically hypnotic. It helped to have her there; helped take the pressure off him, calmed his nerves. She was right about that too.

Of course, all the reporters *had* to dredge up the old shit as well — he *knew* it — and he got grilled at every interview. The weird thing was, instead of ridicule, he now received sympathy, though he didn't trust it — he knew the way tides turned in an instant. He felt such a dick each time he talked about it, but he had people coming up to him in the street and telling him their own stories of ancient humiliations and traumas, swallowed down or overcome. It was like being on *Oprah*; like *being* Oprah. An Oprah opera.

On the day of his dad's departure, Will took him to the airport in Dean's car. He promised to come over in the holidays, although he knew he probably wouldn't. He wanted to be with *her*. He stayed to watch the plane take off, then headed to the hospital to check on Hunter. DS Gilroy stood guard outside his room. The door was closed.

'Wow, I take it Bruce is here?' Just the thought was freaky. How the hell must Hunter feel?

'That kid's a lot more forgiving than I'd be,' Gilroy said. 'We'd stopped Bruce from making contact, but Hunter insisted — and on his own.'

'Yeah, he told me he planned to. You sure he'll be okay?'

Gilroy nodded. 'I doubt Bruce will want to make any more fuss. Thanks to your uncle's information we've passed his dealings onto the Serious Fraud Office and they're going to investigate. They gave us the nod this morning. Our friend in there has just run out of luck.'

'Will he go to jail?'

'Without a doubt. Hunter's given us a very thorough statement about the other day and past assaults. Between that and this SFO investigation, I doubt we'll see him around for a good few years.'

Will nodded but said nothing. Probably wasn't a good

idea to dance for joy when he was due in court again himself.

'I saw you with the orca on the news,' Gilroy said. 'Pretty amazing connection between the two of you. I kind of get it after seeing that.'

'Thanks.' Will laughed. 'You know you've blown all my preconceptions about cops. Who am I supposed to rage against now?'

'Yeah, well you've blown all mine about hippies, or goths, or whatever you are.'

'Come on. If I *was* a goth I'd be wearing make-up.'

Gilroy grinned. 'See? Just the fact you know that proves my point!'

The door wrenched open and Bruce staggered out. He didn't look well, his colour patchy, face a sweaty neon red. He froze when he saw Will.

'You!'

'Okay, Bruce. Remember your bail conditions.' Gilroy leaned into the doorway. 'You okay in there, son?'

Will wormed into the room behind Gilroy.

'I bet you think you're pretty clever, eh?' The venom in Bruce's voice was toxic.

'Not really. But just so you know, he's told me everything. *Everything.*' He looked right into Bruce's snake eyes. Shut the door on him, and wished it had a lock. He slumped against it, eyeing Hunter. 'How'd it go?'

The poor bugger was white, totally wrung out. 'It's done.'

'You trust him?'

Hunter nodded. Pointed to his mobile phone. 'I got it all on there. If he ever tries to screw us over, I'll send it to the cops.'

Will sat down beside the bed, knees a little weak. 'Impressive. Remind me not to piss you off!'

'You think *I'm* tough? You stole a boat and drove it through a gale in the bloody Cook Strait, you crazy townie!'

Will shrugged. 'Guilty as charged, Your Honour.'

'Yeah, well, by tonight I think you'll find those charges have been dropped.'

Relief dawned slowly. Trickled in. 'I owe you big time, man.'

'Forget it. Thanks for being here.'

'Did he apologise?'

A short, bitter snort. 'Rack off! He *never* apologises. But he went as white as snow when I told him I'd remembered. Had to hold onto the chair.' Hunter wiped a bloodless hand across his brow. White as snow.

'Looks like you need to rest. You want me to stay or come back tomorrow?'

'Would you mind just sitting here till I drop off? I know — I'm such a pussy — but it kind of shook me up.'

'No sweat, man.' He grinned. 'Want me to sing you a lullaby?'

'Yeah, go on then.' Hunter didn't look like he was joking. He closed his eyes. 'Can you do that one you sang the night we stayed out at Gleneden?'

Surprise blanked Will's mind. What on earth had he sung? He pictured himself back in the cove. Listened for the soundtrack to his thoughts. Oh yes, of course, from *La Bohème*. He crooned it quietly, not just for the sake of the patients in the other rooms, but his throat was still not right. '*Che gelida manina, se la lasci riscaldar . . .*' *Your tiny hand is frozen, let me warm it with my own . . .*

Poor Helen. What a shit of a life. A good reminder not to settle for second best. To think she could've had Dean. Such a waste — for both of them.

He stopped. 'You know, it's like you've finally avenged your mum.'

'Yeah, I know.' Hunter opened one eye. 'Feels good. Now shut up and keep singing.'

'*Aspetti, signorina, le dirò con due parole chi son, e che faccio, come vivo. Vuole?*' *Wait, mademoiselle, I will tell you in two words, who I am, what I do, and how I live. May I?* Who'd have thought, the first time he saw this great lump, that he'd one day sit beside his bed and sing Puccini to him at his request? Life sure delivered up some strange surprises.

~

TWO NIGHTS LATER, WILL PICKED up Pania and they walked down to the wharf together. The Cat hadn't come back yet, though Dean had been to check it out; he said it was fine, just a few dents and scratches. Will and Pania sat down in a gap between the boats and rolled up their jeans, dredging their feet through the high tide. It was a still night. Perfect. He'd learnt a lot about the weather since he'd moved down here; had never really noticed before how southerlies rolled through with such clockwork precision — three days of total crap and then a clump of perfect days. Pity he'd timed his mission for the worst of the crap ones.

'So, Gilroy rang today and said that all the charges had been dropped.'

'Oh my god! What happened?'

'I guess I must have charmed them with my winning ways.'

She slapped at him. 'Yeah, right. How really?'

Will tapped the side of his nose. 'Top secret. Let's just say Hunter made Bruce an offer he couldn't refuse.'

'Hunter did? Wow, good on him.' She leaned into his shoulder. 'Viv rang to say she's jacked up another interview. Some "save the ocean" website.'

'I can't stop thinking about Helen,' he said, trying to deflect where this was going. 'If she hadn't been pressured into marrying Bruce, she'd probably still be alive — and probably be with Dean.'

Pania frowned. 'I don't get the connection. Is this 'cause you don't like the fact Viv's with him?'

'It's not that. I think Viv's great for him. It's just the pressure of the interviews . . .'

She leaned down and sifted water through her fingers. 'What, you've had enough of trying to save the whales?'

He laughed. 'Course I haven't. But I want my life back. It's all too hard.'

'But look at all the money pouring in. It's not just us any more — lots of people are doing what they can.'

'Yeah, I know. I'm not saying pull the plug altogether — I'd just like to be left alone for a bit. Sort my head out. Plan what the hell to do next.' He picked her hand up and licked the sea off her index finger. 'Tasty!'

She shook her head. Murmured, 'Idiot!'

The tide was on the turn, sucking the ribs of the wharf. Somewhere behind them two cats fought, wails cutting through the settling darkness. Will sighed. 'God, I miss the little bugger. Every night I hear him singing in my head.' He hated that he'd never get to hear Min in the flesh again. Look into those eyes.

'You remember when Min first came? And Nanny said Kingi's spirit had come back?'

He nodded. Couldn't speak. The thought of Min had brought a lump into his throat.

'When I was with him that night you stayed with Hunter, I felt like Kingi was there. I know that sounds stupid, but it was comforting.' She sniffed and he realised she was crying.

'It's not stupid.' He scrabbled for her hand. 'Sometimes when I was out here I felt like there was a great circle of ghosts around me — most human, but some not. There's something about him. He taps you into a whole different dimension.'

She knuckled the tears out of her eyes. Hiccupped. 'After that night, I hated knowing I'd never see him again. It pressed all my buttons, I guess; didn't even know I had any until that night. That's why I keep saying yes to interviews, hoping someone might offer to take us out to be with him again. I keep thinking, what if Nanny's right and Min *is* somehow connected to Kingi?'

'What do you think?'

She sighed. 'I dunno. But it haunts me, Will. Even though Kingi was hardly ever home, I feel like a big chunk of my family's missing now. Mum and Dad are still so sad. I have these dreams where he's walking towards that village and I'm yelling at him to stop but he can't hear me. I wake up feeling like it's my fault he died.'

'Oh, Pans, you know it's not.'

'Course I do, logically, but it doesn't stop it hurting.'

He lifted her hand to his lips. Felt all his defences fall away. 'Why didn't you tell me this before?'

'I thought you'd think I'm nuts. Dad says most Pākehā wouldn't know an ancestor's spirit if it jumped up and bit them.'

He snorted. 'Thanks.'

'I didn't say you were like that. It's just a hard thing to admit, okay? I'm the sensible scientific one, remember?'

'Yeah? Well, I'm the flaky arty one, remember, so you should've known I'd understand.'

'Look, what if we say no to more interviews for now then,' Pania said. 'I don't care. I've got to concentrate on my internal assessments anyway. But if a really interesting — important — offer comes up, let's talk it over, eh? We don't want to regret that either. How's that?'

He nodded, incredibly relieved. '*Damn*, you make life hard for me.'

She frowned. 'In what way?'

'I'm trying to be more sensible like you, not always jumping in the deep end, and you're so adorable you're forcing me to fall head over heels!'

She laughed. 'Oh right, that's *my* fault is it?' He could tell she was pleased. *Thank god.*

'Yep. And there's only one thing for it, Pania Huriwai, you'll have to agree to be my girlfriend. You know, hang out? Step out with me? Date? Fill my dance card? Go steady? Go walkies? Go—'

'Shut up!' She leaned closer, puckering up, but instead of a kiss slurped from his chin to the stud between his eyes; a great big doggy lick. 'Yes, I'll go walkies, you total bloody idiot!'

Will reared back, laughing. He wiped his face, then wagged his finger at her. 'Uh oh! Nanny M's ears will be burning.'

'I guess I'll have to bribe you then.' She grabbed him by the collar and pulled him to her. Kissed him. Left him breathless when she pushed him back. 'Listen, I'm still going down to Canterbury. It's been my dream for years.'

'Of course. Though I *do* hear there's this thing called the phone — and, even better, Skype! Great new-fangled inventions! And you know what they say about absence making the heart grow fonder? I look forward to getting fond with you!' He waggled his eyebrow hardware; was glad to have it back. 'Anyway, I'm gonna be busy too. If I do okay, I'll go and study overseas when I'm finished here. You know, I kind of like the idea of telling people I date a brainbox.'

'Yeah, yeah.'

He could feel her tense up. 'What? Did I say something—'

'Nope. It's just— I'm a, you know . . . I've kind of been too busy to—'

'What?' Was she talking about sex? Hoped so. It meant she had to be considering it!

'If you're expecting me to—'

'Would it help if I admitted I'm a tragic *"you-know"* too?' *Oh shit.* 'Not that I'm saying you're tragic, just—' He didn't bother finishing, she was laughing again now.

'I thought all boys were obsessed by sex? Nanny warns me every summer when the tourists come.'

'Obsessed, yes. Successful? Nah.' He took her hand again; kissed each finger. 'Sounds like what we both need is a bit of private practice.'

'Sleazeball!'

'Schweetheart.'

'What would you be singing if Min was here?'

Where did that come from? 'I dunno. Maybe a little Gilbert and Sullivan. He really seemed to like that.'

'Go on then.'

'What?'

'Sing some.'

'Why?'

The corner of her mouth twitched. 'Because I asked.'

'You sure? It's kind of weird if you're not used to it.'

'So are you!' She lay back, hair splayed across the timbers of the walkway. 'Go on. Please.'

On the spot, the first song off the rack wasn't even for a male voice. Classic *Mikado*, though; lots of yearning. Why not? He stood up, looming above her as he drew in breath. '*The sun, whose rays are all ablaze with ever-living glory, does not deny his majesty — he scorns to tell a story!*' She was smiling up at him, a strange concentrating smile. '*He won't exclaim, "I blush for shame, So kindly be indulgent." But, fierce and bold, in fiery gold, he glories all effulgent . . .*'

As he sang, she first sat up, and then stood. It took him a moment to hear what she was doing. Winding around his song with haunting wordless harmonies — the same kind of harmonies Min would use. She had the tone down almost perfectly. It was so beautiful he had to swallow hard.

'*. . . There's not a trace upon her face of diffidence or shyness: She borrows light, that, through the night, mankind may all acclaim her! And, truth to tell, she lights up well, so I, for one, don't blame her! Ah, pray make no mistake, we are not shy; We're very wide awake, the moon and I.*'

THIRTY-ONE

*Wishing He
Would Wend
My Way*

Seasons had shifted, the sun starting to scorch the ice, and I was tugged towards my Song Boy in our summer seas. Yet, when we went, passing places we were pulled to by The Pulse, I felt my fear follow me, my mother's murder still so fresh. But now my family fussed around me; helped fend off those youthful fears.

We made it to the shingle shelf that edged those dark delicious depths, but now I ached, not for my mother, but for my forsaken Boy. I spent the summer seeking him, wishing he would wend my way. Dear friends, did you know the Fates will grant the wild wishes of a Being who hopes so hard, if truly felt? This too I learned in that long summer so far gone.

Forgive me now. I tire. Many times already I have sung this story, chronicled to every corner, every Being who listens with an open heart. Some strive to teach the ins and outs of solid skills; we Chronicles are tasked with touching every Being we encounter with our words, with unwinding every wisdom we have winkled from our world.

Songs, you see, are often far more weighty than first meanings seem. They start as simple sounds, one thrust, but as the ages roll around, such understandings shift and twist, grow wings. Soon many thoughts are tumbled into one, until each song can speak with untold tongues. Sense splinters, opens out. It is this double-dealing, many-meaning, truth-thwarting trick that makes a meaty meal for the mind.

But now my time is eking to its end I had hoped to tell you more. Instead, my breath grows weak. I long to latch onto the light. To seek the sweetness of the open air. Stay. Sing this one last loop of my long song with me . . . my days of telling tales are almost done.

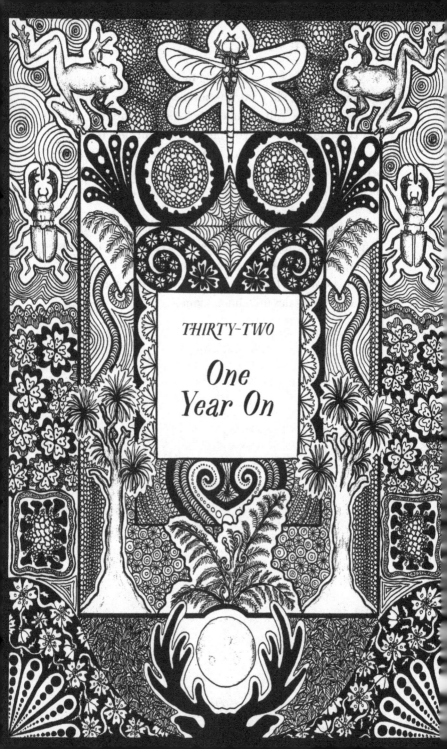

THIRTY-TWO

*One
Year On*

The ferry crossing was smooth; the sea as flat as glass, no indication of the hell it could become — and *had* become, this time last year. Will had busked in Cuba Mall two days in a row to pay for this trip down. He was slowly regaining performance confidence; the headaches were gone, mostly, and his nerves more settled (so long as he didn't feel cornered). Though he'd grown more used to people gushing about his song with Min, he still craved space.

Public fascination hadn't waned. Almost every month, Pania told him of further interviews or requests for information. He'd avoided them, found weak excuses, and by the time he shifted up to Wellington she'd given up and sometimes did them on her own. It wasn't that he didn't care, or didn't desperately want to make a difference; he just needed time to come to terms with being public property. He had yet to trust the switch from being an object of ridicule to show pony; still had a few last wounds to lick. His singing was helping, but he missed Pania's confidence in his ability to pull it off. Even so, the YouTube clip now had well over thirty-seven million hits (he'd stopped looking). Min's fame was cult-like — young Japanese had picketed the supermarkets and restaurants that sold whale meat, both of Norway's major parties were under pressure to halt their annual kill. Of course, Min's popularity had put him and his pod in danger — people were offering thousands of dollars (and doing the most stupid things) to seek Min out. The local Department of Conservation and Whale Watch guys had been forced to set up round-the-clock surveillance to protect Min and his pod until they disappeared back to Antarctica, and even Will and Pania were now arguing for Harley's 'wall'. Thank god, so far no one had managed to break it down.

The ferry arrived in port at Picton, and Will caught the train down to Kaikoura. He was due to reach there just before the others arrived. As the afternoon slipped by, the hills glowed gold. Bright yellow gold. Incredible. Whole hillsides of flowering broom. He thought about how life had changed since he'd been down here last. Pania, for one. They'd taken things slowly (or, at least, that's how it felt), though they *had* crossed the '*you know*' hurdle — incredible, miraculous — but everything changed with this new year. She headed down to Christchurch, full-on with her job and studies, while he moved north, accepted into the vocal stream of the School of Music up at Vic. To be singing again under Marilyn's expert eye helped to take away his angst — though not the sting of missing Pania.

He hadn't seen her now for nearly four months. Sure, they Skyped and texted, but he couldn't touch her, kiss her, and it drove him nuts. At times his head filled up with paranoid jealousies, convinced she was seeing someone else, but in his heart he knew she wouldn't, just as he'd never do it to her.

He wasn't miserable. His parents were happy, both finally finding office jobs in Sydney to escape the mine, and Dean was content with Viv. Will loved his course, and his voice was stronger every lesson. To be immersed in music all day long was total heaven. But always, at the back of everything, was the loss of Pania — and Min. He often dreamed of him, long rambly sequences where he was swimming, singing underwater, at Min's side. He'd wake filled with the burn of regret — like homesickness, as if the dream was his real home and not the other way around.

So when Hunter emailed and said they should all meet to celebrate the anniversary of Min's farewell, Will jumped at it. The icing on the cake came in the form of a message from the guys at Whale Watch. They'd seen his pod last week! Will tried not to let his hope run wild; it would be like searching for a needle in a haystack. But he hoped all the same. Longed. Bargained with the Fates.

Once the train pulled in at Kaikoura, he bought himself a vegan roll and walked around the coast to where they'd organised to meet. The tide was out, fat fur seals sunning on the rugged limestone as tourists shrieked and clicked cameras. Gulls whirled in the updraughts; shags dropped like darts into the prismed sea. It reeked of kelp. *Of Min.*

When Hunter's airhorn started turning heads, Will scrabbled back across the rocks towards the hotted-up Corolla, which had one of the big farm tinnies hooked on behind. They were out of the car and stretching by the time he reached them. He scooped up Pania, twirled her around before he kissed her. Would've kept on going but

Hunter slapped him on the back.

'Jesus, dude. Get a room!'

'Sorry, man.' He wrapped his arms around Hunter's meatloaf chest and tried to pick him up. Failed miserably, but got him laughing. Gave him a smacker on the cheek. 'It's good to see you too!'

'Your face looks naked.' Pania stroked across his eyebrows.

'Yeah, Marilyn said if I wanted a shot at the competitions I had to lose the metal.' He grinned and pulled up the sleeve of his shirt. 'Didn't say anything about tattoos though!'

Pania leaned in to see his new addition: Min leaping across his bicep, complete with tiny bullet hole on his fin. 'Oh, wow!'

'Very cool,' Hunter said. He put an arm around each of them and collected them into a bear hug. 'That's from Dean and Viv.'

'How is the old bugger?'

Hunter shook his head like an overindulgent parent. 'I don't know how the hell they stay together with all their bitching, but they seem really happy underneath.' It was worth keeping Hunter's secret for that. All it would've done was stir Dean up and complicate things. Will liked Viv, she made Dean come alive. And she was gutsy too. He liked the way she fought so hard, even if she didn't always understand Will's need for space.

They drove to the motel. Checked in, with Will and Pania in one room, Hunter in another, and walked down to a café overlooking the sea. Ordered burgers, chips and beer. Clinked their bottles against Pania's glass of water and all said 'cheers!'

Hunter sculled half his bottle straight away. 'Ah, I needed that. I've been working since five this morning.'

'How's business?' Will pressed his knee against Pania's, needed to touch her, not a minute wasted.

'Haven't gone under yet, so I guess that counts for something. And now Mike's lot have come on board we're moving forwards.'

'Good work, man. Have you heard from Bruce?'

Hunter shook his head. 'No, but when I moved into Dean's, he primed Bob Davers to give me stick. No loyalty, blah, blah.'

'Have you fired him?'

Hunter grinned. 'Yep. Dean made me do it — said I had to know how horrible it felt, to make sure I only did it when I *really* had to. It was pretty hard.'

'What, to fire Bob?' Pania laughed. 'I'd have done it no sweat!'

'Me too.' Will nudged him in the ribs. 'Lucky most people don't know what a big girl's blouse you are.'

Pania side-swiped him. 'Shut up! From what Mum says the girls in Blythe don't think so, eh Hunts?'

His ears reddened. 'Dunno.' It was nice to see the little smile that lurked behind his eyes.

'What happened to Simone? I thought you had a thing with her?'

'You won't believe it, but *I* dumped *her*. She was driving me nuts, always on Facebook or the phone. And she had no bloody idea how hard I have to work; always wanting to do lame stuff like shopping.' He rolled his eyes. 'I've been going diving with Willow Hannifer a bit. She's nice.'

'Good on ya, mate.'

He certainly looked happy — and well. Was seeing a counsellor to sort the crap about his mum and dad. Will might've thought his own counselling sessions sucked, but in fact they'd helped him heaps. When he moved into the hostel in Wellington, he'd gone again a few times, just to help him get his head around the stuff with Min. His counsellor had cried when she saw the clip, but he was used to that; there were as many soft-hearted people out there as total shits. Maybe more. It was heartening. Drove away the ghosts.

'So, what's tomorrow's plan?'

'Duncan is going up in the spotter plane just after seven. If he finds them he'll text me where. If he doesn't, I reckon we just go out anyway. Have a good old sing and see what shows.'

'What if we find him and he doesn't recognise me?'

'Come on,' said Pania. 'Of course he will.'

'You think?' If they found Min and he *didn't* respond, Will would be more gutted than not finding him at all. 'So how's my dear friend Gabby?'

'Gone,' Pania said. 'She took off for Australia as soon as she'd saved enough. Reckons she's not coming back.'

'Good for her,' Will said. The final months down in Blythe before he'd shifted north, he'd made an effort — and had to acknowledge she'd made one too. How could he stay mad at someone who got such hell at home?

'And Harley?' When everything came out the locals rallied around him; forgave him for his lapse. Dean and Mike talked his boss into refusing his resignation. A clever move. Now he went to bat for them every chance he could. Same old game, just nicer people. *Did that make it okay?*

Hunter popped the top off another beer. 'He's just put in a really great report for our new consents. We're gonna trial an integrated polyculture system — they're top of the range — and clean up that bloody mess.'

'What the hell's an integrated polyculture system?'

Hunter groaned. 'Dude, I'm on holiday. I'll send you through some links. Let's just say, if we can pull it off we'll lead the pack.'

'Good on you, man. Well done.' It was so nice to see him confident. *And well done, Dean.*

By eight-thirty they'd scraped the barrel dry of local gossip and all Will wanted was to get Pania alone. They strolled back to the motel in the silver evening, Will's arm around her waist.

He faked a dramatic yawn. Hammed it up. 'Time to turn in?'

Hunter grinned. 'Yeah, you look *real* tired!'

As Pania unlocked the door Will picked her up. Flung her across his shoulder like a sack of spuds. She shrieked as he carried her over the threshold. Inside, he kicked the door shut and put her down. Went straight in for a kiss, clothes flying as they rediscovered each other, wasting no time.

Later, as they sprawled across the ransacked bed, Will revelled in the scent of her. *Fresh, like the sea.*

'Hey, I need to talk to you.' She sat up and fluffed the pillows behind her. 'I've had this really great idea.'

'Oh yeah? If it's a proposal the answer's yes!'

'Dork!' She kissed his nose. 'I don't want you to get shitty with me. I want you to listen first. Okay?' A double-quaver in her voice undermined her casual pose.

He roused, nerves rustling. Propped himself up next to

her. Kissed her lovely naked shoulder. 'Spit it out.'

'You know how I've been learning to design experiments?' He nodded. 'Well, I've learnt how to set up long-term ones. Over lots of years.'

'So?'

'Look, I know you hate doing the interviews about Min, okay? You didn't even bite at that guy from Hawai'i who wanted to do the research—'

'He wanted to exploit Min. That was just a smoke-screen.'

She gave him a long look that made his stomach tighten. 'Is that why you said no? You really thought that?'

'He was a vulture. Just cashing in.'

'He *so* wasn't.' She sighed. Ran her finger around his new tattoo. 'Anyway . . . it got me thinking how amazing it would be if someone followed Min's progress right through his life. No one's ever done anything like that before. I don't mean just seeing him every year — if he shows, that is — but actually recording how he grows and changes, do blood tests for things like mercury, pollution, watch how contact with us affects him over time — like, what he learns from us, and what we learn from him.'

She paused. Checked his face. He held it blank. She wasn't wrong; he just felt nervous about the direction this was heading. But she went on. 'Yeah, well, then I thought why not us? You could do recordings of his songs — learn if he adds to them and how they change as he gets older, that kind of thing. And there wouldn't have to be anyone else — just you with Min and me doing the lab work. Hunter's keen to sort the boat and do the filming. We wouldn't even have to broadcast right away if you didn't want to, we could hold off for a bit, but I reckon it'd be really interesting — and we'd have a perfect excuse to see Min every year! I talked to my tutor and he said we'd possibly even get some long-term funding to meet our costs — then, once you're singing overseas, there'd be money to bring you home.' She blew out a long breath. Studied him closely.

'You've already talked about this to Hunter?'

She blinked. 'Yes. We *did* have a two-hour drive. Why?'

'Nothing.' Nice she had faith that he'd be singing overseas. And the thought of staying in contact with Min — well, that was amazing. But wishful thinking. 'What about the law? We're not supposed to approach him, let alone get in the water with him. You think if we're here every year we won't get caught? I'm buggered if I'm going through *that* again.'

'I think if I set up the research properly, we'd be entitled to a dispensation.'

'Wow, you've thought of everything.' He couldn't quite keep his old defensiveness out of his voice. Felt all his old anxieties rushing back, sneering at his naivety for thinking he could ever banish them for good.

She pulled the sheet over her breasts. Crossed her arms. 'For goodness sake. Are you going to go on hiding forever? I know what happened was awful and you were really messed up but it's *over*. Look at Hunter; he's been shat on — but he doesn't give up, run away. He's out there making a life. He's put the past behind him.'

Apart from his drinking. 'I thought that's what I'm trying to do.'

'Yeah, but you're denying a whole lot of really incredible stuff that could change your life for the better. I'm sick of saying no. People care, they want to know. And if we don't do it, carefully and scientifically, then it won't be long before some other crazy idiot will — and who knows what'll happen to Min then?'

His chest tightened as a tug-of-war commenced inside, one team (captained by Will of the Living Dead) pulling him towards the path he'd already walked, littered with all his shredded fears and pains — but familiar, safe, controllable, known. The other team (spurred on by Pania, Min, Hunter and Viv) was strong and ripe with possibilities — but risky, no security, no guarantees, no map. Pure unadulterated heart. He'd hoped if he ignored it all, put his bond with Min out of his mind, life would simplify and, by default, the external expectations on him would ease as well. Or disappear. The trouble was, deep down he knew that while he'd buried himself in uni, and worked hard to convince himself the other life was gone, inside he ached for Min and Pania — and a life not defined and restricted by his own weaknesses. If he said 'no' to this, he may well lose them all. *That* thought made him panicky. What was the point of peace of mind if he lost the very things he loved the most?

'I'm sorry,' he said, clearing uncertainty from his throat. 'I'm being a dick. My stupid default mode — getting better, mostly, but still a dick.'

'I know. I try to remember that — not that you're a dick — shut up! — but your panic thing. It's just that sometimes it makes me panicky too, and I feel like we're running in different directions.'

God, he loved her. She was so straightforward. So *real*. 'You really think we could do that without it turning into a circus?'

'I don't know, but I really want to try. And I think

if we're doing research, proper research, there's a much better chance.' She rubbed her head against his shoulder. '*And* they might even pay for us to come and see him!'

'What did Hunter say?'

'You know Hunts. He's up for anything.'

It was crunch time. Not in a dramatic way, like singing Min home. This was far more fundamental. He'd been the one who'd started the whole thing off. Did he really want to walk away from it? From her? *No way.* He didn't want to let her down. He might be screwy — he hoped not —but he could still support her. Do like she'd suggested a year ago and really, truly, get a life — and not just the half-life he was living now. He should've learnt it from his time with Min, that sense of pleasure in putting something else — someone else — ahead of his stupid hang-ups and doing the right thing. And this *was* the right thing. Plus, if it worked, he'd get to see Min every year! Why on earth had he been so guarded? The only one he'd avoided hurting was himself — though, come on, even *that* wasn't true. Every week that went by without Min and Pania hurt like hell.

He took a deep breath, as though about to dive into a fathomless sea. Panicked, stepped back from the edge . . . *No, idiot! Do it!* Sometimes bravery wasn't facing up to warring hordes, or even psychos like Bruce, it was peering into your own quaking heart to find the one undamaged seed of strength and letting it grow. 'Okay. Let's do it.'

'You mean it? You said that last time.'

'I really mean it.' He raised two fingers to his brow. 'I swear. Tenor's honour! It's a bloody good idea.'

'Thank you!' She kissed him, her nose cold against his.

'Jesus, girl, you're freezing. I think I may have a

cunning plan to warm you up.'

'Again?' she said.

'Yep. And tomorrow and tomorrow and . . .'

He slipped the sheet back off her breasts. Gently pulled her down the bed. And, there, he etched his love onto her with his lips.

~

IT WAS AS THOUGH THEY sat on the belly of the sea, breathing in and out below them. The boat wallowed in a long slow swell, in the position Duncan had given them. So far they'd seen two sperm whales, all squared-off edges, like surfaced submarines. They upended right in front of the boat, huge winged flukes sliding into the water with hardly a splash.

'Time for another song?' Hunter said.

'I guess.' *Where are you, Min?*

'It'd better be the last try. If we don't find him soon, we'll have to give it up. I've gotta pick up something for Dean and get it back to him by five — and you've got a ferry to catch.'

'Okay.' Will stood again; shifted his feet to find his balance. 'Any requests?'

Pania shrugged. 'You haven't done "Amazing Grace" yet. I know the words too.'

She joined Will first, then Hunter came in too. His voice was breathy, undisciplined, but his tone was good. Such a different person from the one Will met last year. Pania was right: Hunter should give him hope. *Did* give him hope. His resilience was totally impressive, booze or not.

Will swept his gaze across the water, eyes weeping from

~ *324* ~

its glare. He felt so disappointed. The whole thing was pointless. Duncan may've spotted a pod this morning, but they could be anywhere, and it could have been any pod. So why couldn't he give up?

He sat down when they'd finished the song. Nothing. Tried one last bid to stall for time. 'Come on, I'll teach you a round. We've still got an hour before we really have to go.'

In the middle of the second run-through of 'Dona Nobis Pacem', Pania shrieked. 'Oh my god — look!' She pointed over his shoulder.

He swung around, saw a forest of fins, straight, high, distinctively orca, cruising their way.

'Min!' He launched himself back to his feet. Nearly overturned the boat. Began Min's signature call, heart so fast his hand flew to his chest to hold it in. *Be Min. Be Min. Be Min.*

A small orca breached near the head of the pod, so high it spun in mid-air before it dropped. Could that be him? He tried to spot the bullet hole. Couldn't see one, yet the little guy was heading straight for them. Maybe all orca babies were that bold?

But then he heard him, recognised him calling back! He glanced at Pania. Her hand was plastered to her mouth, shoulders shaking.

'You bloody little beauty!' Hunter grabbed the camera. Started filming seconds before Min reached the boat.

Min thrust himself towards Will's outstretched hands, clicking, whistling, wailing. Did his demented Donald Duck! Will couldn't stop blubbing; didn't care. He wrapped his arms around him and kissed his salty head. 'Gidday, mate. I've really missed you.'

'Holy crap!' Hunter's tone verged on panic.

Will looked up. Min's pod was spy-hopping, lined up, front-seat to the show. Fifteen he counted, two teenage, three small like Min, the rest really bloody huge next to their tiny boat. They'd be pitched overboard if any of the big ones got it in their head to try. Could bite them right in half.

Min was whining like a shitty kid; slapping on the water as if to say, 'Get in!' Will looked from him to the watching adults, then to Pania — who eyed them open-mouthed — then back to Min.

'D'you think it's safe to go in?'

'Up to you, dude.' Hunter's focus never left the camera. 'But I don't reckon they're gonna hurt you.'

Will turned to Pania, her face a tear-stained mess. 'Pans? What d'you think?'

'I don't know. They're really big.'

He couldn't decide. Wanted to — god, he wanted to — but was he kidding himself he'd be okay? And what about the 'wall'? He stared down at Min, who bunted at Pania's hand like a lamb searching for a teat, and got hooked up in the depth of his eyes. Felt his pleading. Warmth. What if this was his last chance? He'd spend his whole life yearning, haunted by regrets. He didn't need any more of those.

'Bugger it!' he said. 'I'm going in.' He tore off his shirt and jeans. Didn't look at the big orcas. Kept his eye on Min. 'I hope you get all this on camera, man, in case they need it at my inquest!'

'Very funny.' Hunter wasn't laughing.

Will slipped into the chilly water and there was Min, clicking, rubbing against him, nudging just the way he always did. He'd grown at least half a metre, fat and healthy as he tried to herd Will over to his pod.

'Hang on a mo!'

Min was singing their favourite tune, kept nudging, so Will let rip with some Handel to distract him. *'Hallelujah! Hallelujah!'* He got so caught up with the singing, especially when Min joined him, he didn't notice what was happening until he heard Pania's nervous shout.

'Will! Look out!'

One glance at her horrified face sent him spinning around. There they were! The whole damn pod, snuck up on him. He was so small beside them, powerless, but — strangely — he felt safe. Goodwill poured off them, warmth streaming from their eyes.

Min was still singing, his call an eighth tone lower than this time last year. As Will trod water, eyeing the adults, one by one they started singing too. Their voices rose up in a complex orca aria, so resonant it permeated right through him, until he *was* their song. Any last resistance he had towards Pania's scheme evaporated. He'd be a fool to say no to this. Their song wrapped him, dug down deep into the hurts he'd suffered and dredged them right up to the surface. And, as their chorus reached its peak, he was finally set free.

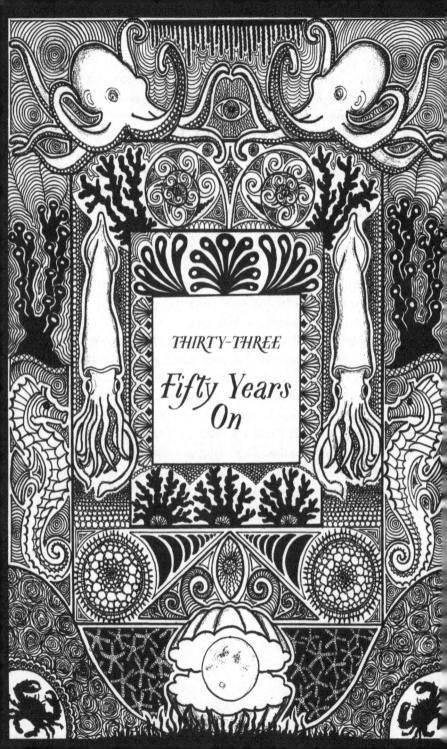

THIRTY-THREE

*Fifty Years
On*

Ah, so here we are at last, winding this tale of love and woe towards its end. Your turnout truly touches me; that you would travel from the far-flung waters of our beset world to hear my song, and take its teachings back to all your tribes, so thrills my heart. Late solace for the side-shows, when I was a Being alone amid the startled scores of Hungry Ones who came to hear the soulful sounds of Song Boy's voice melding with mine. Today the tide has turned: the throngs of you who gather here to heed my call are witnessed only by my Song Boy and his loving clan of five on land.

Swim closer now, share your strength, hold me as the light looms and my life leaks out.

For fifty shining summers I have sung at Song Boy's side; come to know him as no other Being has ever seen inside a Hungry One before. Hark him here beside me now, swimming, singing still, his sounds so meshed into my mind they steep my sleep — a comfort in the seasons we were set apart. When I awake, wracked by longing, loss, I take great comfort in the knowledge that he keeps on coming, summer after summer, keen to hear my call.

Oh, how he has changed since we first met: his long obsidian locks leached to silver shades of misty mornings; his wash of worries, hurts and hungers waning long ago. But the heart of him, his kind and caring core, is ever unwavering; he has loved me all this time with the same depths he loves his dear Good Girl — has a way of building bonds so tough they still have heft to hold us in his thrall. When he sings, my heart flies feather-light, all pains forsworn, all losses flown.

Good Girl, too, I have loved. Her kind concern has sheltered me, bolstered by her backbone; by her brave and honest heart. She is the rock my Song Boy clambers back to when the day turns dark. They have withstood the storms, stood side by side, but never has their merging left me lonely — love, dear friends, is ever limitless; it knows no edge.

See her standing on the shore as I sing you my farewell; Broad Boy too, with his white-haired woman and their two tall sons. They form my Human family, our summers shared in songs, in sea, in full-grown feelings, cosy caring, though the Watchers' eyes were ever on me as we wallowed in the warming waters of our world.

Oh, what a wondrous, worrying life to live, dear friends, swimming on Great Mother's bountiful back. I have seen stars fall from the sky, sinkholes swallow sand and winds sweep seas so high they steal lives. Humans fighting evil; baby Beings born. My clan has gifted me great comfort as I loved and lost and loved again. But no Being ever held my heart like Song Boy has. He was my shelter in that long lost storm of sadness and he soothes me still.

Ah . . . how to wrap my mind's weak witterings? Too many tales end with anger, shame, or hopelessness. Not so mine. True, I had my taste of troubles. I mourned my mother, and my dear aunt's death, too, truly tested me. She, who took me in, taught of life and love and how to last the loneliness on the days that dawned too dark, died mid-life, struck by a ship. We bunched around her battered body, floated her back home. In truth, on listless summer nights I still hear her songs.

But though I've lived with losses, great gifts have I been given too. And simple gems, no less sweet. The sigh of wind on water, flocked geese sent flying by our Mother's brimming breath, light-shows in southern skies, a spiral shell, a frigate's floating feather, the look of love in every mother's eye.

While I have swum Her great oceans, much has changed. Tides suck away the shores, foul flotsam fetches into floating islands, the seas fill up with poisons purged from spilling lands to deal death to many more than just my kind — corals killed, reefs rumbled, seabirds starved, lives lost. And now my boisterous body fails, not from old age but through the blight of seaborne Human spoils. Quicksilver queers my meat, stiffening movements, stealing strength, miring the thinking of my tired mind.

My friends, how Song Boy and his clan have tried to help me shake this from my brittling bones, but all for nought — death whispers on the wind for me as Good Girl lifts her voice from land to call me home. 'Ka heke i ngā huihuinga, ka heke i ngā kawainga . . . Ka moe ki Whare-rimu, ka moe ki Whare-papa . . .' I sense the strength inside her song; her words of mourning gather meaning, as if I learned them in another life. Depart in *company, depart whence the dawn arises . . . Sleep in the House-of-seaweeds, sleep in the House-of-the-reef . . .*

Yet, in spite of creeping sickness, I helped to speed a shift, build brotherhood, bridge blindness, bring together Beings to trade the lessons I have lived — just as Song Boy surely shed some loving light on his clan too. And so our work has brought about the greatest of all gifts: for over thirty turnings of the seasons now, no Being has been slain by Human hands. Good gains. A fair and fitting deal amidst the foul. A fruitful life.

Yes, yes, travellers, I know my pride bobs back, blustering on, as in my youngest years. But, for once, I feel this outburst has been earned: Song Boy and I breached the battlements between Beings and Man. We picked a path. Proved a point. Shone a loving light upon the possibilities for peace. Of that I'm proud.

Only one sadness still sticks like sucking fish: no offspring have I spawned, no small Being to slip into my mantle after me. Perhaps my heart was only ever Song Boy's, so full of feeling for him there was little left for my own kind. This closeness we have fostered fills me up; and when we are apart he darts into my dreams. We swim a shoreless sea, share times of happy heartfelt hush; trust to each other brave bare-bellied truths.

Watch how he holds me, strokes me, soothes me now, my Boy. Make space, squeeze in, give him your ears, your thanks. I feel his heart so heavy, his horror at my dawning death already merging into mourning as he helps me on my way. And, though it troubles him to sense my spirits rise with this unstinting joy — the Hungry Ones fear death, gulp life — even in his grief he gives me what I want.

How I pine for this unshackling from the sea, long to meet my end in open air. He senses my release and sings of all the joy that bubbles up in me, his love so strong his words wash in my mind and settle there: his mind shouts out *Mik-ah-doe* as his lungs let loose this anthem to my exultation. I feel its meaning melt into my brain to bolster me, as you, my friends, weave your mellow mourning voices with his own. '*Then let the throng our joy advance, with laughing song and merry dance, with laughing song and merry dance, with laughing song . . .*'

Oh, fellow Beings, hear his earthborne song and feel this flow of lasting love. No other lesson matters more than this: souls can be the same, albeit that the worlds we wander are as unalike as air to sea, as he to me. It is our hearts that speak . . .

Enough. I have no more.

Lift me now, lighten my load. Take me, thrust me, throw me landward till my bony bag breathes only air; no sea to float my fatness, solid stones to sit beneath my rest. I do not fear my death. My life has been a pulsing path that peaks with this. I pray you push now, press me, prod me, pass me in. Send me on a swash of swell to shore, with Song Boy by my side. To die with his long limbs wrapped around me answers all.

Do not mourn my end, dear friends. My many years of wandering, of telling this true tale, are done. New Chronicles arise, snatch up my songs; swim on and spread this story of our rebirthed bond. Tell it, take it, use it, own this yarn about the yokes that bind all Beings of the sea to those who walk the wooded land.

Song Boy, farewell, my dearest friend. Be blessed. Good Girl, hug him to your side and hold him safe. Broad

Boy, my blessings flow for you and your fine family too.

    I feel the shift of stones, wind swiping skin, as up ahead my faithful Humans herald me back home. So weary now, weight wearing me down. Such a struggle now to sing . . .

    I am lapped in light

            I leave you all with love

                I am The Chronicle

                      and my life's song is sung

                          I am in air

                                in air

                                      in

ACKNOWLEDGEMENTS

MY GRATEFUL THANKS TO Jenny Hellen and the team at Random House New Zealand for their ongoing support, and to Jolisa Gracewood for her expert editing eye, humour and enthusiasm for the project. I owe a great deal to the encouragement and wisdom of Mal Peet, and to the rest of the Masterclass of 2013 for all their help. Enormous gratitude and love to my daughter Rose Lawson, for her beautiful drawings and her thoughtfulness as my first reader. Much love and thanks to Brian Laird for his heroic support of me in every way, and to Nicky Hager, Debbie Hager, Belinda Hager, Julia Wells, Liz Love and everyone else who has helped me on this journey, including Whitireia for their research support. Aroha nui.

www.mandyhager.com — go to the *Singing Home the Whale* tab for links to orca information and music.